PRAISE FOR JULIE KENNER'S
BREAK-OUT CODE-BUSTING SERIES

The Givenchy Code

"A fabulously fun heroine with a math-geek's mind and a passion for fashion outwits and outplays a ruthless killer in this latest ingenious literary creation from Kenner, whose sharp sense of wit is the perfect accessory for this chic blend of chick lit and thriller."

—*Booklist*

"A fantastic, sexy, fast read, full of intrigue, humor, and murder."

—Reader to Reader Reviews

"Did you enjoy *The Da Vinci Code?* Then you simply MUST read this! Do you love thriller novels that keep you glued to the pages? Then you simply MUST read this!"

—*Huntress Book Reviews*

The Manolo Matrix

"Julie Kenner has me hooked on this series! With her ability to build the thrills and chills to a climactic crescendo, Ms. Kenner keeps the action hot, tense, and very unnerving. . . . Not to be missed."

—Romance Junkies

"The plot is inventive, complex and kept this reader engaged from start to finish. . . . The puzzles are outstanding."

—Fallen Angel Reviews

The Prada Paradox IS ALSO AVAILABLE AS AN EBOOK

Also by Julie Kenner:

The Givenchy Code
The Manolo Matrix
The Spy Who Loves Me
Nobody but You

THE *Prada* PARADOX

JULIE KENNER

Downtown Press

Naughty Girls

New York London Toronto Sydney

An *Original* Publication of POCKET BOOKS

DOWNTOWN PRESS, published by Pocket Books
1230 Avenue of the Americas
New York, NY 10020

ISBN-13: 978-0-7434-9615-5
ISBN-10:   0-7434-9615-9

This Downtown Press trade paperback edition April 2007

10 9 8 7 6 5 4 3 2 1

DOWNTOWN PRESS and colophon are trademarks of Simon & Schuster, Inc.

Manufactured in the United States of America

For information regarding special discounts for bulk purchases, please contact Simon & Schuster Special Sales at 1-800-456-6798 or business@simonandschuster.com

Dedicated to my friends in Los Angeles.
Thanks for the good times!

ACKNOWLEDGMENTS

To Steve, research assistant extraordinaire.

THE
Prada
PARADOX

Chapter 1

Someone put a bullet in my boyfriend's brain!

As I race down the street, propelled by terror, I can still see the image in my mind, and the thought of it makes my stomach turn. The blood and gore on his pillow. The gaping hole above his ear.

My heart stutters, and a stitch burns in my side. Move, Mel, I think. Just move! I'm barefooted, and tiny stones poke into the soles of my feet. I ignore the pain and press on toward safety. Toward home.

I'm almost there, and I keep my focus on that simple green door. Reach the door, open the door, through the door. After that doesn't matter. Not yet. Which is good, because right now my brain can't process any more than those three simple commands. It's too filled with terror and rage and confusion to digest rational thought.

Around me, bright light from fixtures hung precariously on steel poles casts dark shadows, giving this Manhattan street an eerie quality. I barely notice. Just as I barely notice the people standing nearby in clusters, walkie-talkies and cell phones silent in their hands. I glance over them, searching the crowd for the killer. I know deep down that he's not there, but I shove that knowledge away and search. I have to be thorough. I have to be certain.

No one suspicious jumps out at me, and I allow myself one tiny glimpse of hope. My door is *right there.* Twenty yards. Fifteen. Ten.

And then I'm there. My hand closes around the doorknob, the metal cool against my hands. I twist the knob violently, then shove the door open. One step and I'm over the threshold and—

"Cut!" Tobias Harmon, the director, yells from across the street. "Beautiful, sweetheart! I think we got it this time! That was brilliant. Absolutely brilliant."

I nod acknowledgment, but don't look at him. I'm too busy shaking off the fear that I've been wallowing in for the last five takes.

My name is Devi Taylor. I'm an actress. And for me, this part is the role of a lifetime.

"This bit here," I say to my assistant, Susie. "Does the dialogue sound cheesy to you?"

She takes the script and reads it, her mouth moving as her eyes skim over the words. After a second, one shoulder lifts daintily. "I dunno."

"O-*kay*," I say, patiently. "But what's your gut impression? Did it feel natural? Do you think that's really the way the conversation between Mel and Stryker went?" The scene we're talking about is on schedule for tomorrow, our second day of principal photography. It's the scene where they first meet, and Melanie Prescott (aka *moi*) is absolutely certain that Matthew Stryker (the hero) is trying to kill her.

"Um, I guess so?"

I silently count to three, then tilt my head back so that I have a full view of her face. Wide eyes, lanky legs, overly bleached hair, completely vapid expression. Honestly, the next time my manager asks me to do him a favor and hire his wife's cousin's daughter's college roommate as an assistant, I'm going to run as fast as I can in the opposite direction. Except, of course, he posed that question while we were at the Ivy on Ocean Avenue in Santa Monica, and the opposite direction would have had me body-surfing without a board.

In other words, I chickened out when I had the opportunity, and now I'm stuck with Indecisive Barbie.

"There's not a right answer," I say, hoping I sound encouraging. "The dialogue just sounds a little off to me. So I want to get your opinion, too."

"Right. I get it. Thanks."

"And?" With great restraint I manage not to make twirling "come on already" motions with my hand.

"I . . . well . . . um . . . Have you asked Blake?"

"No," I say, unable to dodge the invisible steel bar that immediately straightens my spine. "I haven't talked with him today." A fact that I was particularly proud of since he'd dragged his sorry ass down to the backlot today, despite not being on the call sheet. I'd managed to avoid him since I arrived for my five a.m. makeup call, and really hoped that my winning streak would continue.

Another shrug from my wishy-washy assistant. "It's just that, you know, since you play Mel and he plays Stryker, maybe it makes more sense for you to be asking him about the dialogue."

Out of the mouths of babes. And I mean "babes" in the total Hollywood sense of the word. Blond. Stacked. You get the picture.

The irritating truth is that she's right. I should be talking to Blake. Except, I don't want to act opposite Blake, much less talk to him. Not anymore, anyway.

"So, like, do you want me to go see if Mr. Harmon needs you anymore today?"

"Sure," I say, suddenly thrilled with the prospect of being left alone. "And could you do me a fav? I'm completely parched. Go track down an Evian and some lemon for me." I happen to know that craft services ran out of lemon slices around eleven. She'll be gone for hours.

She gives me a mini-salute and then leaves. I sigh and close my eyes, my thumb idly rubbing the edge of the script as my mind begins to drift. The reason I'm so pumped up about making sure the dialogue is perfect is that I know this scene's going to be a tough one. Not only because of the emotional intensity required to nail a scene like that, but because of the personal history between me and Blake Atwood.

In the movie, Blake plays Stryker, an ex-marine turned reluctant bodyguard to Mel. In real life, Blake is my ex, a little fact that you probably already know if you've gone grocery shopping recently. Because despite my best efforts to keep my private life private, our entire relationship—from courtship to our recent pyrotechnical breakup—was played out on the covers of magazines ranging from *Entertainment Weekly* to *People* to *Us*. My mother doesn't even bother to call me anymore to find out what's new in my love life. She just reads the *Enquirer* while standing in the checkout line at the grocery store.

And the coverage wasn't limited to the tabloids and the weeklies. No, even the "classier" mags got in on the buzz. When we were cast to star in the movie together (and still quite cozy with each other), Blake did an interview with *Maxim*. I let my publicity team talk me into doing an interview and photo spread with *Vanity Fair*. (That, of course, was a Very Big Deal, since everyone in Hollywood knows that I've been Miss Ultra-Private these days.)

All in all, our romance blossomed within a circus of tabloids, Internet rumors, and obnoxious paparazzi. And then when we broke up a little over two weeks ago . . . well, that's when the press really went crazy. There was speculation, gossip, innuendo, and the inevitable interviews with former costars and directors. The works.

All in all, a major headache. Especially for someone like me who has a hate-hate relationship with the tabloids.

I didn't always feel that way. Once upon a time, I was the tabloids' favorite It girl—the young hip celebrity who bebopped to all the clubs, had a good time with my friends, and was more than happy to let snippets of my life show up in the *Enquirer* or on *E!*

That all changed five years ago when a deranged fan attacked me in my house. He stripped me, touched me, hurt me, and completely humiliated me. He whispered things and called me his "darling Devi." Then he left without a trace, the police completely unable to find him.

Survive something like that, and it alters the way you look at the world.

Immediately after the attack, everyone expected me to be a basket case. Even me. But then time passed, and my friends and colleagues started suggesting that maybe I was obsessing a bit.

That the move and the alarms and the moratorium on publicity were overkill. That I should simply "move on" and be the same happy-go-lucky party girl again.

Like hell.

Still, maybe they were right. I don't know. But I couldn't do it. All I knew was that I was scared. And I was a complete emotional wreck. I started popping antianxiety meds. I slept with the light on. And I absolutely, positively went ballistic if anything was published about me that didn't originate from my own PR team.

And since it's near impossible to keep the paparazzi from snapping pics if you're out in public, I pretty much stopped going out. I turned into a recluse, hiding out in my newly purchased Beverly Hills home (complete with state-of-the-art security measures and a realtor who swore on her mother's grave that my address would never be revealed).

Of course I still went out into the world, but I was careful. I shopped in the Valley instead of on the Westside. I wore baggy clothes, sunglasses, and baseball caps. I did everything I could not to stand out.

The good news: it worked.

The bad news: it worked.

Not only did the paparazzi forget about me, but so did the industry. I didn't work for three years while I sorted it all out. For a while, I even considered quitting the business. But I don't know any other life. When you start out at age four as the fresh new face in a Spielberg movie, star in a few blockbusters after that, then bounce to a television show that lasts six years, you realize that fantasy is the only life you know.

The thing is, I may have been in some major blockbusters as a kid, but once I emerged from my three-year cocoon, I was no longer the hot young thing. I'd moved from being an "actress" to being a "celebrity." And not even an A-list celebrity.

Honestly, the whole situation sucked, especially for a girl like me who just wanted to act again. I'd like to say that this business is all about your acting chops, but the truth is, it isn't. Yes, I landed some parts in low-budget indie films after my seclusion, but they hardly broke box office records, if you know what I mean. Once you disappear in Hollywood, it can be hard to come back with a bang. That one, I learned the hard way.

But like I said, this is the only world I know . . . and the truth is, I like it. And, yes, I'm competitive.

I want the blockbusters. I want my old career back.

And that's why I jumped when Tobias came knocking. This movie, *The Givenchy Code,* is set up to be the studio's tentpole blockbuster. It's a flick that can put me back on the map. And I leaped at the chance to star in it.

I didn't hesitate even when Tobias made it absolutely clear that I had to shed my disdain for the whole publicity machine. He didn't go so far as to say that I had to put on a happy face and smile, smile, smile for the paparazzi, but he really didn't need to. I knew what he wanted from me. *Buzz.* And boy did he get it, in spades.

And the truth? I didn't really mind. When he signed me on, it had been over four years since the attack, and I knew that I needed to lighten up. So when Tobias announced that he wanted Blake to play Stryker, I loosened up even more. After all,

I'd been dating Blake for months by that time. And how cool that I was set to costar against my boyfriend?

Besides, *Givenchy* is Blake's first movie. He's been behind the scenes for years, choreographing fight scenes and doing the technical consultant gig for martial arts sequences. But he's never been on camera until now. And what good is your big Hollywood break without tons of publicity? (Not that my opinion mattered too much in the long run. Elliot Kelly, Blake's manager, was absolutely adamant that his boy make the cover of every gossip rag in the country. Elliot, in my opinion, is a total ass. But he knows how to handle a career.)

So there we were, basking in the warm and loving glow of the camera flashbulbs and the entertainment reporters' congratulations on our hot-and-heavy romance. Gossip was swirling, pictures were posted, and I wasn't even freaking out. I had a great part, a great career, and a great boyfriend. I was back on my feet and back squarely in the public eye.

Finally, I'd put the assault behind me.

Or so I thought.

Things changed when Blake and I broke up. Suddenly the tabloids that had seemed warm and friendly were harsh and invasive. Bits of my life were sneaking into the press that had no business being there. Personal things that I longed to keep private were being discussed in break rooms all across America. Bloggers speculated about my career and my love life. And whenever I was out in public, cameras snapped as the paparazzi tried to get a candid shot of my broken-hearted face.

I desperately wanted to call for a second take, but life doesn't work that way. Life happens once, and then it's in the can. So I was stuck. Stuck playing against an ex-lover. Stuck with my life plastered over newsstands across America.

Most of all, I was stuck with the fear that by letting my relationship back into the tabloids, I'd opened a door. I'd attracted attention.

And I'm afraid it's going to start up all over again.

Chapter

3

Devi Taylor.

She surrounded him, filled him. Her energy meshed with his, and they were one.

He didn't understand how she could not know that. How she could move through the world without him. Or even why she'd want to.

Five years ago, he'd given her the chance. But had she come into his arms as she should have? Had she opened herself? Welcomed him?

She hadn't. And even now the pain of her rejection cut him like a knife.

She'd been blinded somehow. Damaged. And the knowledge that she didn't understand their connection had come close to destroying him.

How she could be so distant? So unaware of the truth? Especially since he'd known for years that they had a connection. Known from the first time he'd seen her. A tiny bit of a girl, her dark hair in a pixie cut. Her cheeks rosy. Her wide mouth beckoning to him. She'd been barely five, but he could see deep into those liquid brown eyes.

She'd known.

She'd known what she was doing, and she'd set out to seduce him. She'd tempted him like a minx, like a whore. And he'd fallen for her completely.

He'd been barely fourteen then, and he'd seen her first movie over and over, spending his entire allowance on a ticket to the first showing, then hiding in the bathroom and sneaking into every showing that followed.

He'd gone to the theater armed with a box of Kleenex and wearing loose shorts. He'd sat in the back, keeping his low groans to himself, his mind absorbing the girl on the screen. She was there for him, and only for him.

Each time he went into the theater excited and desperate, and each time he left ashamed. *She* did that to him. His sweet little whore who tempted and teased and knew that she was driving him crazy.

If he'd been caught, there would have been trouble. *They* wouldn't understand. His parents. The theater staff. Even his friends. He'd been going steady with Amy Myers, an empty shell of a girl from his homeroom, and she'd wanted to go see the movie together. He'd tried to explain why they couldn't go. That the movie was his alone. She'd stood in his bedroom and seen the magazines and photos and articles about Devi.

And then she'd called him a freak.

Two years later they'd found themselves in the same homeroom. Amy had teased him again. Asked if Devi Taylor had grown up and fallen in love with him. She'd told her friends about his bulletin board. About how he'd made a collage of Devi's face. About how he got off by looking at pictures of a little girl.

Her words had shocked him. He'd let her see the pictures because he'd wanted her to understand why he couldn't be with her. He was already committed to Devi. He'd let her down easy. He'd been *nice*.

And there she was, turning it into something sordid. Something dirty.

He wasn't the dirty one. Amy, however . . .

Well, obviously, Amy was obsessed with him. How else would she know about his sessions in the theaters? About what he did at home under the covers with Devi's picture pressed to his chest?

She'd been spying on him. The bitch. The little cunt.

She'd been spying, and she had to pay.

In the end, it had been remarkably easy. Their town was small, and parents didn't worry about their kids. Girls walked home alone all the time. And the park adjacent to the town square had lots of bushes abutting the walking paths.

Of course, once her body had been found, it had become the scandal of the century. A straight-A high school student knifed in the park. Dead. And absolutely no evidence pointing to a killer.

The police had interviewed him, but that hadn't been any big deal. They'd interviewed all the kids. And the cops never once mentioned Devi, so presumably the other students hadn't told them about how Amy had razzed him. In that, he took special satisfaction. It had taken all of his self-control, but he'd waited a full six months before killing her.

He'd stayed home. Played computer games. Watched movies with actresses less stellar than his Devi. And when they did meet, he was nothing but polite. Hardly a man with a motive. And during that time, he'd never once mentioned Devi. Never once let any other student see him with her picture or a magazine with her on the cover. Did nothing that would remind anyone of Amy's hurtful words.

The waiting hadn't been easy, but he'd considered it a test of his endurance. The wait to eliminate Amy had been nothing compared to his wait for Devi. But wait he had, and patiently. Because he'd known that, ultimately, she would be his.

And then, he'd seen his opportunity. Realized that the time was right for them to consummate their love. He'd gone to her, expecting to be welcomed. Hell, he'd gone out of his way to find her, jumping through all sorts of ridiculous hoops designed to keep pathetic fans away. But not him. Never him. *He* wasn't pathetic. He was hers.

And when she saw him, he'd been certain that they would be joined forever.

She'd been late that evening, and he'd spent the time getting to know her even better. Opening drawers. Touching her clothes. Inhaling her scent. He'd strewn rose petals on the bed and lit candles.

He'd expected her to love him. To want him. To cleave to him with joy in her heart.

It hadn't happened that way.

She'd been distant. Cold. And though her distance had enraged him, he'd also been calm enough to realize that he'd waited too long. She'd been damaged. He'd done everything he could to remind her of their bond, their connection, their *love*, but she refused to open up to him.

In the end, he'd fled, then hid, fueled by a fear of the system that wouldn't understand his passion should they find him. But he never gave up on possessing Devi. And, yes, she would need to be punished, too. She'd turned away from him, after all. Brought other men into her bed and gave herself to them despite the bond between them.

Her behavior, of course, was unacceptable. Which left only the question of what to do . . . and when.

He'd had no answer, but he'd waited and watched, secure in the knowledge that what was meant to be would come to pass. His destiny was with Devi, no matter how twisted the path to get there.

The answer had come from the most unexpected of sources. And yet it was absolutely perfect. As if fate had been building to nothing more than this single moment. The moment that he possessed Devi, body and soul.

With a thin smile, he looked at his computer, nestled in the heart of the room. The bright screen seemed to wink at him, as if they shared a secret. For years, he'd used it to peruse the Internet to find pictures and articles about Devi. Occasionally, he'd log on to a computer game or slip into a chat room. But for the most part, his computer served only one purpose. Just like the room itself—hell, just like him—the sole raison d'être was Devi.

He got up and walked slowly to the nearest wall, running his hand reverentially over the collage mounted there. A tribute to her beauty. Her eyes. Her mouth. Her wondrously thick hair.

His fingertips danced over her features, his cock hardening even as he touched her in his mind.

Soon, my darling. Soon.

He'd been renting the place for years, ever since he'd moved from Oklahoma so that he could be closer to her. He'd learned about the place from the e-mail loop for a Devi Taylor fan club. The building's owner was a fan, too, and had been advertising for a tenant. The apartment was perfect, with just enough space. A place where he could be with Devi. Where he could count the minutes until they could be together.

He'd outfitted this room before furnishing the rest of the place. Blackout shades to keep out the sun and prying eyes. Corkboard over all the walls so that photographs and articles could be easily displayed. Images culled from magazines, newspapers, printed from the Internet. Even a few special photos he'd taken himself on the rare occasion that he'd caught a glimpse of her in a restaurant or at an event.

Built-in desks lined each wall of the study, and the evenly spaced televisions played Devi's movies and network appearances on a constant loop. The sound was off, but the room was not silent. Instead, the sound tracks from her movies played softly in the background.

He moved to the computer, his hand caressing it like a lover as he read the message addressed to Janus, his gaming identity. An historic message. One that not only started the game, but ensured that he would soon possess what he had coveted all his life: Devi Taylor.

He'd read the message over a dozen times already, and he'd followed the instructions to the letter. Everything was in place. *He* was in place.

He'd been chosen. Just as he'd chosen Devi so many years ago.

He breathed deeply, relishing the feel of cool air filling his lungs. Like the ancient Roman god, he boasted two faces. One seen, one hidden. And now it was time for the hidden to step from the shadows and into the light.

He was Janus.

And he was going to win the game.

I stand up and start to pace my trailer. I've actually gone quite a few months without thinking about the attack, so it's frustrating that these thoughts now swirl around in my head. I thought I had better self-control. Hell, forget *better*. I just thought that I *had* control.

The phone rings, and I jump, then curse my own antsiness. I find my cell phone in the small sofa's cushion and flip it open, not bothering to check caller ID. I don't give out this number to just anyone, so I know already that the caller must be on my approved friend list.

"How did it go?" the voice at the other end asks.

I frown, trying to figure out who it is.

"Devi? Are you there? It's Mel."

"Oh!" I say, and then feel stupid. I'd spent two weeks in Washington, D.C., with Mel researching the part, and then she'd flown out and spent a week at my house, all expenses paid by the studio, of course.

The second trip was ostensibly for research, but the truth was, I would have been fine without it. No, I'd invited her out because we'd hit it off. Mel's scrappy, and I like that. She's also scarily smart, but since she can shop with the best of us, I don't hold that against her. (And for the record, I'm no slouch academically. I just don't have a bunch of initials after my name.)

"Sorry," I say. "I didn't recognize your voice. But it went great. I mean, we only did a few scenes today, but we did the race-away-from-Todd's-killer scene, and you can imagine how traumatic that one was."

"Trust me," she says. "I don't need to imagine."

"No. I guess you don't." Mel went through real hell. Fortunately, I'm only playing a role.

"And you're happy with the script? Andy was so gung-ho for you to star, but then once you really did sign on, I think he was nervous that you wouldn't like the script." Andrew Garrison is our story consultant. From what I understand, he was the brains behind shepherding the whole project through the Hollywood quagmire.

"I think the script is awesome," I say, meaning it.

"Well, good. He's had nothing but good things to say about you and the writers and the producer."

I give her the blow-by-blow of the day's shoot, plus some gossip about the production as a whole. After that we move on to other subjects like fashion and travel and her new husband, Matthew. I'm grateful that she doesn't ask about Blake. She knows the story of our breakup; and she also knows that it's not exactly high on my list of favorite conversation topics.

After a good twenty minutes of chatter, we finally say good-bye, and when I hang up the phone, I realize I'm smiling. I like Mel, and the fact that we've become friends means a lot to me.

I'm standing there thinking sappy thoughts about friends and stuff when there's a tap at the door. Since this is a closed set—with airtight security—I know it must be someone from the cast or crew, and I holler for the person to come in. After a brief pause, the door opens a crack and Mackenzie Draper slides in. She's my stunt double, and when she's in full makeup it's like looking in a mirror. Even now—when she's not the least bit made up—the resemblance is uncanny. "You okay?" she says.

I blink, because that's so out of the blue. "Of course I am. Why?"

"Just a vibe."

"A vibe," I repeat, but I'm really not surprised. I'd been thinking about the attack earlier, and Mac is damnably intuitive, especially about me. Or maybe it's just that after working on five movies together, she knows how to read me.

"Is it the story?"

"Huh?"

"The movie," she says, one hand reaching out to vaguely indicate the movie set. "A freaky assassin targeting one specific girl. You know. I thought it might have . . . well . . . you know."

"Creeped me out?"

"It does seem like a rather odd project for you to choose. I mean, considering what Janus did . . ."

Janus. My attacker had told me he'd had two faces. *The one you see, and the one I show to the world.*

I shiver with the memory I'd tried so hard to suppress. Even now I can feel the whisper of his breath on my ear as he bound my hands. "I am like the god Janus, and I have come for you, my darling."

He'd made me plead for my life, plead for him to stop the pain. And once he'd completely humiliated me, he'd simply disappeared.

I'd given descriptions, succumbed to medical tests so they could take DNA, the works. But so far, no sign of him. It's like he moved into a cave.

I've blocked many of the details, but the humiliation and the fear have stayed with me. I still wake up in a cold sweat, certain he's in my house.

The name stayed, too, and even now in my dreams I hear him calling to me, whispering his name and urging me to come. *Janus. You belong to Janus.*

Bile rises in my throat, and I choke it back down. I'm past this. I just need to keep remembering that I'm past this.

Janus may have turned me into a victim, but with this role, *I'm* the one who wins.

Not that I intend to go into all of that with Mac. Instead, I just shrug and say, "It's a good role."

"It's a great role," she agrees. "But—"

"It's a great role," I say again, only more firmly this time.

She looks at me for a second, then nods and heads to my fridge. I sigh, because she's right. The role did get to me today. It took me a good two hours to get my mind back after shooting the race-down-the-street scene this morning—and that was just me. No bad guy. No assassin. No dead bodies.

For a second I wonder if I've gotten in over my head. I push the thoughts away, though. The role is awesome, my career needs a jump start desperately, and I'm grateful beyond words that Tobias brought it to me.

Tobias and I have done two films together—one when I was ten and another more recently. The one from age ten earned me an Oscar nod. The one three years ago? That one barely broke even. But Tobias is a great guy. He believes in me, and he supported me through my personal hell. More, he went to bat for me with the studio.

Before this project, I'd been deep in career-resuscitation mode. My agent and manager were both on the case, and I read every script I could get my hands on.

Nada.

I don't know if there are no good scripts in Hollywood or if they were just circumventing me, but about a year ago, I was reaching the point of desperation. I debated the value of an extreme makeover, firing my manager, or sleeping with an A-list director. (Just kidding on that last one. Sort of. After all, I went into rehab for meds, not sex.) Then along came this role. Literally the answer to my prayers. Not only does the script itself seriously rock (with the minor exception of a few bits of clunky dialogue), but the story is based on fact. And not *just* fact. No, this story is based on absolutely mind-blowingly unbelievable fact.

Play. Survive. Win. Ring any bells?

It's an amazingly popular online multiplayer computer game. The whole thing takes place in a computer version of New York City, with three players running around trying to win the game and survive. There's a target, an assassin, and a protector for each game, but there can be an infinite number of games going on at any one time, which is one of the things that made the game so popular with your average computer geek gaming dude, or so the material they gave me with the script said. The players do pretty much what the role describes. The target is the player that the assassin is trying to kill. And the protector is trying to keep the target safe. And if the target makes it to the end, the prize is real money. Lots of it. And when the game hit the cyberworld, it was an instant hit, with millions of players around the globe.

All by itself, PSW was news. But the story underlying our screenplay wasn't news at all. Instead, it was secret . . . and damn scary, too. Because someone started to play the game in the real world. And Melanie Prescott—a graduate student with a passion for math, codes, and all things Givenchy—suddenly found herself on a scavenger hunt across New York with a killer on her heels. An assassin who was just as determined to kill Mel as she was to stay alive. Her only help came in the form of Matthew Stryker, a very hunky, very competent ex-marine.

A true story. A crazed killer. And a computer game brought to life in the real world. *That* kind of platform is what gets a movie buzz.

In other words, this movie has all the markings of a pivotal role for me, and I knew that from the get-go.

It wasn't just about my career, though. It was about confronting my own demons in the safety of a celluloid bubble. And Lord knows I've got the emotional depth to pull off Melanie's terror.

None of that, however, is something I want to chat about with Mackenzie.

Fortunately for me, she's lost interest in the conversation. Once she decided my "vibe" wasn't too bad, she turned her attention from my refrigerator to my cookie stash, and now she is down on her hands and knees, rummaging through the box I keep under the little sofa in my trailer.

"I should never have told you that was there," I say.

She makes a rude noise, but keeps rummaging. I sigh and tell her to toss me one of the packets of Fig Newtons.

"See? That's why you told me. The more people who know this is here, the fewer treats there are for you to pick through."

"Are you suggesting I have no self-control?"

"Honey, I *know* you have no self-control. Anyone who's ever read *Entertainment Weekly* knows that."

I very politely shoot her the bird, but I smile while I'm doing it. There's something about Mackenzie's laid back yet straight-shooting manner that always puts me at ease.

"So did you really come because you felt a vibe, or did you just want cookies?"

"Gummy bears," she says, holding up a packet. "And none of the above."

"Really? Then what's up?" That she just came to hang out isn't in the realm of possibility. We get along great, but for whatever reason we've never crossed the line to being true friends. I actually kind of regret that—and I've made overtures—but she always keeps her distance. Tobias says it's a work ethic thing. She's more crew than cast, and I'm the Star. I think that's a load of crap . . . but at the same time I fear he may be right.

She looks distinctly uncomfortable, so I ask again. "Mac?"

"I just wanted to let you know that Blake's on the lot."

"Well, yes," I say, trying for professional. "He is in the movie."

She rolls her eyes. "You cannot possibly be so dense."

"Fine," I say. "I'm irritated beyond belief that he's here today."

"Well, I hate to add more bad news to the pile, but he's here for an interview."

"An interview," I repeat, dully. I'm not a big fan of Blake giving interviews. Somehow, I always seem to get screwed in the process. "With who?"

"Not sure," she says. "I just saw them setting up."

I give a nod and try to act unconcerned. If I can't actually *be* unconcerned, acting is the next best thing.

From a purely intellectual standpoint, it's fascinating how far I've come in just the last few months. When Tobias hired Blake, I was over the moon. Not only were Blake and I already happily ensconced in romance-land, but Blake happens to be perfect for the role. He just *looks* marine, if you know what I mean. And he's a natural with the martial arts stuff. He started out teaching karate (or some kung-fu-type stuff), then segued to choreographing it for movies and television. That's how we met—on the set of my last movie, a B-level action flick that really was a lot of fun to make even if it did nada for my career. And since he'd dated one or two celebs before me, Blake was already front and center with the tabloids.

Once we started dating, of course, his tabloid-coolness factor bumped even higher. And when he actually got cast, his status with the paparazzi skyrocketed. A little bit weird considering the man hasn't even been on-screen yet, but that's the way the industry works these days.

Originally Tobias had hired him as a consultant for the action sequences. But then Tobias let the camera roll during one choreography session. He watched the footage at home that night and canceled the scheduled screen tests for Stryker. Blake, he said, was the guy.

He got no argument from me. Which in retrospect turned out to be a mistake, since we broke up almost exactly one month after Tobias signed Blake. And as much as I begged Tobias to fire Blake's sorry ass, he has that irritatingly smug director mentality, and thinks that he knows best. And since I'm not Angelina Jolie (although I do look a bit like her, what with the long dark hair and wide mouth), I don't have the clout to tell Tobias to dump Blake or I walk.

The clout or the guts, frankly.

And, yes, Blake *is* a decent actor, but this movie is supposed to be my vehicle. A way for me to prove that I'm back in the game. Not a centerpiece for Blake to get his jollies with the press.

"So, you okay?" Mackenzie asks through a mouthful of gummy bears.

"Sure. Of course." Although to be honest, I'm not okay. Because I shouldn't be worried about Blake and publicity. I shouldn't be worried about Blake at all. After all, I'm a professional, right? Just because I used to date my costar doesn't mean—

Tap, tap, tap.

The sharp rapping at the door draws my attention, and Mac and I both swivel our heads in that direction.

"Susie," I say. Then, louder, "Come on in. Did you track down lemons?"

"Depends on what you call a lemon," comes the response, in an oh-so-familiar voice. And then the door opens and there's the man himself, his broad smile and dancing eyes still more than enough to make my knees go weak. "That convertible I bought last year was a piece of shit."

"Well, gee," Mackenzie says brightly. "These trailers just really aren't big enough for three people." She aims herself like a bullet for the door and squeezes past Blake with a "catch you later." He steps inside, the door closes behind him, and we're alone for the first time in weeks. Little needle stabs of pain zing my heart, but I can't help the little leap of joy, too. Because he's Blake and I do love him. Love was never a problem. (Neither was sex, for that matter, but that isn't really an issue at the moment.)

"You should have listened to me," I finally say. As repartee goes, it's pretty lame. But it's the best I can come up with.

"About the car?"

"About a lot of things," I say, looking him straight in the eye.

I push myself out of my chair and head to the refrigerator. It's mostly empty, but I have a stash of Diet Cokes and a box of divinity, which has been my absolute favorite candy since some appeared in my Easter basket at age five. Each day I allow myself only one Diet Coke (the carbonation makes it harder to lose weight, according to my trainer, and the caffeine makes me jumpy) and two pieces of divinity. I grab a soda and eye the candy, which is now a hell of a lot more appealing than my Newtons. Unfortunately, I ate my allotment earlier (my reward for both surviving the scene and nailing it).

I'm still holding the unopened snack-size package of Fig Newtons, and I'd been secretly proud of myself for not ripping into them despite temptation. Now, though, temptation be damned. I toss the package aside and dive for the divinity. Because if it's a question of fortitude by sugar or facing Blake unarmed, I'm going for the candy.

He watches but doesn't say anything, and I give him points for that. He knows about my divinity rule. And he also knows that I invariably snarf my allotment after nailing a scene. So he has to know that he's driven me to this—it's his fault I've fallen off the candy wagon.

Frankly, I hope he's wallowing in guilt. But at the same time, I'm grateful that he's wallowing quietly.

"What's up?" I ask, after I've swallowed. I'm silently congratulating myself on not leaping on him immediately and demanding to know what the heck he's doing coming on the set when he doesn't even have scenes scheduled today.

"Interview," he says.

I narrow my eyes. I know him too well, and something's up. This is more than just an interview. "With who?" I say, cautiously.

"Letterman," he says, and I immediately bristle.

"That isn't even funny." I'm impressed that my voice comes out normal despite my shock and anger. I never dreamed Blake would be that cruel.

"I'm serious," he says. He gestures vaguely toward the north. "They're setting up on the set."

"Why are you doing this?" I ask. Letterman shoots in New York, so I know he's just being a prick. But I don't understand why.

"Satellite feed," he says.

"Bullshit. Letterman doesn't do satellite feed."

Blake just shrugs. "I guess he does now."

I just stare. I'm honestly not sure if he's telling the truth or lying. Frankly, I can't imagine why he'd do either.

"Apparently the producers thought that since my last appearance was about landing my first movie role, my second appearance should be from the set."

"Uh-huh." I lick my lips and fight for control. "And you thought that would be smart? Or was this Elliot's idea? Either way, I can totally see the appeal. I mean, you got so much publicity with the first appearance, another one should go over even bigger. Too bad you haven't got a new girlfriend. You could break up with her on television and really pump up your PR quotient."

"Dammit, Devi. I didn't break up with—"

"Don't even start with me."

"Devi—" His tone is harsh, warning. And I really don't give a damn. *Technically* maybe he didn't break up with me on television, but the hurt is still the same. And the humiliation.

"Just go." My throat is thick, and tears are starting to well. If he doesn't get out of here soon, I'm going to lose it. And I *really* don't want him to know that I'm still a basket case. As far as he's concerned I am *so* over Blake Atwood.

"Would you just listen? I thought we could do it—"

I hold up a hand. *"Go!"*

A myriad of expressions play across his face, so fast that I'm unable to catch and latch on to one until his face freezes into neutral and one hand raises in a dismissive fashion. "Fine. I'll go."

"Good."

And then he turns, like he can just waltz in here and drop a bombshell any old time. An unexpected burst of anger rips through me and everything just spews out. "You son of a bitch!" I grab the Fig Newton package and toss it at him. It's too late, though. He's already gone, and they smash ineffectively against the door.

I'm a complete emotional mess, and I shatter, too. The tears flood out, warm against my cheeks. Tears for what I could have had with him, and tears for what we'd lost.

But most of all, they're tears of anger and frustration. Because our relationship ended on *that* show. No warning. No hint that anything about our relationship was bothering him.

Just *boom.*

And now he's doing a segment here? On the lot?

He's just cavalierly throwing it all back in my face?

The thought makes me sick to my stomach, and I want to lash out. I want to do something.

I want to humiliate him the way he humiliated me.

Maybe I was reluctant at first to get back into the PR game, but I'm in it now, and I'm more than capable of upping the ante.

I stand up, my body thrumming with anger-fueled adrenaline. It's time to pull out the red stiletto pumps and go have a chat with the boys from *Letterman.*

I haven't played the diva for years . . . but that doesn't mean I don't remember how.

Chapter

5

"I found the lemons!" Susie trots alongside me, breathless, a mesh bag stuffed with lemons swinging in her hand. "But they're out of Evian."

"No problem," I say, without breaking my stride. "Considering my mood, sucking on a lemon will do me just fine."

"Oh."

Since I've clearly thrown her for a loop, I take pity on her. "I'll take these," I say, reaching for the sack. "You can head home if you want. Unless you have some rotten tomatoes?"

I can't resist the last bit, but I probably should have, because I think I just fried her brain. I wave the comment away. "Never mind. Really. I'll see you tomorrow."

" 'Kay." She takes a step backward, then stops and nods in the direction I'm heading. "So, um, what's with Blake?"

"What do you mean?" I ask warily.

"They had all the lights and stuff set up for some interview, and now they're striking everything."

"So?"

"So I don't think they did the interview."

That stops me. "You have to be wrong. They must have done it already."

"Dunno," she says. "Maybe." Which is incredibly *un*helpful, but in this instance, I can't really fault her.

Apparently Susie isn't up for speculation, though, because she trots off, a lot faster in her tennis shoes than I can handle in my blood-red pumps. (And, yes, I really did change clothes. I'm wearing skin-tight distressed jeans that I bought at a charity auction, a white blouse with a plunging neckline contrasted by innocent eyelet material, and my favorite Prada pumps. If I'm going into a confrontation, I'm going to damn well look my best.)

As I watch her leave, I spot Elliot beside the wardrobe trailer. He sees me and starts to walk in the other direction, but I'm having none of that. "Elliot!" I call in my most self-important voice. "Hold up a second." (A command, not a request. Am I good, or what?)

"What is it, Miss Taylor?" he asks, tapping his watch. "I'm running late."

"I won't keep you. I just wanted to find out where Blake's shooting the *Letterman* segment. I thought it might be good for the movie if they do a snippet with the two of us together." I flash my widest smile. It's phony, manipulative, and he totally knows it. I, of course, expect an equally phony yet polite response.

"You conniving bitch," he spits, which isn't polite at all. "What did you say to him in your trailer? What the *hell* have you done?"

"Are you out of your mind? I haven't done a thing!" I'm completely unnerved by his rage. Elliot and I have never gotten along well (I think he's a charlatan, and he thinks I've fallen too low on the celebrity totem pole for his newly hot client). So I didn't expect him to be excited about my offer. But this? This is psychotic!

He points a finger at me. "This interview was essential to Blake's career. And I swear, if I could get Tobias to fire your skinny little ass, I would!"

I hold up my hands in defense. "What did I do?"

But he just shakes his head and walks away. I'm tempted to go after him, but honestly, I'm too baffled. What the hell was he talking about?

Clearly my diva has nosedived, and I'm left standing on the backlot utterly flabbergasted. At a time like this there's really only one option. I pull out my cell phone, hit number 2 on the speed dial, and tap my foot impatiently.

"I need retail therapy," I say, the second I hear her pick up.

Lindy's delicate laugh seeps through the line, and I picture her sitting at her desk, wire-frame glasses perched on her nose, a coffee cup within arm's reach, and a forest's worth of paper spread out on the desk in front of her. "You're rich and famous," she says dryly. "You're not allowed to have bad days."

"Fuck you," I say, but oh so politely. She laughs, of course, because she's been my best friend since age three and knows me too well. We lived next door to each other growing up. I had the celebrity shtick. She had public school. We played at each other's houses, our moms were friends, and when I got my Academy Award nomination, she spent her allowance to buy alcohol-free champagne and told me that if my head got too big she'd never return my Malibu Barbie.

That sealed it. We were friends for life.

Seriously, I love Lindy like a sister. In a business where knowing who your real friends are can feel a lot like you're playing a real-life game of *Deal or No Deal,* it's nice to have someone who would love me even if I were serving weenies at Tail O' the Pup.

"So what's up?" she asks, serious now. "Blake?"

"Yes," I admit. "But not the way you think. In fact, I'm not even sure what to think."

"You should just get back in bed with him. Not only is the man total eye candy, but he loves you. And you two were good together."

"*Were* being the operative word."

"Devi," she says in the mom-tone she acquired after giving birth to my godchild two years ago.

I hold up a hand to silence her, which is ridiculous since she isn't even there. "Don't even start," I say, and hear her very loud silence in response. "Damn it, Lindy!"

"What? I didn't say a thing!"

"I heard you thinking."

"You're paranoid," she says. "I would never think a critical thought about you. You are perfect in every way."

I roll my eyes and try not to snort. It's a bad habit—I snort when I laugh. Fortunately, no one has caught that on tape yet.

I'm reaching the end of New York Street, which means that I'm almost to the lot where I left my car. "So what do you say?

Will truth, justice, and the Hollywood movie machine collapse if you take the rest of the afternoon off?"

"They'll survive," she says. "My boss, I'm not so sure about." Lindy is an attorney for Universal. Her boss, Richard, is an absentminded professor sort. He's absolutely brilliant, but also absolutely scattered. Lindy isn't exaggerating when she says the world as I know it might collapse if she leaves him unattended. After all, in the current state of the industry, lawyers are just as important to the movie-making process as the actors, the director, and the script.

"So you can't?" I am crushed. I'm suffering from severe Prada withdrawal, but shopping by yourself when you're depressed is just pathetic. Shopping with a friend, however, is therapeutic.

"What time?"

"I can be there in thirty."

"Make it an hour. And meet me at the bar."

She means the bar in the Regent Beverly Wilshire, of course. Just a stone's throw from Prada. And because she's my best friend, she also knows that *has* to be my intended destination. "Will do."

"And I need to get some stuff for Lucy. So let's hit the children's boutiques, too."

"Retail therapy is an adult shopping experience," I say, but just for form.

"Hey," she says. "It's for me. Those little baby capris really show off my calf muscles."

I tell her she's a loon, then sign off. As I slip my phone back into my bag, I realize I'm somewhat happy. It feels nice, too. Considering that my morning started off with terror (albeit fake), then moved to frustration, anger, and complete bafflement, a little bit of friendship is just the ticket. And friendship with a martini or a Cosmopolitan would be even better. And, yes, I gave up alcohol when I gave up the pills, but I'm still going strong with the virgin variety. Fortunately, the bartenders at the Beverly Wilshire make one mean nonalcoholic Cosmopolitan.

"Devi! Wait up!"

I turn and see Andrew Garrison hurrying toward me. I like Andy, but I wish he hadn't called out to me. Because when I turn, I get a full view of Blake strolling down New York Street. He sees me, too, and holds up a hand in a tentative wave. My chest tightens, and I fight the urge to go toward him.

Then I see that he's with Elliot, and I no longer have to fight—I'm staying way the hell away from that one.

Not that I have much choice. Elliot shoots me a fierce look, takes Blake's elbow, and starts walking with him in the opposite direction. As I watch, I see Blake jerk away. Then he turns and points to me. He puts his fingers to his ear in the universal symbol for "Call me."

No way, Jose.

I turn away, unnerved, baffled, and thinking the kind of lusty thoughts that I really didn't want to think about Blake. Not anymore.

I shake off the thoughts and try to focus on Andy, who is now breathless beside me, a book of Sudoku puzzles tucked under his arm as usual.

No luck; I'm still thinking about Blake. And Lindy's right, of course: I still love him. But like I already said, love really isn't our problem. Trust and commitment, however . . .

I sigh. Damn Lindy for putting the thoughts in my head. And damn me for falling for him in the first place.

"Heading out?" Andy asks, obviously completely uninterested in either Blake or my lust.

"Meeting a friend for shopping," I say, my voice as reverential as if I were talking about a religious experience.

"You must be heading toward Prada."

"Yeah," I say. "How did you know?"

He just laughs and shakes his head. "Devi, your fascination with Prada isn't exactly breaking news."

Okay. He has a point. And I would blush, except that I'm not in the least bit embarrassed by my Prada-lust. Prada, I figure, is totally worthy.

"You did great today," he says. "Your performance was dead-on."

"Thanks. That means a lot." I'm not lying when I say that. Andy is the one person on the set who has personal experience with Play.Survive.Win. Not only was Andy forced to play the game—and almost died doing it—but he's been working with Mel for a few years now, trying to locate other game survivors. Apparently he was some kind of tech-head before he got sucked into the game. In other words, he's a total computer geek, and I know he's been a lot of help to Mel, investigating Web sites and stuff that have been used as clues in the real-life version of the game. More important for my purposes, though, he's the movie's story consultant. And that means he's been working closely with Tobias, the screenwriters, and the producers for months.

"When I first suggested to Mel that we turn her story into a movie, I told her you'd be perfect for the role," he says. "And then when we started negotiating with the studio and Tobias, I kept pushing. I mean, I've seen all of your movies, so I knew you could nail the part. I'm really pleased to see that I was right."

Okay, *now* I'm going to blush. "That's really sweet, Andy." I'm not sure what else to say. I mean, I'm glad that he thinks I'm good in the role. *That* part is flattering. But I can also tell that Andy has a little bit of that fan-boy thing going on.

Normally, that would give me pause. Clingy obnoxious fans freak me out (for obvious reasons). But Andy is of the polite breed. He's also part of the production team, which makes him safe. All of which means that his fan status is charming rather than creepy.

Even so, I can't help but feel a little bit self-conscious. Which is yet another downside of the whole celebrity thing. People know all about your life even without you ever telling them one single thing. It takes some getting used to. Trust me on that.

"So, I was wondering if you wanted to go get a coffee," he says, a little bit hesitantly. "Tomorrow's scenes are intense. And I, well, I thought you might want someone to talk through them with."

"That's sweet," I say, wondering if he's just doing his job, or if he knows how awkward the whole me-Blake thing is. Or if, like Mackenzie, he's worried about my emotional well-being. Whatever the reason, it's a nice gesture. "Normally I'd take you up on it, but I've got these plans . . ."

"Shopping. Right."

Suddenly my need for retail therapy sounds so trivial. This is a career-making movie for me. But am I running lines before a major emotional scene? No, I'm planning to drown my sorrows in a flurry of Prada paraphernalia.

I debate whether I should call Lindy and cancel. Except if I do, then I'll feel guilty, since I'm the one who begged her to take off early from work. Besides, I really want to shop.

I'm weighing my options when Susie trots up, breathless, a small package in her hand. "Hey! This just came for you!"

I hold out my hand to receive the package, and Susie shoves a festive green gift bag stuffed with pink tissue paper into my hand. Inside, I see an envelope peeking out, as well as a silver foil box. I pull out the envelope first. It's on T-H Productions stationery, and the return address of Tobias's office bungalow on the studio lot is embossed in the upper left corner. Inside, I know I'll find a single sheet of paper with Tobias's neat handwriting. At the top, he'll compliment me on one aspect of my performance. And then he'll fill up the rest of the sheet—front and back—with both criticisms and suggestions for nailing tomorrow's scenes.

I barely glance at it—I'm *so* not reading notes in front of Susie and Andy—then slide it back into the bag and pull out the small foil box. It's a little bit wider than a ring box and significantly taller. Inside, I find a very plump strawberry covered in white and black chocolate, designed to look like the strawberry is wearing a little tuxedo.

"Awww," says Susie. "It's so cute."

"Darling," I say. Then I put the lid back on and slide the box back into the bag.

"Aren't you going to eat it?" Andy asks.

Susie rolls her eyes. "Teeth."

"Excuse me?" Andy shoots her a baffled look.

Susie points to me, giving me the floor. "She means my teeth," I say, aiming a solid glare in her direction. "I never eat unless I can brush my teeth."

Andy looks taken aback. "Really? I never heard that."

"That's because I'm careful to keep my personal quirks out of the tabloids," I say, directing the comment to Susie, who at least has the grace to blush.

"I gotta get back," she says, probably afraid I'm going to chew her out. And then she scurries away.

I stifle the urge to roll my eyes and turn back to Andy. "It's an old habit," I say, by way of explanation. "If I ate full meals on the set when I was a kid, I'd be too sleepy to get through all the takes. So they let me snack pretty much all day. But I had to brush my teeth after everything. It wasn't that anyone cared so much about the health of my teeth. But if they had to redo a scene because I had chocolate on my front tooth . . . well, then that would be an expensive chocolate bar, you know?"

"I had no idea," Andy says.

I shrug. "No one does."

For that matter, no one knows I hate chocolate. That's another one of my little quirks that I've never revealed to the public. It's stupid, but I just want to keep some personal details secret. If anyone asks in an interview, I always say that I love chocolate just like every other girl on the planet. Just recently, in fact, I'd claimed that chocolate-covered strawberries gave me more of a rush than sex. (Not that this is a red-hot interview subject, but you'd be surprised at the mundane stuff that some of these reporters want to know.)

Although . . .

I frown a little. Because Tobias *does* know about my chocolate issues. But he probably just forgot. Or, more likely, didn't tell his assistant when he asked her to buy me a trinket to go with the note. She'd probably read the *Vanity Fair* article and decided that a chocolate-covered strawberry was just the ticket.

Tobias wouldn't care what she bought. From his point of view, the only purpose of the package was to deliver the note and pump up my ego after my first critical scene and before the next one tomorrow.

There it is again: another reminder that tomorrow's scenes are critical. I can practically feel my credit cards crying, knowing that they're not going to get a promised workout.

"Listen," I say to Andy. "Maybe it would be a good idea to run lines after all."

"I thought you were meeting someone."

"I was. I am. I mean, there's no reason why I can't do both," I say, even as the idea enters my head. "Do you mind meeting up later?" It's still early. I can shop for a few hours with Lindy, and easily be finished in time to get in a few hours of rehearsal.

"Sure," he says. "Do you want me to come over to your house?"

I hesitate, because for years, my number-one rule has been to not get too close to fans. Fans, after all, can be scary.

But this is different. This is Andy, our official story consultant. He's not only on the payroll, he's a genuinely nice guy.

Plus, he's been a victim, too. So we already have that much in common.

"Sure," I say, coming to a decision. I pull a notepad out of my purse and scribble my address, directions, and my phone number. "How does eight sound?"

"Perfect," he says with a glance at the note. "I think this will be really productive."

"Yeah," I say. "Me, too." But I can't quite conjure a matching smile. I've just broken my own hard-and-fast rule. And I can only hope that I don't live to regret it.

>>http://www.playsurvivewin.com<<<

PLAY.SURVIVE.WIN

WELCOME TO REPORTING CENTER

PLAYER REPORT:

REPORT NO. A-0001

Filed by: Janus

Subject: Status update.

Report:

- Toxin delivered as per instructions. Awaiting confirmation of infection.
- Delivery of additional systems established and scheduled as per introductory instructions.
- Game currently proceeding on schedule.

>>>End Report<<

Send Report to Opponent? >>**Yes**<< >>No<<

Block Sender Identity >>**Yes**<< >>No<<

Chapter

7

Blake clenched his hands into fists at his sides, trying to keep quiet as his manager went off on his latest tirade.

"Are you *trying* to fuck up your career?" Elliot howled. "That's what I want to know. Because if you're trying, then I owe you a congratulations. You're doing one hell of a good job."

Blake stiffened, reminding himself that he'd known this was coming. For that matter, considering the strings Elliot had pulled to arrange the satellite feed, the man had every right to be pissed. Except for the tiny little detail about Blake not wanting the interview in the first place, and Elliot damn well knowing it. "Last I looked, this was still *my* career," he said. "Or did I miss a memo?"

"Dammit, Blake, you just don't get it."

"No, *you* don't get it," he spat, trying to keep his temper in check. Now wasn't the time or the place for a knock-down, drag-out. Not with the press on the set and the crew still wandering around. In this day of camera phones, anyone could snap a picture, and three hours later it would be all over the Internet. He could see the headline now: "Fresh from Breakup with Darling Devi, Bad Boy Blake Breaks Down on the Set."

"Well all right, then," Elliot said, his Brooklyn accent sneaking in around the edges. "You tell me what I don't get." He aimed a fat finger at Blake's face. "You tell me why I've managed to keep every one of my clients at the top of his game, but for you, I don't know what the fuck I'm doing. You wanna tell me that?"

"Honestly, no," Blake said. "I don't want to talk about it. I made a decision. It's done. End of story." He knew why Elliot was pissed, but the decision was a good one. He hadn't meant to, but he'd hurt Devi in that last interview. He'd been unprepared to talk about his personal life, and when Letterman had asked him if wedding bells were in the future, he'd shot off an answer without thinking. Because at the time, he *hadn't* been thinking about marriage. Why would he be? Sure they were serious, but marriage? Not on his radar.

So, yes, he could have handled the question better. But dammit all to hell, Devi knew he was an idiot in interviews. But had she cut him some slack? Not even a tiny bit.

For that matter, neither had the media, and "Trouble in Paradise" headlines popped up everywhere. Suddenly every ex-girlfriend had something to say about him, and all the gossip rags started speculating about how he'd only gotten together with Devi in order to land the part in *Givenchy.*

The whole situation was fucked up, and he hadn't had a clue how to make it better. He'd gone back to Los Angeles expecting

Devi to commiserate with him, maybe even laugh at the press and his own stupidity. Instead, she'd cried and told him to get the hell out of her life. Something that was easier said than done, considering they were scheduled to start shooting the movie.

Yes, he'd screwed up, but she'd overreacted, too. But none of that changed the fact that he'd hurt her, however unintentionally. That one reality haunted him. He'd grown up with an absent father, a mother he adored, and two impish little sisters. It simply wasn't in his nature to hurt a woman, especially not a woman he cared for.

Having the *Letterman* crew on the lot was like rubbing salt in her wound. Which was why he'd gone to her trailer to see if she wanted to come on the segment with him. She'd pissed him off by not hearing him out and assuming the worst, and he regretted the way he'd stormed out without telling her why he'd come in the first place.

At least he'd had the wherewithal to cancel the damn thing. He might not completely understand women—with Devi at the top of that list—but he knew enough not to make the same mistake twice. No matter what Elliot Kelly might think.

Of course, since Elliot made no secret that he thought Blake should date a star with more box office bang, Blake's attempt to save Devi's feelings probably wouldn't pull much weight with his manager. A manager who was currently pacing, his jaw working back and forth as if he were trying to chew something really unpleasant.

As he stalked about, the scalp under his comb-over started to turn red, a sure sign his blood pressure was rising. "So I guess I should just quit," he finally said. "Why not? You don't need me. Not if you got a fucking death wish."

"A death wish?"

"Yeah. A death wish. You're gonna kill off your career. And my reputation, too. You remember that the next time you pull a stunt like this."

Usually Elliot's histrionics just rolled off Blake. Not today. Today, he wanted to hit something. Or someone. "Give it a rest, Elliot. They're rescheduling."

That stopped Elliot's pacing. "Rescheduling? For when, exactly?"

"It'll get done," Blake said. "Trust me." The truth was that he'd be perfectly happy if the damn interview never went forward. He liked the work just fine, but the trappings that came with it? All the damn publicity and people sticking cameras in his face? *That* he hated. Especially since he seemed to be miserable at it. He'd sure as hell shoved his foot firmly into his mouth on more than one occasion.

Elliot's fat finger came out again, and his mouth opened, but Blake cut him off. "I said it'll get done."

"They're still on the lot," Elliot said, suddenly perking up. "If you don't have a time already set to reschedule, then let's just do it now. Get this out of the way, and you can concentrate on your performance. Trust me, that's the way to go."

"Give it a rest."

"She's not worth it, Blake," Elliot said. "She's not a girl who's going to make your career."

"Maybe not," Blake agreed. "But I'm not going out of my way to upset her. I hurt her once. I'm not going to do it again."

"You're a damn pansy-ass. Honestly, I don't know why I keep working with you."

"Because I'm such a charmer," Blake said, and this time the grin was real.

"That must be it." Elliot looked at his watch, then pulled out his cell phone, a sure sign that the conversation was over. "You got a big day tomorrow. Get some rest. We'll clean this mess up later."

"I'm sure we will." But the sarcasm was lost on Elliot, who was already telling someone on the other end of the phone to "Get him on the horn now, baby. We got things to talk about."

Blake just shook his head, not sure if the gesture was exasperation or fondness. The voice from behind startled him.

"You got a live one there."

He turned to find Tobias, his gaze fixed on Elliot.

"Don't I know it." As much as Elliot drove him crazy, though, he couldn't completely fault the man. He'd signed with Elliot back when his only interest in Hollywood was getting fight-scene choreography work. And even though Elliot's clients had been limited to actors, he'd taken Blake on simply because they'd gotten along and because Elliot thought that someone needed to show those effeminate action hero types how to really kick some butt.

When Tobias had offered Blake an on-camera role, Elliot had truly stepped up to the plate, negotiating a sweet contract and making sure that the public knew damn well that there was a new star in the Hollywood sky. Blake still wasn't entirely sure he was comfortable with being labeled a star months before his first movie even opened, but he couldn't argue with Elliot's results.

He'd already landed foreign commercials, follow-up roles, and several endorsements.

He'd accepted the role because he'd been financially strapped. Not so anymore, and that was in large part due to Elliot's advocacy.

The man might drive him crazy, but he was damn sure effective.

"Let's walk," Tobias said.

Blake fell in step beside him. With his scruffy beard and teddy-bear build, Tobias Harmon usually seemed like the least dangerous man on the planet. But he was also the kind of guy you didn't see coming. In a town that watched carbs more carefully than the stock market, Tobias's well-known glutton tendencies made him a bit of an anomaly. He was invariably invited to all the best parties. And yet he never quite fit in.

Blake had liked the man from the first moment they'd met. "What's on your mind?"

The director glanced at him, but didn't break stride. "Do you know when I met Devi?"

"Years ago, I assume. You did *Taming Lily* when she was, what? Ten?"

"I met her five years before that. She was five. Just finished with Spielberg, and I wanted her in my next project. We met at a hotel while she was doing the publicity dog-and-pony show. Her mom looked wiped out, but Devi was as fresh as a flower."

One of the production assistants waved at them, then rushed over with a clipboard.

"She's a professional," Blake said, as Tobias started to scribble his name on various sheets in the mile-high stack of papers. She'd grown up in the loving glow of camera flashes. There'd been a few catty remarks from the occasional reporter, sure. But for the most part, she'd never had a reason to do anything but soak in the attention. Not until that son of a bitch assaulted her, anyway.

Just thinking about it made Blake's blood boil. They hadn't been dating at the time—hell, they hadn't even met back then—but he'd seen the damage that the bastard had done to her. It both broke his heart and made him want to lash out and hurt someone. No, not someone. *Him.*

And so help him . . . if the police ever managed to track the guy down . . .

Well, a background in martial arts could be damn useful at times.

Of course, if he was going to kick anyone's ass, he supposed it should be his own. After all, Devi had mostly recovered from her attack. She was off the drugs, back out in public, and she hadn't even balked at Tobias's mandate to promote the hell out of herself and the movie. He knew it hadn't been easy on her. But thankfully the glare of the spotlight had been soft-focused. They were the romance du jour, after all. The reports were extravagant, but generally kind. From a PR perspective, the situation couldn't have been more perfect.

So what did he do? He went on national television and slapped a big red target on the two of them.

God, he was a jerk.

The production assistant babbled a thank-you, then hurried off to her next task. Tobias turned back to Blake. "So there I am," he continued, as if they'd never been interrupted, "bonetired from shooting pickups all day, and this little slip of a girl marches over and shakes my hand. 'So you're our brightest new actress,' I say. And do you know how she answers?"

"No idea," Blake said, even though the question was mostly rhetorical.

"She says, 'I guess I am, sir. But what I really want to do is direct.'" Tobias shook his head, chuckling. "She's never wanted to direct a day in her life. But she knows how to play to an audience. *That's* her special talent. And it's a rare one."

"I know it," Blake said, not sure where this conversation was going, but suddenly more nervous about it than he used to be when his army colonel father would come home from a trip overseas and spend an hour grilling him on how well he'd taken care of his mother.

"She's like a daughter to me, and I don't want to see that spark in her fade. She's been through hell twice already. Real hell, and then that crap you pulled on her."

"With all due respect, she's the one who broke up with me." It was a ridiculous comeback and he knew it, but Tobias had got his defenses up.

"You want to know the truth? I don't give a shit who dumped who. At the moment, all I care about is protecting this picture."

"You won't get any argument from me."

"Good. Because I've been talking with the publicity folks over at the studio, and they want to turn this thing around."

"This thing?"

Tobias shot him a sideways look. "Whatever you may have heard, all PR is not created equal. Your breakup's going to affect our bottom line. Folks want to see a movie starring a couple in love. A movie starring a couple at each other's throats? Not so much. Gossip may go up, but breakups don't sell tickets. I've seen it happen to lesser couples than you two."

"I'd love to help you out there, Toby, but let me state the obvious. We *are* broken up."

"I never was good with the details, kid. I'm a big-picture man, myself. And the picture I see is filled with happiness and joy. You get what I'm talking about? I want every rag in this city talking about the chemistry between you two. How you made up, and now it's hotter than ever. We need to do everything to make sure that you two are the golden couple."

"And this all because of the box office? You're just looking out for the bottom line? This isn't about Devi at all?"

Tobias met and matched his gaze, but didn't answer the question. He started to walk away, then turned back. "I'll say this much. You do anything else to hurt her, and you're going to answer to me. You understand?"

"I'd never do anything to hurt her."

"Blake, you already have. What you need to do now is make it right."

"I know." The only problem was, he didn't know how.

Chapter 8

"So you really mean it?" I ask for the eight-hundred-and-seventy-five-millionth time. "I can handle it, right?" There's a lot of things we could be talking about. At the moment, though, I'm focused on tomorrow's scenes with Blake. Because after the way my heart skittered in my chest upon seeing him today, I'm more than a little nervous about working with the man.

Lindy signals for the check, but ignores me. I skim my fingers around the rim of my glass and try my best not to scream. The Beverly Wilshire is posh. Primal scream therapy really isn't welcome here.

The bartender slides the check in front of us, and I make a grab for it. Lindy gets it first, but I manage to snag it between my thumb and forefinger. We're locked in a desperate tug-of-war to see who gets to fork over forty-two dollars.

"You're ignoring my question," I accuse.

"Um, yeah," she says. "Duh."

"Fine," I say, letting go of the bill. "You pay."

She snaps the paper toward her and pulls out her wallet, completely unperturbed. "I've already answered you. At least nine times at last count."

"Do me a favor and answer me again. Just one more time," I plead. "It's the neurotic actress in me. I need constant reassurance." I also need food, but I'm not going to touch the bowl of nuts sitting just six inches away from me. Too many calories. Too much salt. My trainer would have a fit.

What the hell. I snag a handful and pop them into my mouth before I can change my mind.

I close my eyes, reveling in my little corner of cashew heaven. When I open them, I see Lindy grinning at me. "Protein," I say.

"Uh-huh."

"Answer my question," I demand, but she just smiles. I'm about to press the point when my cell phone rings. I snatch it up, check the caller ID, then ignore it.

"Who is it?"

"Larry," I say, referring to my agent. "He's calling about the *North by Northwest* thing. I just know it."

"So just tell him you don't want to do it."

"I should," I say. "But I'm still waffling."

I've been offered the lead in a big-budget remake of that famous Hitchcock film. Apparently the producers think I'd be great in the Eva Marie Saint role. *I* think it's a sin to mess with Hitch. I would have assumed that after the whole Gus Van Sant psychosis, everyone knew that.

At the same time, though, it *is* a big part. And Larry thinks that since my star is on the rise again with *Givenchy,* we need to jump on the role.

He's probably right, but my head hasn't managed to convince my heart. Which is why I now tuck my phone back into my purse, ignoring the chirp that signals that he's now left a voice mail.

"So," I say to Lindy. "Where were we?"

"Time to shop," she says brightly, completely ignoring the fact that five seconds ago I was elbow deep in angst. Then she heads out of the bar and into the ornate lobby.

I sigh, then trot behind her, aiming needle-like glares at the back of her neck. I played a superhero two movies ago, and I had the power to force the truth out of my enemies with a single glance. That kind of power would come in real handy right about now.

The doorman holds the door open for us, and we step out into a balmy Los Angeles afternoon. The hotel opens onto Wilshire Boulevard, just steps from where that street intersects the fabulous Rodeo Drive.

I rummage in my purse for my sunglasses, then slip them on. Lindy does the same. We stand there for a moment. I don't know about Lindy, but I'm taking stock. Because right in front of us is a shopper's nirvana. "Shall we skip Via Rodeo?" I ask, referring to the ostentatious new walking street. Relatively new, anyway. And, in my opinion, tacky.

You reach Via Rodeo by climbing a set of stairs that rise from Wilshire. Then the road curves around until it meets up with Rodeo Drive proper more or less at Dalton Way. It's a nice piece of real estate—and home to some of the ritziest stores on the planet—but I happen to like what I call the "old" part of Rodeo

Drive best. And the stores along Rodeo aren't slouches by any means. Tiffany's (technically on Rodeo *and* Via Rodeo), Harry Winston, Versace, Dolce & Gabbana. You get the picture. And, of course, there's Prada. Which, to my way of thinking, is the ultimate Beverly Hills destination.

Since Lindy knows my personal agenda well, she doesn't argue. We walk the fifty or so yards to the crosswalk, then wait for the light to change. (*Always* wait for the light in Los Angeles. We're a car culture here. Pedestrians are only good for target practice.)

I'm itching to start shopping. Although my bank account runneth over, I rarely buy anything on these outings (well, except at Prada, but that's because of my own personal weakness), but I'm a die-hard window shopper.

The light changes, and we cross with the rest of the throng, a combination of locals and tourists. A few do a double take when they see me, but most are oblivious. I look cute, but compared to most of the shoppers, I'm hardly dressed to the nines. And I scrubbed off my makeup before I left the set. Hard-core fans and paparazzi will know me on sight. Everyone else, though? To them, I'm just another face in the crowd.

I know it's not cool to be in love with your town, but I really do love Los Angeles, and Beverly Hills most of all. I mean, there's an *island* of tall trees right in the center of Wilshire. Clearly, this is a town concerned about aesthetics.

We reach the other side, and Lindy stops dead, making me (and a dozen or so shoppers) almost stumble over her. "What the—"

"Here," she says, taking me by the arm. She turns us around so that we're facing Wilshire again, right back the way we came.

"Hey! We haven't even shopped yet."

"Just read." One elegant finger extends, indicating the Panic Button sign that someone has helpfully mounted where the standard Push to Walk should be. "Total Crisis Panic Button," it says. For the standard white walking man symbol, you're instructed, "Start running . . . Danger is imminent!" When the hand starts to flash, that means, "Don't think! Stay fearful and alert!" And when the red hand stays solid, you need to "Obey orders."

It's a professional-looking sign, printed on thick metal and firmly attached with screws. In Beverly Hills, it seems, even the grafitti has style.

I'll admit the thing amuses me, but I manage to keep a straight face. "And you're showing me this because . . . ?"

"You're panicking," she says, as tourists flow around us. "And you don't need to be." She turns around, takes my arm, and starts walking up Rodeo. For a moment, I walk beside her in confused silence. And then I realize: she's talking about tomorrow's scenes with Blake.

"You're just trying to make me feel better."

"I'm a hard-nosed bitch lawyer," she says with a perfect deadpan. "I don't do touchy-feely."

"Yeah," I say, hiding a smile. "I noticed."

The truth is, just by reassuring me, she is doing touchy-feely. She knows how weird I get about my acting. Couple that with my general neurosis about Blake, and I'm a walking time bomb.

She hooks her arm through mine and gives me a friendly squeeze. "Dev, sweetie, all you need to nail a scene is an actor to play against that you trust. You may not trust him in a relationship anymore, but I know you trust him professionally. Blake's a good guy. He's solid. And you two are going to sizzle on the screen."

I want to press her for more, but I don't. Because she's right. I *do* trust Blake. Or at least, I did. Before Blake, I'd never truly had a real, serious relationship with a man. It was just too hard getting past all the celebrity stuff. I love my life—don't get me wrong—but finding the time for a relationship was just as hard as finding a guy who wasn't either jealous or awed by my money and fame. I'd been burned a couple of times early on, and by the time I hit twenty-two, I realized there just weren't that many men out there that I could put my faith into.

After the attack, I didn't even try to date. I was nervous and jittery around everyone, but men especially. Blake, though . . . Well, somehow he eased in through the cracks in my heart. Slowly at first, and then so much that I let down my defenses. He was there. It felt right. And I truly believed that I had finally found a man who truly loved me. A man who could soothe my fears and share my life. A man I could trust with my heart.

I was wrong, though, and that miscalculation was one of the reasons it hurt so bad when he betrayed me on television. But even now, I know that I can work with him. I might hate him, but I can definitely work with him.

"You're right," I say. "But I still feel . . . I don't know. Antsy."

She looks at me appraisingly. "Is it the scene? Coming home and finding a stranger in your apartment?"

"You sound like Mac," I say. "She said pretty much the same thing earlier today."

"Maybe we're right."

"Maybe . . ." I trail off with a shrug. "At any rate, whatever the reason, I *am* nervous about it. So I guess it's good that Andy's coming over tonight to rehearse."

"To the house?" Her brows rise a bit with the question.

"Yes," I say, feigning casualness. I know she's not fooled, though. Lindy knows me better than anyone, so she knows just how few people I've opened myself to since the attack. I've had like zero new friends, so inviting Andy over is a big step.

Blake, actually, is the only new person in the last few years who has squeezed through my walls. And look how *that* turned out. I'd opened my heart to him—shared things I'd never shared with anyone else. I'd believed it was for real and for forever. And then he'd gone and twisted the knife.

Lindy flashes me an understanding smile, then hooks her arm through mine and tugs me along. "Come on, my insecure friend. Let's go spend money."

Since that sounds like a truly fabulous idea, I walk with her in silence for a good ten seconds. But this whole invite-someone-over thing is now on my mind, and after a few moments I can't take it any longer. I pause in front of Tiffany's extravagant windows. "I didn't screw up or anything by inviting him over, did I?"

She smacks me in the arm with her purse, and that shuts me up. "Oh, honey. He's a working member of the team. That's why you invited him over in the first place. He's not Janus. You know that."

"You're right. I know you're right."

"Besides, Andy probably understands what you're going through better than anyone. I mean, wasn't he stalked himself? Isn't that what you told me?"

"Sort of," I said. "He got sucked into the game as a protector."

"Explain that to me again? I still don't get this whole Play.Survive.Win thing." Considering that she has an IQ high enough to be the gross national product of an emerging nation, I don't believe her. But I do appreciate what she's doing. So I humor her and give her the rundown of the game, explaining about the target, protector, and assassin roles.

"And that's just the structure," I continue. "It's the actual scavenger-hunt part of the game that makes it really cool."

"That's right. I remember from the script you let me read. The target has to follow clues around the city."

"Exactly," I say. "But the really neat part is that each of the clues is based on a profile that the player fills out the first time they play the game. I think some early players lied—I mean, who doesn't in cyberspace?—but later folks realized that the clues keyed off their interests."

"So doctors would have medical lingo, and attorneys would have legal clues to follow?"

"Exactly," I say. "And after people started putting down the truth, the game's popularity grew even more. The guy who invented it became hugely rich. Scary rich."

"What's he doing now? Does he have any ideas about who started playing the game in the real world?"

"Nope," I say. "He's dead." Archibald Grimaldi had started out a poor, abused kid who'd been failed by the system. He'd climbed out of the muck, though, and made a fortune at a very young age by inventing and marketing PSW. None of that money did him any good in the end, though. He disappeared one night, sucked into the sea. Finis. Game over. For Grimaldi, at least, but not for the millions of players around the globe who kept pumping energy into the PSW machine.

"How sad," Lindy says when I tell her all that.

"I know. Very."

"You played once, didn't you?" she asks. "In real life, I mean?"

"Once," I admit. "Lost right off the bat."

"I can't even win at Spider Solitaire. PSW sounds like it's way out of my league."

"Mine, too."

"But back to Andy," she says, twisting the conversation back to where we started.

"He was sucked in as a protector," I say.

"But something happened," she prompts. I can't remember if I've told her the whole story or not, but she definitely knows where we're heading.

"Andy took a bullet trying to save his target, but it didn't matter. In the end the assassin killed the target, and Andy . . ." I trail off with a shrug. Because what can I say?

"Wow," Lindy says.

"Exactly."

"He must be a mess."

"I think he's dealt with it pretty well," I say, feeling the need to stick up for him. "He was in an impossible situation, and he did his damnedest to keep the guy alive. And once it was over, he found Mel, and now they're doing whatever they can to help other folks who get caught up in the game."

"What do you mean?"

"Mel used the money she won by surviving the game to fund a kind of project. She and Stryker and some other folks who survived now visit computer gaming conventions and post on bulletin boards and generally do all sorts of investigation to try to find other people who've played and lived to tell about it."

I shudder a little. The whole thing just sounds too horrible. Getting caught up in some maniac's version of a good time. I mean, how terrifying is that? (Actually, considering I'd gotten caught up in Janus's version of a good time, I suppose I could answer that. And the answer is: *way* terrifying.)

"So, a lot of people must survive, right? You said she's got other people helping her?"

I lift a shoulder. "I don't think so. Last I heard there was just Andy and two others. Jennifer Crane and her fiancé, an FBI agent named Devlin Brady."

"Jennifer," Lindy says, her forehead scrunching up. "Why is that familiar?"

"Because you read the script," I say. "She's my roommate. Or Mel's roommate."

"Oh, right," she says. "So is the movie all part of Mel's grand plan? To get the word out, I mean?"

"Apparently," I say. "Andy's the one who's actually been shepherding the film rights through, though. I guess he convinced Mel that getting her story out there and clueing the public in to what's been going on would not only bring more players out of the woodwork, but also might put a stop to the whole thing."

"Shine a bright light on the fungus and kill it," Lindy says.

"That's one way of putting it," I say, as we start walking again.

"So do you feel better?" she asks after a moment.

I stop and squint, because I don't know what we're talking about. "About what?"

She just laughs. "You're so predictable! Not five minutes ago, you were totally second-guessing yourself for inviting Andy over. You need to stop that. You do it all the time."

"I do not," I say, but that's a big fat lie. I *do*. I always have, but it got worse after the attack. And doubly worse after the breakup.

"You told me yourself you did it today," she argues. "Kicked Blake out of your trailer and then raced after him to do the interview yourself."

"Oh, that is so not fair," I counter. But I start walking again, which my therapist would undoubtedly say is my attempt to move away from the truth.

Lindy rushes to keep up with me. "You'd totally decided that he was the love of your life, and then he goes and makes one mistake, and you do a complete one-eighty. I mean, sweetie, Olympic gymnasts don't flip that fast."

"*Hello?* Are we talking about the same man? He dumped *me*. And on national television, no less."

"He didn't dump. He hedged."

"Hedged," I repeat. "Well, that makes sense. Because that way he was safe if someone better came along." We'd been hot and heavy, or at least I'd thought we were, especially since we'd been talking about moving in together, buying a stereo system together. Commingling our DVD collections . . .

The kind of stuff I'd never done before. Not with any guy.

But I found out at the same time that the rest of the viewing public did that we were "dating, but not yet locked into any sort of commitment." His words, not mine. And that was news to me, let me tell you. Painful, humiliating news.

He'd been on *Letterman* at the time, so that's what? Umpty-million viewers? And when Letterman asked—in his oh-so-

Letterman way—if Blake was waiting for something better to come along, he'd laughed uncomfortably and got this little-boy-lost look. "Hoo boy," Letterman had said. "Devi's got a drifter on her hands."

The next week, guess what the *Entertainment Weekly* headline was? And two points to you if you guessed "Hoo Boy. Blake's a Devil."

I mean, come on!

"He didn't mean it, and you know it," Lindy says. "Letterman put him on the spot, and he said something stupid. And now you're punishing you both because he ran off at the mouth. The boy was acting under the influence of Elliot. Obviously he was spouting nonsense."

That makes me laugh, but I try to stifle it.

"So you're telling me that the exact instant you found out about it, you fell out of love with him?"

I stop, my arms crossed over my chest, and stare her down. We've reached Dalton Way, where the curve of Via Rodeo meets up with Rodeo Drive. Around us, well-dressed tourists glide past, along with some well-heeled locals. I catch a glimpse of someone who looks remarkably like Paris Hilton making a bee-line toward Gucci. She sees us and waves. Duh. It *is* Paris.

"I'm not saying you should have forgiven him," she says, oblivious to the fact that we're only yards away from a power shopper. "I'm just saying that you didn't react to what he did or to what he was feeling. You looked at *you*. You learned that he wasn't ready to put a ring on your finger, and suddenly *you* decided that *you* were totally wrong to have fallen in love with him in the first place."

"God," I say, suitably awed. "No wonder you're a lawyer."

She shoots me the finger and continues walking. I hurry to catch up, my mind in a whirl. To a certain extent she's right, and I know it. But what she doesn't understand is that I had no choice. I couldn't just sit there, knowing how he felt, and wait for the other shoe to drop. That would make me the victim in our little love story, and that simply wasn't a role I could play again. Not ever.

Lindy slows down enough to look hard at me. "Just give the guy a second chance, okay?"

I think about the way he looked in my trailer doorway earlier today, the soft light from the early afternoon sun filtering around him. "I'll think about it," I say. "But don't place any bets on it yet." Good looks are one thing, but he hurt me to the core.

"That's all I ask," she says.

"I don't even know why we're talking about Blake, anyway," I say. "We're here for shopping, and he was always lousy at that."

"It's an X-Y thing," she says, and I roll my eyes. She lets out a breath of air, then turns to scope out the street. "I'm becoming old and pathetic," she announces. "There's not one store here that has something I want."

"You are old and pathetic," I say with a laugh. "But I love you anyway. And I know exactly what your problem is, too. She weighs about thirty pounds and has curly blond hair and thinks I'm the coolest person ever."

Lindy raises an eyebrow.

"Okay," I correct. "She thinks I'm the coolest person next to her mommy and daddy."

"Will you kill me if I beg to hit the kids' boutiques next?"

"No," I say, because my mind isn't really on shopping at the moment either. "Except we can't leave without going to—"

"Prada. I know." She gives a little nod of her head. Our destination is about half a block up and over, just past the crosswalk. "Let's go."

As I've already mentioned umpteen thousand times, Prada Beverly Hills is my absolute favorite store in the universe (next to the Manhattan locations, of course). And before you go all "Celebrities should be more responsible with their money and not bow to the god of designer fashion" on me, let me just say that I am the last person who has to leave the house decked out in designer labels. My current outfit should be proof of that. Yes, my shoes are Prada, but the jeans and the funky eyelet shirt are eclectic, not designer. Which I think proves my point. I'm not a slave to fashion. I'm a trendsetter. Seriously. *Entertainment Weekly* said so just last week.

About Prada, though, I'm a total fan girl. There's just something about the way form and function mesh, which sounds like I watch too much *Project Runway* or something, but it's true. I'll confess that my loyalty lies primarily with the bags (purses and totes), but that doesn't mean I'm not a sucker for the clothes, too.

Here's my neurotic celebrity secret: If Prada wanted me to be their spokesgirl—like Liv Tyler did for Givenchy and Demi Moore did for Versace—I would *totally* do it in a heartbeat. Hell, I'd even negotiate down my usual wage (assuming I got to keep the products). I love the stuff that much.

Today, though, I'm not getting my bags gratis. And I do plan to walk away with a bag (or ten). I've had my eye on a classy black tote for a week now. I'm thinking today's the day to take the plunge. I've recently bought a new laptop computer, and I want to be able to easily schlep it with me. (I'm not a computer geek or anything, but my assistant syncs all my appointments electronically and forwards drafts of all my fan-mail responses for me to review and send on. So like it or not, I'm attached to the laptop. And, yes, I have been known to type my name into Google and surf the Web looking for fan sites. I know I shouldn't, because I invariably find a blog or a Web site run by some perv, and then I spend a week being freaked out. But I can't help it. It's insecure and pathetic, maybe, but I have to know what's going on.)

"Are you going to pry open your checkbook?" I ask Lindy, as we pause at the crosswalk. "Or am I the only one indulging?"

"We'll see," she says, with a tiny little smile. She makes a nice living, and since her husband is an attorney, too, they're doing just fine financially. Lately, though, her purchases have been geared more toward the under-five set. Honestly, it's put quite the crimp in our shopping sprees. Like me, though, she has a weakness for Prada. And I'm guessing that, like me, when she walks out she'll have at least one shopping bag hooked on her arm.

The store entrance is technically anonymous in that there is no signage announcing that it is Prada. You'd have to be brain-dead to miss the place, though. It's conspicuous merely by its simplicity. A gray facade, sleek and modern, juts out, forming what I like to think of as an Huxleyesque entranceway. You're entering a brave new world of fashion here.

The entire width of the store opens onto Rodeo, so even without any sort of sign, it's not like you're going to miss the store. Although some people think the store is weird-looking or even tacky, I think it's a tribute to style and fun. It's different. And in my book, different is good.

Case in point: To get inside how many stores do you have to walk *over* the window displays? But that's just what Lindy and I do. Our heels click on the wood entrance area as we pass by and over the futuristic pods that display decked-out mannequins below our feet. It's incredibly bizarre and totally fun, and I've loved it since the first day I saw it. Which, thank you very much, happened to be at the opening party. And, yes, Miuccia Prada, the doyenne of high fashion herself, invited me to the opening. I'd arrived in heel-to-head Prada, and looked amazing. But I was no match for Miuccia, who had arrived for the event resplendent in a wooden skirt (yes, wooden). It clacked when she walked and was absolutely fabulous. I'd never wear it, mind you, but in theory it totally rocked.

At any rate, today I have tote-bag-and-purse tunnel vision, so I don't waste a lot of time scoping out the display pods. Instead, we head straight into nirvana.

An impressive staircase fills the center of the room, leading up to the second floor and the clothes that I know Lindy craves. She calls it the stairway to heaven, and immediately abandons me. I call it a distraction. After all, why get all muddled about clothes when there are perfectly good purses right there on the first floor? Purses that fill that nearly unfillable void in a girl's life. Purses like that one right there in the nearby glass case. The black bag, with the buckles and the oversize straps.

The floor is made up of black-and-white tile in a checkerboard pattern, and I play my way across the room, absolutely certain of my next move. I lift a hand and signal toward Armen, my favorite sales associate. He sees me, and his eyes go wide. He rushes over, not too fast, but with a definite spring in his step.

"Miss Taylor!"

"*Devi*, Armen. How many times do I have to tell you?"

"At least half a dozen more," he says. I don't even bother to argue. He's too well trained. And I want my bag too much to waste any more time. "You should have come in through the VIP entrance," he scolds. "I had no idea you were here."

"And miss walking down Rodeo Drive? No way." There's a VIP door tucked in the back. It actually has a sign and everything. But it's just not the same. If I simply wanted to open my checkbook, I could send Susie. I want the experience.

"That one," I say, pointing at my precious baby, tucked away in the glass case. "That one looks like it needs a good home."

"What?" he teases. "No trying it on for size? No walking down the street for a test drive? You're not even going to give our other bags a chance? Darling, you're breaking my heart."

I laugh. "If it will make you feel better, I'm happy to stroll down Rodeo with that bag over my shoulder. And you know as well as I do that the odds of me getting out of here with only one purse are virtually nil. But you may as well wrap it up for me now, because we both know I'm getting it."

"I already have."

I cock my head, sure I've misunderstood. "Pardon?"

He lifts a finger, signaling for me to wait, then disappears into the back. After a moment, he returns, a familiar Prada shopping bag hooked over one finger. He extends his entire arm and presents the bag to me with as much ceremony as if he were passing off the crown jewels.

I look inside and see the tissue-wrapped tote. I use my fingernails to pry the tissue away and reveal my bag in all its glory.

Considering all the pomp and circumstance, I can't say that I'm surprised. What I am, though, is baffled. "Did you set it aside for me the last time I was in here?"

"I wanted to, but you told me not to."

I had. At the time, I'd still been wavering. I have an entire closet in my house devoted to purses, after all. Then again, a girl really can't have too many bags.

"Then why is it already wrapped up?" I ask.

"Because you are one lucky lady." He cocks his head. "Or did you pull a few strings?"

He looks so eager, but I don't have a clue what he's talking about.

"Huh?" (How's that for articulate?)

His face seems to fall. "Well, damn. I was so sure that you're the one who arranged this."

"Armen! What *this?*"

"The bag," he said. "It's a gift from the producers. Apparently the order of the day is Givenchy—what with the movie title and all. But you, my dear, are getting Prada, since everyone knows you love us so much. Well," he adds, hedging a bit, "I think you're getting something Givenchy, too. I really didn't get all the details." He waves a hand, as if he's moving the conversation along. "Anyway, I was supposed to deliver it to you tonight, but since you're here, I don't see why I can't give it to you now."

"Really?" I peel away the rest of the tissue and pull out my oh-so-fabulous bag. I am in awe. Truly. It's not unusual for studios or production companies to buy cast and crew gifts, but usually I get an engraved box. Or a hat with the name of the movie embroidered on it. Or I get to keep my director's-style chair.

But Prada? And Givenchy, too? Be still my heart!

"Did you tell them which bag was my favorite?" I ask.

"Of course," he says with a smile. "I did good?"

"Armen, darling, if I didn't think I would fall in love with you forever, I'd lean over and kiss you right now."

He laughs, and even blushes a little.

"You know," I add, "this just proves what I've been saying all along. My love of Prada is a force to be reckoned with. You guys really need to think about letting me be a spokesperson."

"Looks to me like you already are," he says, then winks. "But I'll send a memo."

I sigh, then rewrap my tote in its tissue and nestle it snugly in the shopping bag. Then I sigh again. As usual, retail therapy worked—even better than I could have imagined, actually.

My day is definitely looking up . . . and I can't imagine anything bringing me down now.

>>>http://www.playsurvivewin.com<<<

PLAY.SURVIVE.WIN

PLEASE LOGIN

PLAYER USER NAME: *PlayToWin*

PLAYER PASSWORD: * * * * * * * *

. . . *please wait*

. . . *please wait*

. . . *please wait*

Password approved

>>>Read New Messages<<<   >>>Create New Message<<<

. . . *please wait*

WELCOME TO MESSAGE CENTER

You have one new message.

New Message:

To: PlayToWin

From: Identity Blocked

Subject: Funding

Advance payment deposited your account.

Amount: $20,000.

Client name: Devi Taylor.

Additional funds to be delivered upon successful completion of mission.

Game commences: 12:01 a.m.

Rule Refresher: Involvement by police or other authorities is **expressly forbidden.**

Good luck.

>>>*Player Profile Attached: DT_Profile.doc*<<<

Chapter

11

"Life is good," I say, hugging my Prada shopping bag close to my chest. We're back on Rodeo Drive, heading toward our cars.

Lindy raises an eyebrow. "No more angst about inviting Andy over? No more nasty remarks about Blake?"

"Maybe a few nasty remarks," I say. "But they can wait until tomorrow. For the rest of the day, I'm basking."

"You're too easy."

I hold up the shopping bag. "Easy? Or expensive?"

She laughs. "Both, apparently."

"I still can't believe it. A tote bag. And not the kind with the name of the movie silk-screened on the side. I mean, how classy is that? I didn't know Tobias had it in him."

"It probably wasn't Tobias," she says, and for some reason, that comment gives me chills.

"What do you mean?" I ask warily.

"Just that Tobias doesn't really seem like the Prada type. More like the McDonald's Happy Meal type, if you know what I mean."

I do know, and I can't help but laugh. (Well, snort, actually, but let's not go there.) "Marcia, probably," I say, referring to Tobias's assistant. "She's saved him from many a social and fashion faux pas."

"Trust me," Lindy says. "Marcia has *never* saved that man from a fashion faux pas."

She has a point.

"Listen," she continues. "I know you want to get home and switch everything from your purse to your new bag, and I want to get back home before the traffic gets truly insane. So let's do the Lucy shopping later."

I heave a sigh of relief and agree. I love my goddaughter, but that plan is fine with me.

We part ways, Lindy to maneuver her way down to Manhattan Beach through the four p.m. traffic, and me to drive the fifteen or so relatively traffic-free blocks to my house in the hills of Beverly, as they say in the *Beverly Hillbillies*.

In other words, ten minutes later I'm home. Lindy, I'm sure, is still listening to talk radio while idling on the 10. Like I said—I love Beverly Hills.

I also love my house. Before the attack, I lived in a darling little bungalow tucked away in the hills just off Laurel Canyon. Pretty and charming, with a great view and little critters that visited me at night, like raccoons and possums and the occasional coyote.

Those critters didn't bother me.

It was the two-legged vermin that forced me to move, and even though I loved that house dearly, I love my very secure new home even better. This baby is wired for action, and even has a guardhouse complete with three guards on rotating shifts provided by the security firm I hired. (Lucas, Tom, and Miguel, all three of whom get really great Christmas presents from me.)

I'm all about security and privacy these days. You hardly have to be a celebrity to be the victim of a freakish crime, but all the information that had been in the press about me over the years must have fed Janus's fixation. And probably helped him figure out how to get to me.

That's one big downside of being a child star. Folks see you grow up on television and in the movies, and they think they own you. Couple that with a psychopathic personality, and you have a whole I'll-assassinate-the-president-to-prove-I-love-Jodie-Foster thing going.

It's bizarre. And, yes, it's a little scary. (Okay, it's a lot scary.) And that's exactly why I decided to start keeping a tight grip on the personal information that gets leaked out about me. And why I moved to a house with security roughly the equivalent of Fort Knox.

Too little, too late, you say? Well, maybe. But it helps me sleep at night.

The house was built in the twenties by Greta Garbo, although she never actually lived there. (That little tidbit made for tons of tabloid fodder after I became a recluse. "Spirit of Garbo Infuses Miss Devi, Who Simply 'Vants to Be Alone.' " Puh-lease!) And although the house is older than my old bungalow, it's been more thoroughly updated. State-of-the-art kitchen. State-of-the-art electrical system. Fully landscaped. Fabulous privacy fence (complete with security, of course). Video monitors all around the grounds. You name it.

And whereas my old house had been just off the street, my new place is tucked up against the hills and set back away from traffic. The driveway is more like a private road that winds around until you reach my house, tucked in against the hills. The guards check and announce all guests on the property intercom, and then send them through the gate after I give my okay.

A high fence surrounds the property, and it's under twenty-four-hour video surveillance. It's also got some voltage running through it, but I don't advertise that.

The bottom line? I feel safe there. And for someone like me, that's saying a lot.

Lucas is on shift when I arrive, and I pause to do the chitchat thing.

"How'd the first day of shooting go?"

"Great," I say. "And the shopping afterward was even better."

He grins, then nods toward the gate. "Go relax. And have a good night, Ms. Taylor."

Lucas is an odd bird in Los Angeles—a man who wants absolutely nothing to do with the movie business. He used to be a plumber, but he went back to school to get an engineering degree. He likes the job because it gives him time to study. (That's his basic overview, at any rate. I know a lot more about the man. Believe me. The background check I ran before I let the security company put him on-site would put the FBI to shame.)

My first order of business when I come home is to switch purses. My new Prada bag is a little bit tote bag and a little bit purse . . . and one hundred percent perfect. I slip my new laptop in it just to be sure, and it fits like a charm, with two interior pockets for my wallet, makeup, and other girlie things. It even has a pocket on the back that is just the right size for a script, and two additional pockets for sunglasses and a cell phone.

I take my time making the transfer, and when everything is switched over, I center the bag on my kitchen table, take a step back, and just look at it.

Perfect.

And, just in case I sound way too pathetic, might I point out that most women come home from a clothes-shopping spree and try on every single item in front of their own mirror. So my bag adoration is a long way from neurotic or abnormal. Really.

Everything from my old bag (also Prada) fits nicely into this one, and the stuff I don't need to transfer I leave on the breakfast bar. Since I tend to only carry the basics, nonessentials include the present from Tobias, the parking ticket from the Beverly Wilshire, and the cocktail napkin on which I'd doodled some notes for tomorrow's scene.

I take the strawberry box out of the bag and put the whole thing in the fridge. I'd meant to give it to Lindy, but I'd forgotten. Now, I consider just trashing it, but that seems a shame. I'll pass it off to Miguel in the morning as I'm leaving for the set.

The only thing left in the gift bag is the envelope, and I open that now. Inside I find a card monogrammed with Tobias's initials. I open it to find a block-printed note:

Good job today. The real fun begins tomorrow.
Some notes for you:
http://www.YourGivenchyCodeMovieNotes.com

I have to laugh. Because about two weeks before filming began, I was giving Tobias grief for being the most computer-illiterate person on the planet. Looks like he decided to get literate fast, just to show me up.

For a second, I'm tempted to head over to the Web site, but my laptop is already packed away neatly in my new bag, and honestly, I'm just not in the mood to think about work. My script is on the countertop, and so I shove the card inside to deal with later.

Then I step back and consider my options.

In actuality, I should study the script, but all I really want to do is take a shower before Andy comes over. I'd been in such a hurry to shop that I hadn't bothered to shower in my trailer. And after a day that began at four and wrapped up with a walk through the summer heat and smog, I'm feeling the grime of the city.

Besides, my bathroom is just shy of heaven, and any excuse for a shower is a good one.

It was, in fact, the bathroom that sold me on the house, even more than the security system. The room is huge, with a walk-in shower with eight vertical showerheads for a full-body effect, and two rain-style heads that spray from above. The shower stall is granite and glass, and the phone and the intercom to the gatehouse are just past the water barrier so that even in the shower you're never out of touch.

The bathtub is insane as well. Lindy swears she's going to teach Lucy to swim in it, and I don't think she's kidding. It's sunk into the floor and surrounded by candles and bath salts and baskets of luscious-smelling soaps. Stacks of fluffy towels are easily within reach, and my maid, Carla, knows that the one thing that will get my ire up (other than rearranging the purse closet) is letting the towel supply dwindle.

One wall is dominated by a plasma television, another by glass bricks that let in light but distort the view, and another opens directly into one of my closets. My exercise bike and some free weights are tucked in one corner (I have more in the weight room downstairs), and the stereo system is elegantly hidden and operated by remotes that I aim at hidden infrared thingamabobs.

All in all, the room is awesome, just like the house. And I thank my mother for it every day. I've earned a lot of money over the course of my career, but my mom is the one who turned "a lot" into "a *lot*." The woman has a knack for negotiating and a sixth sense about stocks. She dumped every cent I made as a minor into brokerage accounts, and bought and sold tech stocks at just the right time.

Today, I forgo the exercise bike (shopping was workout enough) and head for the shower. It's a toss-up between that and a bath, but the idea of getting pounded by steaming hot water appeals at the moment. What can I say? It's been a stressful day.

I get the jets going, strip off my clothes, and step into heaven. I scrub down with a rosemary mint body wash, then slather my face with Noxzema. I'm a fan of the basics.

The stuff is still on my face and I've worked my hair into a good lather when the intercom buzzes, and Lucas's voice echoes through the room.

"Ms. Taylor? You've got a visitor at the—"

Andy. I reach out and blindly slap the intercom button, effectively silencing Lucas. "Lucas!" I shout over the drone of the shower. "He's here to run lines and he's early! But go ahead and send him on to the house. I'll be right there!"

"Will do, ma'am."

The intercom clicks back to silence, and even though I try to do the fastest rinse ever, I manage to get soap in my eyes and it takes me longer than I'd like. I can't believe he's almost an hour early. Finally, I'm squeaky clean, and I bundle my hair in a towel and myself in a big, fluffy bathrobe. I trot toward the stairs, my bare feet leaving damp prints on the hard wood floors.

I reach the front door—breathless—just as the bell rings. I used to have a live-in housekeeper, but having someone else putter around just made me nervous. So it's just me, alone with the responsibility of opening doors and greeting guests.

"I was in the shower," I say, even before the door is open. "Just wait down here while I get dressed, and—"

I stop cold, the words caught in my throat. Because this isn't Andy I'm staring at. It's Blake. And that's just a bit more than my already fried brain can take today.

Chapter

12

He stands there on my front porch, his stance casual, his grin both quick and sincere. He looks perfectly at ease and sexy as hell. And there's not one iota of doubt in my mind that this man will be a huge star someday.

I step back away from the door, instinctively pulling the robe tighter. "What are you doing here?" I ask. I turn and head across my foyer toward the kitchen then, and toss my words back casually as I walk. "If you're coming for consolation that your interview was canceled, you really haven't come to the right place." That's a shot in the dark on my part. I still have no idea why they were striking the set for his interview, but considering Elliot's reaction, it obviously wasn't expected. And I'll admit I'm curious. And I'm not too proud to pry. Surreptitiously, anyway.

"They didn't cancel it," he says. He's right behind me. For that matter, he passes me as we reach the kitchen and heads straight for my refrigerator. He opens it, and his hand automatically goes for the cooler drawer on the bottom where I keep the beer. Since I don't drink anymore, it's for company only. He pulls one out, twists the cap off, then tosses it into the trashcan I have tucked in next to the cabinetry.

I watch in a kind of awed silence. His movements are so familiar it makes my chest hurt, and I have to shove my hands into the pockets of my robe to stifle the urge to reach out and touch him. This man hurt me. And no matter what Lindy says, it's going to take a lot before I trust him again.

I tell myself I'm not going to ask, but of course I do. "If it wasn't canceled, what happened?" I shoot for casual, but when the words come out, I have to wonder why I call myself an actress. I mean, talk about a crappy delivery.

He takes a long swig of beer. He's wearing black jeans and a white T-shirt. Probably Hanes, knowing Blake and his totally unpretentious manner. Whatever the brand, I can't help but think that he ought to be plastered above Times Square as an advertisement for all things male. Honestly, the way his biceps bulge against the thin cotton of that shirt is driving me to distraction. Which, naturally, pisses me off even more. I'm supposed to hate this man. For that matter, I *do* hate him.

I just happen to be in love with him, too.

"I canceled the interview," he says after swallowing. The words come out casually, as if we're discussing the weather or traffic. Just another mundane life fact.

To me, though, it's not mundane at all.

"What do you mean, *you* canceled it? I thought you set it up."

"That would be Elliot," he says, then turns to scour my kitchen with his eyes. "Do you have anything to eat?"

I toss my hands up, not sure if I should be amused or exasperated. From his expression, I can tell he's unimpressed with my histrionics. So I give in and point to the refrigerator.

He opens the fridge and starts to rummage about. After a second, I can't stand it any longer.

"Come on, Blake. Tell me. Why did you cancel it?"

He emerges from the fridge, the little box from Tobias open in one hand. "Who gave you chocolate?"

"A crazed fan," I say, dryly. "Now, *tell me.*"

He takes a step toward me, and I take a step back, which leaves my rear pressed against the kitchen island. He's right in front of me, and there's nowhere for me to go. I'm trapped.

He leans in even closer, and I hold my breath. I don't know what I expect, but I admit that my mind's in a muddle. My head is angry with this man, but my traitorous body is tingly, and I'm painfully aware that I'm wearing not a stitch of clothing under my fluffy bathrobe.

His shoulder brushes mine, and I stifle a gasp. He shifts, comes closer . . . and then pulls back enough that my personal space is restored. "It'll taste better at room temperature."

I blink in confusion and wonder what he's talking about. But a quick glance over my shoulder reveals the strawberry box sitting front and center on the kitchen island. He wasn't trying to get close; he was just vying for perfect food placement.

Isn't that just like a guy?

My reaction to his proximity flusters me, and I edge sideways, then scoot around the island until it's safely between us. I try to do this all casual-like, but I have the sinking feeling that I'm being incredibly obvious. Damn.

"You still haven't answered my question," I say, since my

brain isn't capable of more than stating the obvious at the moment.

"I wanted you to do the interview with me. When it looked like that wouldn't work out . . ."

He trails of with a shrug, and I'm left trying to process this new information that doesn't quite fit inside my current view of reality.

"You wanted me on the interview with you? That's why you came by my trailer?" Even as I say the words, I can feel the ice around my heart melting a little.

"Yup," he says, and his face is perfectly serious, perfectly clear. His eyes never leave mine, and I know that he's not lying. He's a good actor, don't get me wrong. But he's not *that* good.

"Oh," I say. And then, because there's just a little too much hope sneaking in around the edges of my heart, I ask, "Why?"

He shifts a bit, as if he's not comfortable in his skin. Or, more likely, in my kitchen. "I thought I owed you."

The tiny ember of hope dissolves into a pile of ash. "Don't do me any favors, Blake," I whisper, not able to look at him.

"Devi, it wasn't like that. If you'd just—"

I turn away, not wanting him to see the tears pooling in my eyes. "Does Elliot know you're here? Does he know why you canceled the show?" Suddenly Elliot's earlier rage makes a lot more sense to me. At the same time, I'm not really fighting fair. Blake's relationship with his manager was a point of contention throughout our entire relationship. Now that we have no relationship, I hardly have a right to bring it up.

Then again, he hardly has a right to come to my house. So I figure we're even.

Blake tilts his head back, as if he's fascinated by the antique tin tiles that cover my ceiling. When he straightens up to face me, I see resignation in his eyes. And maybe something else, too. Disappointment? I don't know. And now isn't the time to ask. I'm too on edge. And I'm honestly not sure what I want. He hurt me—he really did. But at the same time, I keep hearing Lindy's voice in my head telling me to give him another chance.

It's times like these when I remember why I love my job so much: real life is a hell of a lot more difficult than play-acting.

"We're actors, right?" he says, doing that mind-reading thing again.

"Yeah." But there's a question in my voice. I mean, where could he possibly be going with this?

"Then let's act. Let's forget our fight and focus on the movie. Let's shed our real selves and be pretend-Blake and pretend-Devi."

"Uh-huh. And what exactly are pretend-Blake and pretend-Devi supposed to do?"

"Get along," he says simply. "Work together. Go out in public without the threat of bloodshed."

"Sounds tricky," I say, but with a tiny smile.

"Devi . . ."

"I'm teasing. And obviously I get the work-together part. But the going out in public? That one intrigues me."

"It shouldn't," he says. "Press junkets. Promo opps. You know the game better than I do."

I also know the way his manager thinks. "This isn't coming from Elliot," I say. Could it be that Blake himself is tugging at this proximity string? Manufacturing an excuse to get close to me again?

Just the possibility makes my heart beat a little faster, and I hold my breath, waiting for him to answer.

"Tobias is concerned about fallout," he says, and I concentrate on breathing normally. Damn me. I fell too hard for this man. Even after breaking up with him, I'm still getting hurt.

"Fallout," I repeat, my voice as sharp as the knife in my heart. "Maybe we should just elope. That would be good for the box office." I pause, purely for dramatic effect. "Oh, wait. Marriage isn't even on your radar at the moment. Isn't that how you put it?"

"We had this argument weeks ago," he says, perfectly reasonably. And you know what? He's right.

Immediately, I deflate.

"Fine," I say. "I'm not going to go overboard pretending we're as chummy as we ever were, but I'll make an effort to be seen in public with you without the voodoo doll or the evil eye."

"You have a voodoo doll of me?"

"Of course," I say. "Internet shopping is a wonderful thing. I had it within hours of breaking up." I aim my glance toward his crotch and try out a tiny smile. "Any trouble in that department lately?"

"Sweetheart," he says, the word rolling off his tongue. "You were trouble enough."

Oh my.

I turn away, suddenly discomfited, and head to the fridge. I know I shouldn't drink yet another Diet Coke, but this seems like a day for breaking rules, so I pop the top on one I find hiding in the back behind a bottle of Evian.

When I turn back around, Blake has moved closer to the island and is plucking the strawberry out of the tiny box. "Are you saving this for someone?"

"Apparently, I'm saving it for you," I say. Blake loves chocolate as much as I loathe it. "You'll probably get one of your own tomorrow, anyway."

His brows lift in a question as he bites off a corner of the treat.

"Tobias," I explain. "A 'good job' treat."

"Really?" he asks, holding the strawberry (less one mouthful) in front of him. "Hmm."

"Hmm?"

"Just that I thought Tobias would know you better." He pops the rest into his mouth, then chews and swallows. "Not bad, but not nearly worthy of your performance. The chocolate's a little too bitter."

I laugh. "Isn't there an old saying about gift horses and mouths and such?"

"What can I say? I'm a chocolate connoisseur."

"You're a perfectionist," I shoot back. Which is true. It's also one of the things that both attracted me to him . . . and drove me absolutely nuts.

"Probably true. Right now, all I'm concerned about is the movie."

"The buzz," I say. "I never expected you to be a promo whore." He'd always told me he didn't like the limelight, but I suspect his attitude is changing.

The expression on his face shifts from bland to guarded. "Screw the buzz. I'm not interested in being a star because of who I'm dating." He pauses, then looks me straight in the eye. "Or not dating."

I look away, not sure what to say. Because even though he caused our breakup (and nothing's going to convince me otherwise), I can't argue with the fact that I was the one who said the actual words. And to now hear the regret in his voice . . .

Honestly, it's all a bit too much too fast. And having him standing so close to me is making thinking difficult.

I take another swig of my Diet Coke and try to act casual. "So if you aren't here about Tobias's PR mandate, then why did you come?"

"We've got a scene tomorrow," he says. "I thought maybe we could run lines."

"Oh. Right. Okay." Considering how much I *didn't* want to discuss characters and scenes with him earlier today, the anticipation I'm now feeling is a little disconcerting. I need to get my emotions back on track. Hell, I need to take control of the whole conversation.

"The whole scene?" I ask with a smile. "Or just the part where I hit and kick you?"

"Looking for a little catharsis?"

He says it with such an easy confidence, that I can't help but grin. "Maybe I am."

"Well, all right then," he says, then spreads his arms wide, scrunches up his face, and closes his eyes. "Have at me."

I am not going to laugh. He's my ex. He broke my heart. And I am so not laughing.

He opens one eye. "Come on, already. Don't be a girlie-girl."

Damn it. I start laughing.

"See?" Blake says. "I'm not the spawn of Satan."

"Don't be too sure," I counter. "I have a feeling Satan has a very wry sense of humor."

"You wound me."

"Not as much as you wounded me."

The pain cuts across his face with as much intensity as if I'd slashed him with a Ginsu, and I feel myself crumple inside.

"Devi," he says, his voice as raw as my heart. "I am truly sorry." He reaches out and strokes my cheek, and I want to melt under his touch. I want to press my body up against him and put my arms around him. I want to pull him close and ask him if it can still work between us.

And even while all those thoughts swirl through my head, I want to kick myself for being so insecure and vulnerable that I fall back into the arms of the man who wounded me mere minutes after he walk back through my door.

It's one of those awkward moments. The touch between us, so sweet and gentle. And me chastising myself and dredging up harsh reality. I don't know if I should kiss him or run from him, but the question is thankfully brushed off the table by the buzz of the intercom. "Ms. Taylor?"

This time, I know it's Andy.

"Andrew Garrison, right?" I say, having leaped toward the intercom and away from Blake at the first possible moment. "You can send him on in."

"Federal Express, actually. I signed for it. Shall I bring it up to the house?"

"Yes, please."

Saved by the courier.

I turn back to Blake and shrug. "Probably something from the studio," I say. "We can get down to the script as soon as Lucas drops it off."

What I don't say is how grateful I am to the anonymous sender for timing the package so well. Another minute or two, and I might have actually forgotten that I hate this man. And how awkward would that be?

Two minutes later, though, I'm not grateful at all. I'm confused.

Because the envelope that Lucas just gave me has *my* address as the return. But it doesn't have my name.

Instead, it lists the sender as Play.Survive.Win.

"Is this some kind of joke?" I demand, but I can see right away that it's not. Blake's face is too pale, and he's eyeing the envelope with just a bit too much trepidation. "You didn't send this," I say, and it's a statement, not a question.

"No," he confirms, "I didn't."

"Publicity stunt?" I ask. "Something Tobias cooked up to keep me in character?"

"Could be," he says, but I can tell from his expression he doesn't really believe it. This isn't Tobias's style.

"Maybe I should just throw it away," I say. I'm holding the package in both hands, and I see that they are shaking. I've lived in Melanie Prescott's head for too long. I know that what's in this envelope is Bad News.

Worse, I know that throwing it away won't make it go away.

I look up and meet Blake's eyes. He knows it, too.

"Give it to me," he demands.

I start to, then shake my head. "No. It's addressed to me." I take a deep breath, then swallow, my throat dry. "It's my problem."

"*Our* problem," he says. "I'm in this with you."

Considering I'm the one holding the ticking FedEx package, that point is debatable. But it's a sweet thought, so I don't call him on it. Instead, I just pull the little cardboard strip to open the envelope. As I do, I step back a bit, holding it away from my body as if the thing might explode. It doesn't, of course, and so I cautiously bring it closer, then slide my finger into the opening.

"What is it?" Blake asks.

"Another envelope." I pull it out. This one is standard letter size, with no return address. The only writing is my name printed in block letters across the middle: Devilla Marigold Taylor. (You can see why my mom shortened it for professional purposes all those years ago. What I've never understood is why she saddled me with it in the first place. But when I ask her, all she says is, "Your father." And then she shakes her head and changes the subject.)

As I hold on to this smaller envelope, Blake takes the larger FedEx one. I watch as he slides his hand inside, then pulls the edges apart and inspects it visually.

"I know how to empty an envelope," I say testily.

"Can't hurt to double-check." And since that's just so damn reasonable, I don't even argue. He nods toward my hands. I'm gripping the envelope so tightly that my fingers ache. "Do you want me to do it?"

I shake my head, mentally chastising myself for getting all

worked up over nothing. This has to be a joke, right? Maybe Tobias hired a new PR firm. Maybe one of the producers has a sick sense of humor.

I don't know, but there has to be some explanation. So I quash my fear, then slide my fingernail under the edge of the sealed flap. I'm just about to rip when Blake reaches out. "Wait!"

"Are you nuts?" I say, jerking the envelope back toward me and away from his grasp. "It's not a bomb!"

"DNA," he says, and I gape stupidly at him. "On the flap," he clarifies. "From where whoever sent this licked it."

"Oh." I lick my own lips. "Right." I look up at him, my little bubble of manufactured comfort rupturing with a *pop*. "So you don't think this is just some goofball stunt?"

He doesn't answer. After a moment, I nod. The truth is, I don't think so either.

"Just open it, Devi. We won't know for certain until you open it."

Sometimes that man is far too pragmatic. But he's right, and I do. I rip a tiny bit of the corner and then open the envelope from the end, leaving the flap—and all that lovely DNA—perfectly intact.

I squeeze the edges and peer inside to see a single folded sheet of paper. "Here we go," I say, then pull the paper out. I open it, and then—even though I'm expecting the worst—I gasp at what I see:

PLAY OR DIE
My daughter, my sister, and a crazy old man.
The clue's where he lost it and Jack found it again.
But where to look to find the key?

A house not a home, though used for a fee,
A reflection of grandeur, of good times once seen,
And many have seen her upon the grand screen.
Play or don't play—it's all up to you.
But if you decline, Death will Become You.

Chapter 14

"**N**o," I say. "No way. No *fucking* way." I'm on my feet, pacing, when Blake snags the paper from my hand.

By the time I calm down enough to face him, he's already read it, and I see my own confusion and fear etched in his expression.

"This has to be a joke," I say. "Somebody in Tobias's office has a sick sense of humor. This is a publicity stunt. It has to be."

"Does it?" he asks, sounding a little shell-shocked. "I hope you're right. And if it is, someone is getting their ass fired in the morning."

"I'm calling Tobias," I say, heading toward the phone.

"*Wait.*" He's beside me in an instant, his hand tight on my arm. "What if it's not?"

I shake my head slowly, my brain really not ready to process the what-if-it's-not line of thinking. "It has to be," I say.

"I know. I agree." He hooks a finger under my chin and tilts my head up until he's looking me straight in the eye. "But what if it's not?"

His voice is strong, and firm, and I hate him for being right. "It can't be real," I say, but weakly this time. "But you're right. We can't call anyone until we know for sure." I've spent enough time with the script and with Mel to know that if this really is PSW, then the rules are clear: no outside help. If I call Tobias to ask if he's pulling a prank on me, he might fess up, and all will be well. But if he says no . . .

Well, no matter how hard I try to explain away the reason for my call, he's going to know something is up. And if he gets worried . . . if he calls the cops . . . if he calls Mel . . .

I shudder, because the ramifications are just too horrible.

"There has to be a way to prove it's just a PR stunt," I say, clinging desperately to the hope that it *is* just a PR stunt, even though a tiny part of me keeps whispering that no one I know would be so cruel as to pull that kind of crap. Not knowing what I went through with Janus. That would just be evil, and the people I work with aren't evil. Are they?

"There's one way to know for sure," Blake says, holding up the clue. "We follow the trail."

I shake my head. "No. No." I can't explain why that's so horrible, but, "No. That would make it real. And I can't deal with—"

"You *have* to deal with it," he says. "We both do."

He steers me toward the couch, and we both sit down. And when he takes my hand so intimately, I don't pull away. I'm confused and scared, and I want the comfort, and I'm not too proud to take it. Even from Blake.

"What do we know?" he asks, but gently.

"That I got a weird message from PSW."

"It *says* it's from PSW," he clarifies. "But we both think it's a publicity stunt."

I nod. I'm not entirely sure that *think* is correct. But I'm definitely hoping it's a stunt. Because right then, that little shred of hope is like a thin red thread on which my hold on reality depends. Snap the thread, and I snap with it.

"We can't call anyone and ask," he goes on. "So the only way to know for sure is to start playing."

I look up, my heart pounding, as I suddenly realize that there is another way. "We can check the game," I say. "The real game."

Now it was Blake's turn to look confused.

"We log in," I say. "Remember the script? When Mel played, there was at least one message for her in the real PSW's message center."

He considers that for a moment, then nods. "All right. Let's check. But Devi," he adds, looking at me intently, "if there's something there, it proves the worst. But if you've got no messages, that doesn't prove anything."

I nod, quick and sharp. I know he's right. All that the lack of a message would prove is that I have no messages. But it would calm me down. Give me one more thread to grasp throughout the night. Because I'm certain that if it *is* a PR stunt, we'll find out in the morning when we go to the set. All I have to do is keep my head on straight until then.

My laptop is in my new bag, and we haul it out and set it up on the coffee table in front of the sofa. And even as Blake urges me on, I enter the address in my Web browser, head over to the game, and log in with my user ID. It's been years since I played, but I use the same ID and password for everything I do online. It's not safe, but it makes my life easier.

Sure enough, the information is accepted and access is granted. Seconds later, the message center portal page pops up, and I click over to the one message that's waiting for me.

>>>http://www.playsurvivewin.com<<<

PLAY.SURVIVE.WIN

PLEASE LOGIN
PLAYER USER NAME: *LuvPrada*
PLAYER PASSWORD: * * * * * * * *

. . . *please wait*
. . . *please wait*
. . . *please wait*
Password approved

>>>**Read New Messages**<<<   >>>Create New Message<<<
. . . *please wait*

WELCOME TO MESSAGE CENTER

You have one new message.
New Message:
To: LuvPrada
From: System Administration
Subject: Message Filed by Assassin

Report:

- Toxin delivered as per instructions. Awaiting confirmation of infection.
- Delivery of additional systems established and scheduled as per introductory instructions.
- Game currently proceeding on schedule.

>>>>End Report<<<<

I stare at the computer, not quite able to process the words on the screen. Only two stand out: *Toxin delivered.*

The words seem to pulsate on the screen, mocking me. No way. It's not possible.

And yet there it is, in black and white.

Toxin delivered.

Dear God in heaven . . . it's real.

Chapter

15

I can't stop shaking. My hands. My arms. My teeth.

My entire body seems to tremble from within, and it's all I can do to crumple the note in my fist, then collapse onto the couch.

Dear God, this is real. Someone is after me. Again.

The thought is too much to bear, and I pull my knees up against my chest and press my forehead to my knees. My back is pressed hard against the plush sofa cushions, and I feel like—if I just try a little harder—I can make myself so small that I'll completely disappear.

No one can find me then. I'll just be gone.

Gone.

At the moment, I want nothing more.

An eternity passes, and then I hear a whimper. I've been lost, zoned out in some hidden place in my mind, and it takes me a while to realize the sound is coming from me. I'm rocking, too, hugging myself and moving on the couch. I know I should stop. That I should get up and hold my chin high and say, "Fuck you," to the world or to the bad guy or to whatever asshole thought that sending that note was a good idea.

I can't do that, though. I remember too clearly the press of metal against my neck. The sound of the buttons popping off my shirt as Janus had so casually flipped the tip of his blade against the flimsy threads. The sting on my breasts where his blade drew blood.

And the ultimate horror of his hands on my body.

I feel those hands now, and I thrash, screaming, even though some part of me knows that Janus isn't here. It's only Blake, trying to hold me. Trying to comfort me.

But there really is no comfort to be had.

I'd finally gotten my head back on straight. Surely fate wouldn't be so cruel as to push me back down.

Not again. Please, God, not again.

My whole body seems to tense, each pore seething with longing. With a desperate need to escape into a sweet oblivion. I can imagine the feel of the pills in my hand, their negligible weight ironic when compared to the punch they pack. So easy.

No, no, NO!

I'd flushed every last Valium, Vicodin, Xanax, and Percocet down the toilet months ago. I was clean, and I was staying clean.

Except . . .

I can't do this. I can't survive this without the drugs . . . and at the same time, once I take another pill, I know in my heart there's no turning back. I beat addiction once. I don't think I can do it again.

A hysterical bubble rises in my throat, and I squeeze my eyes tight. I'm losing it, and I don't want to be losing it. I'm strong. Isn't that what my therapist has been telling me for years? I survived Janus. I beat the drugs. I. Am. Strong.

And yet a few little words send me whimpering to my couch.

Clearly, my therapist is wrong. Which begs the question of why I pay her such an obscene hourly rate.

There it is again, that perverse sense of humor. I tell myself I'm calming down. That humor is my way of taking control. But I don't believe it.

I don't have any control here. None at all.

I close my eyes and try to hide inside myself again. Because that, I think, is the scariest part of all.

Chapter

16

Blake had never felt more helpless in his entire life.

He'd watched as she read the message. Watched as her face went white and terror filled her eyes. Watched as she'd curled up on the couch, whimpering like a frightened child.

And then he'd watched, helpless and terrified, as Devi slipped inside herself. He felt lost, impotent, and all he wanted to do was hunt down and kill the bastard who'd done this to her. Since that hardly seemed an option at the moment, he wanted to hold Devi herself. Hold her and comfort her and tell her that it would be okay. That he would never let anything happen to her. That he loved her and that he'd protect her and that if he could erase all the bad stuff between them, he'd do it in a heartbeat.

He couldn't say those things, though, any more than he could break the bastard's neck who'd sucked her into the game. He'd tried. So help him, he'd tried to hold her and pull her close. She'd pushed him away, though, and from the wild terror in her eyes, he knew that he shouldn't force her. She was straddling memories and reality, her body and mind equally in peril. Her body, he intended to protect with his life. Her head, though . . . about that, he hadn't a clue how to help.

She was terrified. And the truth was, she had reason to be. All he could do was love her, and he'd already seen that loving Devi simply wasn't enough.

He knelt in front of her. "Devi," he whispered.

No response. He took a deep breath, then took her hands, hers limp in his tight grip. And then he waited. He moved his thumb softly over her skin until, finally, she gripped back. At that moment, Blake was sure his heart would explode. He could do this. He could protect her.

But then, when she lifted her head and looked at him, her eyes pleading, the bubble burst, and he was lost again. Lost and grasping.

"Devi," he said. "Baby, I—"

"No." The word was whispered, barely even voiced. But he heard it, and he felt the pain behind it.

"Sweetheart, we'll get through it. We can—"

"*What?*" she demanded, and although the fear in her eyes etched deep into his soul, the fire in her voice gave him hope. "What can we do?"

"We can fight. Devi, we can do whatever it takes."

She shook her head, looking at him almost pityingly. "Blake, someone is trying to *kill* me. Someone has fucking *poisoned* me.

It's not a movie. It's not even a game. It's real. And it scares the shit out of me."

He watched, helpless, as her shoulders shook and tears ran down her face. She'd blown whatever courage she'd manage to collect, and now she was collapsing again, lost in a nightmare that she'd never expected. He wanted to believe that the well would fill again. That she would remember how much she loved the life she had, and how much he knew she wanted to fight for it.

He wanted to believe that, but he didn't know if he could. She'd been injured so badly already, and after fighting the battle once, he wasn't certain that she'd want to fight it again.

No matter what, though, he was there to fight it with her. He'd see her through this, whether she wanted his help or not.

He wanted to tell her all that. Hell, he just wanted to tell her that he loved her. But the words wouldn't come. Instead he moved silently to the couch and pulled her into his arms. She didn't hesitate this time, and that probably scared him most of all. Because the strong woman he'd fallen for—the woman who hadn't hesitated to kick his ass out her door—was disintegrating in front of him.

That reality broke his heart. It also pissed him off.

And once he got his hands on the bastard who was behind this, that man was surely going down.

At the moment, though, there wasn't anyone around to hit. There was only Devi, scared and vulnerable in his arms. And if he couldn't make it right, at least he could keep her safe. Or he could damn well try.

He stroked her hair, murmuring soft words. She was scared, he knew that. But nothing could prepare him for the depths of fear he saw in her eyes.

"I can't do this again." The tiniest shake of her head. "I can't be a victim again."

"You aren't a victim," he said, his hands on her shoulders and his eyes looking deep into her own. His instinctive response was to hold her and comfort her, but he'd fought it. She didn't need soft words. She needed to get her edge back. She'd need it if she was going to get through this. And he fully intended to do whatever it took to make sure that she *did* get through this. "This is your show, Devi. You're the one in charge here."

She actually snorted at that, which he took as a good sign. She shifted, then waved at the table and the note he'd dropped there. "How the hell do you figure that?"

"We follow the clues. We win. You can do that."

"I can't," she said. "I can't, and I won't."

"Won't?"

She lifted her chin. "Maybe I don't want to play."

The haughtiness in her tone almost made him smile. This was the diva coming out. But the diva wasn't going to win this round. He knew it, and deep down, he was certain that Devi knew it, too.

"You have to play, sweetheart," he said, gently. "Toxin, remember? The kill switch?" At the start of preproduction, everyone in the cast had been given a summary of the game—both the computerized version and the real-world version that Mel had played. The kill switch was an incentive that was built into both versions of the game. In the computer version, a player that doesn't start to play the game within twenty-four hours basically forfeits their right to play. But whoever brought the game into the real world must have realized that forfeiting a player's right to play wasn't going to cut it. So the real-world kill switch forfeited a player's life. In Mel's case, she'd been infected with a toxin and had only twenty-four hours to follow the clues to find the antidote.

Devi apparently had been given the same incentive. And that really wasn't sitting well with Blake. "Devi," he said again. "You have to find the antidote."

"But that's just it," she said. "I think I must have beat the system."

He just stared at her, baffled. "What are you talking about?"

"No one I don't know gets close to me," she said, her eyes full of hope. "After Janus, that just doesn't happen. I've come out of my shell, yes, but I'm hardly back on the party circuit dancing and drinking and bumping uglies with strangers until four a.m. Not anymore."

"So you're saying—"

"I'm saying that my reclusiveness is my ace in the hole."

Blake could only shake his head, because he knew how much she wanted to believe that. He took her hand, held it tight. "This game isn't about bluffing. If it says delivered, then it's delivered."

The hope on her face dissolved. "You really believe that? I'm infected with something?"

He did, but he couldn't bring himself to say it. Instead, he just stroked her cheek. "We have to assume that you are. But even if you're right—even if he couldn't get to you with the poison—you still have to play the game. You know that, right?"

"Why?" she asked, her voice choked. "If there's no poison, why should I?" She stood up, fear and anger coming off her in waves. "I mean, why the hell do I pay all this money for security if it can't keep me secure? It *can*. I'm safe in here. There is no way in hell he's getting in here."

"And when you go out?"

"I'll take a bodyguard," she said, her tone rising. "I've got money, Blake. I can use it to keep me safe."

He took her hand, understanding that she was terrified, but also needing her to understand reality.

"A bodyguard can't keep you safe from a sniper. A bodyguard can't keep your friends safe."

She cocked her head at that. "My friends?"

"You read the script, just like I did. What happened when Mel said she wasn't going to play?"

He watched her face as she remembered. As the hard, brutal truth set in. "They killed her boyfriend," she finally said. And then he watched as she closed her eyes in defeat. She'd known all along that she would have to play, of course. Now, though, she'd finally accepted what she already knew.

"I can't do it." Her voice was raw, almost a whisper. She opened her eyes and looked at him. "That message is nonsense. Gibberish. I can't play this game. I can't win. I'm not Melanie. I'm an actress. I mean, there's a reason I've got a stunt double, you know?"

The corner of her mouth lifted in the slightest hint of a smile as she said that, and Blake clung to that, desperate for any sign the Devi he knew was coming back to him.

"You could do your own stunts, and you damn well know it.

It's the bonding company that won't let you." That won a genuine smile, albeit small, and the band around his chest eased a bit more. "You're smart. You can figure this out."

She dropped back down onto the far end of the couch, not so much pulling away from him as pulling herself together. He'd seen her do it before. It was the way she attacked a role. And this role was about as important as they come.

He watched as she closed her eyes and took three deep breaths. When she opened them again, the fear was masked. Not gone, but hidden. Behind what, though, he didn't know.

"Devi?"

"No. Not Devi," she said. "Devi doesn't have a clue how to play the game. But Melanie . . . ?" Her eyes were wide, as if she was holding back tears. "Maybe I just need to be Melanie. She knows how to win, right?"

His heart stuttered in his chest, and he stumbled over his thoughts. Yes, it was good that she was getting her courage back. But he wanted the strength to flow *from* her. Not *through* her.

Still, any port in a storm, right? And ultimately, even if she was playing Melanie Prescott, in the end, it was all about Devi.

And the Devi Taylor he knew had the strength to get through anything. She just didn't know it yet.

"*You* can do this," he said. "Draw on Mel all you want, but at the end of the day, it's *you* who's going to make it through this nightmare."

"Or not make it."

He took her shoulders. "You will make it. I refuse to accept any other outcome."

A tiny smile. "Well, now I feel so much better."

"I'm serious, Devi. *We* can do this. We can solve the damn puzzle. We can follow the clues, and we can figure out who's behind this, and we can beat this thing."

"Oh, really?" She shook off his touch and stood up. She was still wearing the white cotton robe, and now she wrapped her arms around herself, looking soft and a little lost. "You're going to help me? You're just going to step up to the plate and save the day?"

"I'm going to damn well try."

"I don't rewind that easily."

"Dammit, Devi. This isn't about me. I'm not trying to win forgiveness. I'm trying to keep you alive."

"Really?" There was a hint of sarcasm in her tone, but underneath it, he thought he heard a legitimate question. And he had to admit that it was a fair question, too. Because if he was going to answer honestly, he had to admit that, yes, in the deep recesses of his mind, he did fantasize that if he could find the bastard who was doing this and pound him into a bloody pulp, then Devi would realize he loved her and come back into his arms.

Dear God, was he really so selfish?

Yes, he probably was. But fantasies of rewarded chivalry aside, the bottom line remained the same. "I want to keep you alive, Devi. Do my motives really matter so much?"

"They do to me," she said, her voice like ice.

He cringed, the force of her words like a physical blow. His chest tightened, his heart breaking with the fear he heard in her voice. She was so fragile. And he hated the fact that part of her wounds had come from him. He wanted to hold her. To assure her that everything would be fine. That she would heal. And that he'd be there to help her.

But that wasn't a conversation she was ready for. So instead, he just told her what she needed to hear.

"Be mad at me all you want," he said, grabbing the note off the table. "I don't give a damn." He held the damn thing up. "Because so long as you're furious with me, you're not being scared of this."

Chapter

17

"**D**on't be too sure," I say, but I can't help the way my heart feels a little bit lighter. I owe that in part to Blake. I know that. He sat here with me while I let myself drown in terror, fighting the whirlpool that would pull me back to the safe comfort of the meds.

Except there *is* no comfort there. Not really. There's just oblivion. I know that better than anyone.

I fought my way kicking and screaming out of that pale gray death, and there is no way in hell I'm going back. I *am* a fighter. Hell, I fought the drugs, didn't I? And I won. The proof is today, after all. I haven't called my shrink, haven't called any one of my friends who could slip me a Valium or two under the table. I've called on nothing but my own strength.

And, slowly, the terror has faded. Not disappeared—I'm still as scared as shit—but I'm not letting it debilitate me. I can't. Not this time.

Not ever again.

I still can't quite believe this is really happening to me, but I know that I'll get through this drug-free—or I'll die trying. After all, I have a secret weapon. *Melanie Prescott.*

I'm not an actress for nothing, and I've spent too many days and nights in Mel's head to let her fail me now. For that matter, I spent too many days with the woman herself. Studying her. The way she moves, the way she thinks. Her sense of humor.

I know Mel. And on the set, I can become Mel.

Now, I just need to become Mel *off* the set. She survived the game. Now she's going to help me survive.

That, at least, is my plan. And, yes, it gives me some small comfort.

And as much as Blake gives me comfort, too, I know that he can't stay. Because I can't hold his life in my hands. I'm just not that strong.

"Devi?" He's peering at me, clearly afraid I'm going to bolt like a rabbit. Either that, or do something stupid.

I wave away his concern. "I'm okay now. I just needed . . ." I trail off, not sure what I needed. I'd pulled away from reality, that much was for sure. But why? And what if I did it again, when the stakes were truly high? Lose it when the killer's nearby, and I'll be losing a hell of a lot more than my pride. I'll be losing my life.

That's not something I can think about. I'm Mel, remember? And Mel is cool under pressure.

I draw in a breath and start over. "I just needed to freak out for a few minutes. But I'm better now." When all else fails, try the truth.

"Good." He puts the note on the table. "Then let's get to work."

"No."

I watch his face, the actor's mind struggling with what expression to show. "No?"

"No," I repeat.

"Devi, are you—"

"I'm fine. I'll be fine." I stand up again, my hands deep in the pockets of my robe. "But I'm doing this on my own."

"The hell you are. If this is the game, then you need a goddamn protector."

I can hear the sharp edge in his voice. Frustration and fear, all there about me. For me. And damned if I don't want to run to him and let him hold me. Because the truth is that I want his comfort. The truth is, I love him.

That really doesn't matter, though. Or, rather, it matters too much.

"You can't be my protector, Blake. You know that. Not unless the game assigns you the role."

"Maybe it did," he says. "Maybe I *am* your protector." He's moving fast now, heading toward my computer and pulling up the game interface. In no time at all, he's called up the log-in screen and typed in his information.

"You play?"

"Once," he said. "Right after I got the role."

I hold my breath, thinking that maybe I'm wrong. Maybe he *is* my protector. And maybe this nightmare is about to turn a corner.

But then his message center loads, and I see that it is empty. And I have to face what I already knew—I'm all alone.

I draw a breath and put my hand on his shoulder. "Blake, you have to go now."

"No," he says, his voice harsh and unyielding. "I'm not leaving you."

"Help outside the game is forbidden," I say. "You know that. You've read as much as I have about Mel and Jenn and the rules of the game. Pull in someone else outside the game, and I put them at risk. I mean, look at Andy."

Blake knows as well as I do that Andy was shot with a poisoned dart after offering help to Jenn. Obviously, Andy survived. But there's no guarantee that Blake would be so lucky. And that's not a risk I'm willing to take. It's not a risk I'm willing to take with Mel, either. So although I can *be* her, I can't *call* her. She already survived the game once. If I somehow caused her to get shot by a sniper's bullet now, I don't think I could live with myself.

No cops, no Blake. No anyone, until I find out who my protector is, I'm all alone, and it's all I can do not to reach for Blake, seeking comfort where I really shouldn't be looking for it.

He watches me, his eyes looking right through me. "In other words, you want me to leave because you care about me."

A shiver courses through me. "Yes," I say, which is more than I really want to. "That's right."

I watch the emotion play across his face, a slot machine that finally stops on pity and self-loathing. "Devi," he says, his voice raw. "I'm sorry."

I blink, spilling the tears that have welled in my eyes.

"Dammit, I didn't mean to make you—"

"No," I say, as he gently wipes my tears. "It's okay. I just need . . ." And then it's my turn to trail off. Because I know what I need. It's the same thing I've always needed. *Him.* But I just don't know if that's possible.

But then he's pulling me close. My body, naked under the robe, tingles with awareness as he brushes my tears away with the pad of his thumb. "I'm not leaving you."

"Yes," I whisper, my voice hoarse through my tears. "You are. If something happened to you because of me, I don't think I could—"

He silences me with a kiss, deep and sweet and erotic and tender. Everything I remember and more. His strength is in that kiss, and as I hook my arms around his neck, I feel myself weaken. I need help. He wants to help me.

I moan a little and press myself against him, my body saying yes even though I haven't quite convinced my mouth to cooperate.

He's warm and familiar, and I want his strength. I need it, honestly, way more than I ever needed a drug. And although I know I should fight and scream and kick to keep him away, I also know that I can't stand the thought of going through this alone. Do that, I think, and I will surely end up popping the lid on a bottle of little white pills.

I pull away, searching his face until I find the courage. "Blake," I begin, my voice tentative and soft. "I want—"

I close my mouth, because in truth, I don't know what I want. Not exactly. Not other than that I want this nightmare to end.

"It's okay," he says. "I understand."

"Do you? I'm amazed because I don't, and—"

I don't finish the sentence, though, because his mouth is on mine again, and this time it isn't soft or sweet. This time it's passionate and wild, and my entire body is burning from the heat that Blake is generating.

His hands, I realize, are inside my robe. And so help me, I want them there. Want them all over me. Want to lose myself in sex, and forget this nightmare. I want to float away. I want Blake. I want him so much I can taste it. Taste *him*.

"Blake," I whisper. "Please."

And then my hands are on his belt, and we're fumbling at clothes and—

"Ms. Taylor?" Lucas's voice filters through the kitchen console. I shift toward the control panel, planning on hitting the mute button, but Lucas is too fast. "There's a man here. A Mr. Garrison. He says he's here to read lines."

Damn.

The kitchen unit has one of the video monitors, so we can see Andy standing by the gate, his entire body tense. I can't blame him. Security checks are for airlines and federal buildings, not friends and coworkers.

"Tell him you've got it covered," Blake says, his hand on my bare hip. I look down and realize my robe is gaping open. I take a step back, then knot the thing. I see the cloud in Blake's eyes, but look away, too chicken to face the issue.

"Not because of us," Blake says, his voice somehow both sad and harsh. "You're dangerous now. *We're* dangerous now."

The game.

I nod, once again going a little numb. "You're right. Of course. I wasn't thinking." I lean forward and tap the intercom. "Lucas, give Andy the headset for a second." I watch as he does, and once Andy has it pressed to his ear, I say, "Listen, I appreciate you coming all this way, but something's come up, and it's really not a convenient time for me."

Wow. I sound so damn normal. There's a reason I got that Oscar nod. I mean, considering the severely *un*-normal circumstances, I must be one hell of an actress.

Or, maybe I'm not so good, because he's still standing there, his back to the gatehouse, his face aimed at the security camera, and the handset pressed tight to his ear. "It's important, Devi. Let me in."

"I'll get the lines down, Andy. I mean, I appreciate the help and all, but I promise you I can handle it."

"It's not about the goddamn lines," he barks. And then he holds up a piece of paper. I can't see any of the writing on it, but my stomach falls anyway. Because somehow, I know what's coming. "It's the game, Devi. And I'm your goddamn protector."

Chapter 18

"What the hell is going on?" The words are out of Blake's mouth before I can stop him, and he's got Andy by the shoulder and is yanking him inside. The whole thing is very cloak-and-dagger, like something out of a movie, and I actually smile. Not because it's funny, but because I'm on that knife edge between reality and the abyss.

I think Blake knows it, too, because he steps away from Andy without pressing for an answer, then moves to take my hand. But not before first brushing a soft finger over my lip and giving me a smile of his own.

Andy looks between us, then takes a tentative step farther into my foyer.

"It's okay," I say, even though nothing is really okay at all.

"Well?" Blake demands.

"What are you doing here?" Andy retorts, his voice sharp. I'm a little surprised at his tone, actually. As far as I know, Andy and Blake get along fine. I know they've had meetings, giving Blake the opportunity to question Andy about the game. And I've never gotten one whiff of gossip about any bad blood between them.

Of course, these are hardly normal circumstances. And neither man wants to yield the role of knight on a shiny white steed.

"I came to run lines with Devi," Blake says

"What a coincidence," Andy replies. "So did I." He looks at me. "We need to talk."

"Clearly," Blake says, before I can get a word out. "So talk."

I take a step forward, my earlier instincts to hide under a rock fading as I'm pushed out of the center of my own drama. Besides, the air's getting a little thick with testosterone. Call me a girlie-girl, but at the moment, all I want is peace. And some explanations.

I point to Blake. "You, be quiet. And you," I continue, the finger moving to Andy, "explain what you meant outside. About being my protector."

He casts a quick glance Blake's way, and I can see he wants to argue. I'm not giving him the chance. "Talk with him in the room," I insist, "or don't talk at all."

For a second, I think he's going to take door number two, but then he nods. He ignores Blake and looks straight at me. "It's the game, Devi. Play.Survive.Win. It's for real. And you're right in the middle of it."

"I know," I say, and his face shifts from concern to surprise to horror.

"Oh, shit," he says. "You've already gotten the first message." He holds out a hand. "Let me see it."

"Whoa there, cowboy," Blake says. "Finish your part. What do you mean, you're her protector?"

"Just that," Andy says. "I was at home. You know, getting ready to come over here. And I thought I'd check my e-mails. And there it was."

Even though I'd known what he was going to say, my stomach drops anyway. This is for real. And if I'm the target, and Andy is the protector, that means that somewhere out there an assassin has been tagged. And it's the assassin's job to kill me.

Suddenly, I'm not nearly as irritated that Blake is taking charge. I'm too lost in my own fears. I move into my living room, the men behind me, then sink into the familiar comfort of my couch and pull a pillow to my chest. Blake is beside me immediately, his hand on mine. "Don't go there," he whispers. "You've already been there once tonight, and that's not a place you want to go back to."

I nod, because he's right. I almost got lost in the black. But getting lost won't do me any good. All that can save me now is to fight. And I'm not alone. I have Blake.

And now I have Andy, too.

The thought gives me strength, and I look up, shifting my gaze between them. "All right," I say. "What now?"

Andy's head shifts just a little bit, and then he says what I already know. "Now, we follow the clues." Then he looks at Blake and adds the zinger. "And we follow them alone."

Blake is immediately up and on his feet. "I don't think so."

"I do," Andy says. "And I'm the only one in this room who's ever played the game before."

"No. I'm in this now."

"Then you're an ass," Andy spits back. "Because if whoever's behind this finds out, you just might end up dead."

The harsh tone scares me as much as his words. And I know they're true. No matter how much I might have earlier justified Blake staying to help me, now that Andy's here, I can't hold on to those selfish reasons any longer. "He can't possibly know, can he?" I ask. My assassin could easily be a woman; I know that. But to me, whoever is out to get me is Janus. Hoarse voice. Broad shoulders. And the scent of old urine.

I fight a gag as the memory washes over me, and I'm thankful when Blake takes my hand, sharing his strength.

"No," Blake says. "He can't possibly know."

Andy's eyebrows raise. "Really? Your security system is electronic. Someone could have tapped in. You're at the base of a hill. Someone could be listening now. Whoever is behind this is serious . . . and seriously supplied. Don't put anything past him. Not if you want to survive."

"He's right," I say, letting go of Blake's hand. I turn away, too, simply because I can't bear to look at him. We'd connected again today, but now . . .

Well, now I have to push him away.

"Devi," Blake says. "Think about this."

"She *has* thought about it," Andy says. "You're the one not thinking." Blake glares at him, but Andy doesn't slow down. "She draws someone else in, she's breaking the rules. She's risking her life, my life. And most of all, she's risking the life of the person she brings in. How do you think she'll feel when your body is on a slab at the morgue?"

"You son of a bitch," Blake says.

Andy holds his hands up in a gesture of self-defense. "Hey,

I'm just telling it like it is. You tell me. Do you really want that on your head?"

I know Blake well enough to see that he's torn. His protective instincts have kicked in. But in this case, I already have a protector. And as much as I'd like to have two, I know what I have to do.

"Blake," I say, putting a gentle hand on his arm. "You need to go."

"Devi, this isn't a game. I can help you. I can—"

"It *is* a game," I say. "And if I break the rules, you're going to be the one who gets killed." I meet his eyes, hoping he can read the emotion there. "I lost you once. I don't think I could stand losing you forever."

He hesitates, but I know I have him. "You're sure?"

I'm not. But at the same time, I am. So I nod. "I'm sure."

"Okay, then." I watch as his chest rises and falls. Then he takes me by the shoulders and bends a bit so that he's looking straight into my eyes. "But if you don't show up on the set tomorrow, I'm calling the cops. Hell, I'm calling the FBI. I don't care about me, but I'm going to do whatever it takes to keep you alive. Got it?"

I shiver a bit, feeling all warm and tingly from his attention. "Yeah," I say. "I got it."

"I'm sorry," Andy says, as we watch the video monitor. Blake's car disappears down the drive and through the security gate, and then he's gone. I feel a pain in my gut as intense as if someone had stabbed me.

"It's not your fault. And you're right. He needed to go. It's the only way to make sure he's safe."

"And now we can concentrate on you. On finding the antidote, and on winning the game."

"Yes," I say. "Let's do that." Before Blake left, we showed Andy both my clue and the message about the toxin. He took it all in, promising that we were going to play the game like pros . . . and we were going to win.

What can I say? That plan works just fine for me.

Since I'm feeling a little self-conscious in my robe, I tell him that my laptop's in the living room, but that he can move it to the kitchen. Then I run upstairs and change into real clothes.

When I come back, I find him at my huge oak table. It's antique and well-worn. It used to belong to my grandmother, and then my mother. My mom passed it off to me when she downsized and moved to Florida. Sitting there gives me strength, as if I know the women in my family are watching out for me. That's a good thing. Especially since at the moment, I need all the help I can get.

Andy is holding the clue in one hand and a pencil in the other. I peer over his shoulder at it before circling around to a chair. I'm disappointed to see that the inscrutable words are still there, despite all my wishes that I'd been wrong and the words had magically shifted into an advertisement for household cleaning products.

"I don't have any idea what it means," I say. "How about you?" I know he's good at puzzles. Hopefully, he's good at riddles, too.

"Nothing yet," he admits. "Let's see if we can't figure it out together."

He shifts his chair closer to mine, then puts the clue down on the table between us. We both huddle over it, trying to figure out what the words mean.

> PLAY OR DIE
> *My daughter, my sister, and a crazy old man.*
> *The clue's where he lost it and Jack found it again.*
> *But where to look to find the key?*
> *A house not a home, though used for a fee.*
> *A reflection of grandeur, of good times once seen,*

And many have seen her upon the grand screen.
Play or don't play—it's all up to you.
But if you decline, Death will Become You.

I read it once to myself, then out loud, hoping that inspiration will strike. It's been about a half hour since I first saw the damn thing, and let me just say that in that interim period the synapses haven't fired any more. In other words, I'm still clueless.

Frustrated, I get up and start to putter in my kitchen. Blake left the strawberry box on the counter, and I move to trash it.

"Teeth all clean now?"

For a second, I'm confused. Then I remember the conversation earlier today. I smile brightly, certain my teeth are clean and shiny. "All good," I say. "But that's mostly because I didn't eat the thing. Blake snagged it before I got the chance," I add, keeping up the faux chocolate-lust.

Andy chuckles—one of those awkward laughs—and I can tell he's not certain if I'm really pissed at Blake for eating my present. I take pity on him by patting my ass. "No big deal. I watch calories pretty strictly when I'm shooting."

"Not that you need to," he says, and I have to smile. Andy's a little geeky with his out-of-control hair and his crooked wire-rim glasses, but I really do like the guy.

I shake off the warm fuzzies because now really isn't the time, then indicate the clue. "So where are we?"

"Well, 'Play or Die' is pretty clear."

"Yeah," I agreed. "I'd say so." I grab two Diet Cokes—I'll own up to my nutritionist if I'm still alive at our next appointment—then sit at the table beside him. "But what about the first line? 'My daughter, my sister, and a crazy old man.' That sounds familiar, but I'm not placing it."

"It's a good sign that it sounds familiar to you, though," he says. "The clues are always geared toward the target's interests. We just need to find that kernel of familiarity in the clue that will unlock your understanding."

"Right," I say. "You make it sound so easy."

He reaches out to give my hand a firm squeeze. "We'll be fine. I know the game. You know the clues. Together, we're going to get through this."

As pep talks go, I have to admit that one's pretty good.

"Let's move on to Jack." Andy asks, "Do you know a Jack?"

I think back, trying to think of all my personal and professional contacts. "I met Jack Black at a party about eight months ago. And my CPA's son is named Jack."

"Him?"

"He's three," I say. "Somehow that doesn't feel right."

"No," Andy agrees, "it doesn't. The Hollywood connection, though. *That* makes a lot of sense."

"Jack Black?" I say.

He shakes his head. "Not if you just met him at a party. But I really think movies are our best bet. Considering who you are, it just makes sense."

I sigh and resist the urge to bang my forehead against the table. He has a point, but we still haven't solved anything definitively. So the announcement that my celebrity is somehow the key to the riddle isn't exactly grounds for celebration. The only good thing, actually, is that I'm not scared—not at the moment, anyway. Instead, I'm frustrated. I'm angry at whoever sucked me into this nightmare. And I'm unreasonably pissed off at Blake for leaving. Considering how much I'd hated the man this morning, my current desperate need for him was either ironic or pathetic. I didn't care which. I just wanted him.

Andy was right about sending him away, but knowing he was safe was small comfort when I wanted his arms around me. Selfish? Maybe. But so very true.

I can feel tears welling in my eyes, and I stand up and start pacing the kitchen. "Okay," I say, because I can't think of anything else to say. "Okay, let's start over. Hollywood. Movies and television."

"And Jack."

"Right. Okay. Sure." I'm babbling, but I'm also pacing and thinking, and Andy is smart enough not to interrupt me. "I know Johnny Depp pretty well," I say, without waiting for him to answer.

"Good for you. But he's not a Jack."

I roll my eyes because Andy is obviously clueless. "Captain Jack Sparrow. It's a huge role for him."

"Okay, so maybe it does refer to a part someone played. *Pirates of the Caribbean,* right?"

"Right," I say, resisting the urge to pat him on the hand and tell him to read the entertainment news every once in a while if he wants to work in Hollywood.

"So there must be a pirate map and all that. Did they follow clues?"

I think back, trying to remember, but of course I can't. Not for sure. "I don't think so. I think they just knew where the treasure was."

"Well, hell."

"What about the reference to *Death Becomes Her?*"

"Was there a Jack in that movie?" he asks.

"Not a lead," I say. "Maybe an extra?"

"Maybe," he says, but he doesn't sound convinced. I'm not surprised. I'm not convinced either.

"We're screwed, aren't we?"

He shoots me one of those looks, and I smile sheepishly, then shrug off the whininess and slide back into character. "Right. Confident." I take a breath. I can feel the black, smoky edges of fear creeping up beside me, and I steel myself. I'm not going to lose it. Not again. Lose it, and I might die. More important, lose it, and he wins. And there's no f'ing way I'm letting him win.

"The first clue is supposed to be the easiest, right? So we're just making too much of this. 'My daughter, my sister, and a crazy old man.' Plus a Jack." I clench my hands into fists because—dammit!—I can feel the answer tickling my brain, but I can't quite—

"Weren't you in a movie with Jack Nicholson? Back when you were thirteen or something?"

"*Chinatown!*" I scream out the title and even do a little jig right there in my kitchen. "Two points for the home team. You are brilliant, and we are *so* smoking."

"You weren't in *Chinatown.*"

I resist the urge to roll my eyes. I can only wish to have been in a classic like *Chinatown.* "No," I say, "but Jack was." I look at him with new respect. "How the heck did you know about that movie? It got no press and disappeared in about fifteen seconds."

"I went over your filmography back when we were casting *Givenchy.* I think I've seen everything you've been in at least once now. Some of them more than once."

"I'm sorry," I say with a laugh.

"Don't be," he says, his tone almost reverential. "You're awesome."

My cheeks warm. "Right. Well. At any rate, it's good you remembered that, because Jack *was* in *Chinatown,* and I'm not sure I would have made the connection if you hadn't blurted out his name."

"My pleasure," he says, his grin wide and his eyes big behind his glasses. "But help me out with the specifics. What does 'my daughter, my sister' mean?"

"That was the thing in the movie," I explain. "Faye Dunaway's daughter is also her sister."

He makes a face. "That explains the crazy old man part."

"Exactly."

"So the old man was played by Jack?"

"Actually, he played the private detective." The pieces are falling into place, and I tilt my head to the side as if that's going to make them fall even faster. "The whole movie was about water, and there's a scene where Jack finds the old man's glasses in a fish pond."

" 'The clue's where he lost it and Jack found it again,' " Andy recites.

"Yeah. But what does that mean?" The part about *Death Becomes Her* is what's throwing me, and I turn toward my laptop, which Andy had moved to the table earlier.

"Google?" Andy says.

"Absolutely."

I drag my finger over the trackpad and navigate to Safari. I bought the iBook after watching those fun Apple v. PC commercials. Am I the ultimate consumer, or what? At any rate, I love it and it's fast, and the page was up in no time. "The clue was in a fish pond. So all we have to do is figure out what koi pond they used for the movie, and go there. Right?"

"Maybe."

He doesn't sound convinced, but I'm not about to be slowed down. Besides, I have to be right. *Chinatown. The clue. Where he lost it and Jack found it.* Obviously, *our* clue is waiting in the same place where Jack found his clue. Figure out that place, and we're golden.

My euphoria soon fades, though, in the wake of the responses Google spits back. Chinatown, of course, is not only a movie, it's also a section of Los Angeles. And to make matters worse, it's a part of Los Angeles frequently used for movie locations. Instead of one nice little answer on Google pointing the way to the next clue, instead I'm faced with a billion (well, several thousand) hits. And no idea where to start.

"Fuck," I say, because it seems appropriate. And then, because that felt so good, *"Fuck."*

"Frustrated?"

I shoot him one of those looks designed to kill, and he gives me a sympathetic smile in return. "Don't worry," he says. "We'll figure it out."

"Maybe," I say, thinking about the poison that's supposedly flowing through my body. "But will we figure it out in time?"

Chapter

20

By some miracle, the Pacific Coast Highway was relatively free of traffic by the time Blake had wended his way out of Beverly Hills and over the surface streets toward the famous highway. The empty road was a blessing. He wanted to punch the accelerator and feel the wind against his face and breathe in the smell of the ocean to his left. He wanted to watch the sun finish its slow descent into the calm waters of the Pacific, and he wanted to believe that life really could be that beautiful even despite the horror that was sneaking in around the cracks.

Most of all, he wanted to get home and switch cars. Because Devi hadn't yet seen the classic black Caddie he'd bought last week. And if he parked it on her street—if he hung back just out of sight—he could keep an eye on her. He could keep her safe.

He hadn't wanted to leave, but he also hadn't wanted an argument. So here he was, sneaking around on his girlfriend, all with the hopes of saving his girlfriend.

Chinatown.

That much of the clue, Blake had figured out, and it had taken every ounce of willpower not to pull over and call Devi right then. Two things had stopped him. One, his promise not to get involved. Two, the fact that the first part of the clue was so damn straightforward that she and Andy had surely figured it out.

And, also, there was the little fact that his cell phone had no service along this particular stretch of PCH. That, most of all, was the defining reason.

Not that any of those reasons mattered. After all, what good was a reference to *Chinatown* without any idea what to do with it? And he had no ideas. None. And that despite the fact that he'd seen *Death Becomes Her* at least three times, and *Chinatown* twice that many. If there was any connection between the movies, Blake had no idea what it was.

Still, there was something so familiar in the clue, and he wished he'd written it down, because he was pretty sure that his memory wasn't doing it justice. The gist, yes. But the devil really was in the details, and if he could just remember, then maybe he could—

What?

What could he do? Call Devi? Even though she'd made him promise to let her and Andy handle this? He considered the question as his foot pressed the accelerator and he cruised through the dusk. Would he call her? If he knew the answer, would he call and share it?

Damn straight, he would.

She was already in danger, so whatever he did wouldn't add to that. And as for his own safety—well, if it would save Devi, he was more than willing to put his own life on the line.

Not that it mattered, since he couldn't figure out the damn clue.

His classic baby blue Buick convertible flew along the road, the salty air stinging his cheeks, the whiz of traffic in the opposite direction merely a drone buzzing in his subconscious. He could almost feel the answer. Almost taste it, almost—

Brrrr-brrrr!

The sharp hum of a police siren startled him back to reality, erasing the epiphany that was just about to burst forth. Blake cursed, then eyed the speedometer before tapping the brake. Just shy of one hundred. Great. Wasn't that the kicker in an already fucking great day?

Trying not to let his irritation show, Blake pulled over, then turned off the ignition. He stayed in the car, the spinning light from atop the cruiser casting the convertible's interior in alternate shades of red and blue.

"Any particular reason you're in such a hurry, Mr. Atwood?" the officer asked, after inspecting Blake's license.

For a split second, Blake considered the truth. *Actually, yes, officer. You see, the woman I love is being stalked by an assassin, but I can't help her. I failed her a few months ago when I fucked up on television, and now I've failed her again because there's not a damn thing I can do to help save her life.*

"No, officer. Sorry. A lot on my mind. I wasn't paying attention."

"Hmmm." The officer shone his light into the Buick, illuminating the passenger seat and the backseat. Since Blake never let so much as a candy wrapper touch the inside of his car, the sweep didn't reveal anything interesting. Even so, the officer shone the light at Blake and cocked his head. "Atwood. You're somebody, right?"

Blake balked. It was the kind of question he still wasn't used to. From his perspective, he'd been "somebody" all his life. But he knew what the cop meant. "I'm an actor," he said simply.

"Right." The cop nodded, the light still shining in Blake's eyes, making him blink. "You're that guy. The karate guy."

Blake gestured at the flashlight. "Do you mind?"

"Oh, sorry." The light came down. "My daughter's been reading all about you. I think she'd line up right now for the movie if they'd let her. She's got some crush." He held the ticket pad firmly in one hand, his pen tap-tapping on the paper.

Blake eyed the pad, pretty sure he understood the subtext. "Shall I give her an autograph?"

The cop laughed. "Sign the ticket, and I'll *have* an autograph."

Blake swallowed. So much for subtext. "Right. Speeding. Sorry about that."

"I'm just giving you grief," the officer said, waving a hand in front of his face. "Truth is, if my daughter finds out I gave a speeding ticket to her movie star crush, I'll never hear the end of it." He pulled a notepad out of his pocket and passed it to Blake. "Do you mind?"

"No, sir. What's your daughter's name?" The officer told him, and Blake wrote a quick note to Tammy, all the while fighting the strangest sense of déjà vu.

"She's gonna love this," the officer said, tucking the pad back into his pocket. "But you slow down, understand? The next cop up the road might not have a daughter." He gave the car frame a friendly pat and headed back to his cruiser. Blake shifted into gear and pulled carefully back onto PCH, this time watching the speedometer even as he remembered what had been nagging at him.

The Getty Museum. He'd gone there with Devi during those first date heydays. They were trying to play it cool, hoping to fade into the crowd just like everybody else. But the tours are docent-led, and their docent was apparently a fan. She'd attached herself like Velcro to Devi's side, then insisted on an autograph. Devi had been sweet and polite, but she'd confessed to Blake later how much she hated the attention. Not if she was in full star mode—which she rarely was anymore—but when she was out and about, just trying to do her thing and be herself.

The worst of it, of course, had been the fact that the tour was docent-led. Which meant they were trapped, with all the others in the tour now staring and whispering. And, of course, snapping pictures. Hardly a miserable experience—or unrealistic for a celebrity—but it still took the shine off their date.

After that, they chose their outings more carefully. Places where they could wander unescorted. The Griffith Park Observatory. Venice Beach. The grounds at the Greystone Mansion. The Santa Monica Pier. Even Magic Mountain, Disneyland, and Knott's Berry Farm.

They'd been like teenagers, albeit teens with flush bank accounts. Going from romantic candlelit dinners to chauffeured trips to Vegas to picnics in private parks.

He tapped the brakes, his mind whirring. Could that be it? Now that he'd thought of it, the solution seemed almost too simple.

He reached for his Sidekick, but then hesitated before dialing Devi's number. Helping her was a risk, no matter what. He should be certain first.

And so, as the sun finished its descent into the ocean, and as traffic whipped past him, Blake pulled onto the shoulder and pulled up the tiny Web browser on his phone, thankful he'd moved from the dead zone back into an area with a signal.

It was a tiny bit of good news in a day filled with horror. But at the moment, Blake was willing to take whatever good he could get.

Chapter

21

"Maybe it's a six-degrees-of-separation kind of thing," I say. We're still in my kitchen, and I'm pacing with a mug of coffee.

"How do you mean?"

"Something connecting *Death Becomes Her* to *Chinatown*."

"Like the actors," Andy says. "Or a location. That could explain the 'house, not a home' reference."

"Oh, right," I say, since Andy is now way ahead of me.

When he pulls out his phone gizmo thingie and starts tapping on the keys, though, I have to grin.

"What?" he demands.

"Why don't you use my computer?" I ask, settling back into my chair. "That thing's gotta be a pain to browse on."

The corner of his mouth curves up, and I feel like a cheerleader who just tossed the class geek a bone. A totally unreasonable reaction, but there's just something about the spark in his eyes as he slides the phone into his pocket, then scoots his chair closer to mine. (And, to be fair, closer to the computer.) "It's a Treo, and it works great. But the computer probably will be faster."

"Want me to type?" I ask.

He waves one hand, indicating the keyboard, while his other arm rests comfortably on my seat back, so that he can lean in and see the screen with me.

"Great." I tap my fingers lightly on the keys, happy to be doing something other than pacing.

"Where to first?" he asks.

"Back to Google," I say as I type *Death Becomes Her Chinatown location.*

I'd looked for locations in my previous Google search, and come up with way too many hits. This time, however, I'm more confident. Adding in the reference to *Death Becomes Her* has to be the key. The limiting factor that will zero Google in on that one perfect clue.

The computer does its thinking thing, then spits back the hits. The very first one is "Hollywood Film Locations," and I think that maybe we've done it. But when I click on the link, the bubble in my chest bursts. Nothing about any commonalities between the movies. Just a list of locations where a whole load of movies have been shot. And nothing odd, either. Only the usual suspects: The Beverly Center. The Greystone Mansion. The Santa Monica Pier. Venice High School. The Biltmore Hotel. And on and on. Great if you want to sit on the side of the road and sell tourist info to the folks from Indiana. Not great if you're me. Especially since not one of those locations was listed for both *Death Becomes Her* and *Chinatown*.

On to Plan B.

Fortunately, I actually have a Plan B. I move the mouse up to the address bar, then type in *www.imdb.com*—the Internet Movie Database. My plan is to compare the cast and crew of the two movies and see what overlaps. Or if I see any connections anywhere. Like maybe the daughter of Robert Townsend—the screenwriter for *Chinatown*—worked as the costume director for *Death Becomes Her.* (For the record, I don't even know if Townsend *had* a daughter, but I'm grasping at straws here.)

Those kind of connections, however, aren't exactly easy to find. You have to know what you're looking for. And after fifteen minutes, I still have bupkiss. Oh, sure, I know who directed *Death*—that was Robert Zemeckis. And I know he directed *Back to the Future,* too. And since *Chinatown*'s an old movie, I thought maybe we could go from there. But, no. Nothing.

"I still say it has something to do with the locations," Andy says. "Places make a lot of money renting themselves out as movie locations, right?" He doesn't wait for me to continue. "That's got to be the 'used for a fee' line."

"Okay, but nothing's overlapping. "

"Then we're missing something," he says.

I start to snap back a retort, but stop myself in time. He's right, of course. I just don't know what we're missing. And my fear is that we're not going to figure it out in time. I swallow, because all of a sudden the ramifications are real and looming. I've screwed things up before, of course, but my publicist always fixed it for me. Even when I went all Gloria Swanson and hid in this house, I didn't really do any permanent damage. I got this job with Tobias, didn't I? And the *North by Northwest* remake offer is still on the table. Which means my career is still alive, no matter how stupid I was in the past.

In other words, career fuckups aren't deadly, even though they might seem so at the time. But screw this up, and it's all over.

I stand up and start to pace again, my mind in a muddle. One chance. One play. And if I can't figure it out, I'm six feet under. And *that* is a career fiasco from which there really is no recovery.

"Andy, I—" My voice catches in my throat. I can't get the words out, mostly because I don't know what I want to say. It's okay, though, because he seems to understand.

He's immediately beside me, his arms around me, and I can't hold it in any longer. The tears flow, and I sag against him, soaking in the comfort that he's so willing to give and I'm so desperate to take.

"I'm scared," I say. "I'm so scared."

"I know. It'll be okay. I won't let anything happen to you." He's stroking my hair, his movements a little jerky and awkward. "I promise, I'll take care of you."

I tilt my head back to try out a smile. "I guess you have to. That's your job, right?"

"A job I'm happy to have," he says seriously. "Especially if it means I get to keep you alive."

He's trying to comfort me, but his words are having the opposite effect. Suddenly the ramifications seem to loom before me. "God, Andy, you shouldn't have to go through this again. You've played the game once. You've—" But I can't say it.

"I lost a target," he says softly, and I have to nod.

He hooks a finger under my chin and tilts my head up. "I

won't lose you. I promise you that right here and now. I am going to protect you, and we are going to win this game."

I sniffle a little, but nod.

"Do you believe me?"

"Yes," I whisper. And even though it's probably foolish, I mean it.

His mouth curves into a smile and he pulls me close. It's nice there in his arms, and for just a moment I can almost relax. Andy's always seemed a bit of a geek to me, but right then, he's *safe*. More, he's there.

And there's no doubt that he cares.

He strokes my back, murmuring soft words to which I don't listen. All I hear is the comforting tone that holds an unspoken promise: He is my protector. And he will see me through this.

We stay like that until my tears dry up and my sense of embarrassment kicks in—that awkward emotion that stems from revealing too much to a man I really don't know. But even though I know my cheeks are burning, I'm glad he's there. And when I pull back, I see more in his eyes than just comfort. I see a startling need that is both flattering and surprising.

I know I should say something, but before I can, his lips are on mine, and I feel such a timid need in him that I can't help be a little sad. Especially since he *is* my hero now. He isn't, however, the man I want as my hero.

And so I gently break the kiss, not wanting to hurt him, and yet not wanting him to believe this is going to go anywhere.

Although I don't want to talk about it, I know that we should. But before I can find the words, my cell phone rings, and I lunge for it, grateful for the interruption.

I glance at the caller ID, then immediately stiffen. *Blake.* A wave of guilt crashes over me, and I force it away.

On this particular day, boyfriend angst is the least of my worries.

Still, when I answer the phone, I can't help the little trill of pleasure that shoots down my spine. Pleasure . . . and then fear.

"Are you okay?" I demand. We'd barely discussed the game. Surely he wasn't in any danger, right?

He hesitates before answering, and in that brief gap in time, my entire body seems to go from cold to hot and then to cold again. Finally, he whispers, "I miss you."

Three little words, but they melt me all the way down to my toes. "Oh, me, too," I say, the words sincere even if a little guilt-laden.

"I've thought of something," he says, his tone leaving no doubt that we're now talking about the game. A subject that is, of course, verboten.

"Yeah?" I try to sound casual. "Well, I guess we'll see each other tomorrow in spite of everything. I mean, the show must go on and all that." I smile at Andy as I speak, trying to pretend that everything's all casual and work-related, and certain I'm failing miserably. No wonder I didn't win that damn Oscar.

"Tomorrow's no good, and you know it."

"Ah, well, hang on. Let me find my markup of the pages." I cover the mouthpiece. "I'm running upstairs," I tell Andy.

"He shouldn't have called you," Andy says, his forehead rippled with concern.

"He knows. He apologized. But he's right. If we don't show up for the movie tomorrow, people will wonder. I might get fired. We'll have reporters speculating what's up.

And how am I supposed to play the game with all of that going on?"

Andy doesn't look happy, but he knows I'm right. And I *am* right. I hadn't thought of it before, but somehow I have to fit saving my life in around living my life.

"Go," he says, then taps the paper with the *Chinatown* clue. "I'll work on this."

I nod, then head toward the foyer and the stairs. I pass my grandfather clock on the way. It's already ten p.m. We have a five a.m. call.

And in the short amount of time in between, I need to figure out what the hell to do about that one simple message: "Toxin delivered."

Fuck.

Time really is running out.

My stomach starts to twist, and I don't know if it's from fear or poison. At this point, I guess it doesn't much matter. Either way, I have to claw my way to survival.

"I don't have time for this," I say as I climb the stairs. I go into my room and shut the door. "I still don't know what that damn clue means, and we really do have to be on the set tomorrow morning."

"If we're together making the paparazzi happy, Tobias will forgive you for missing call."

"We *won't* be together," I say. "Because you're not helping me."

"I'm helping you now," he says.

"No." I can't bear the thought of him getting hurt. "We've been through this."

"Have you figured out the clue?"

I hesitate.

"Because I have."

I take a step backward and plunk myself down on the foot of my bed. "You're serious?" Even as I'm speaking, though, I know I should just hang up. Hear the solution, and Blake is in deep. I don't know how my tormentor would find out, but somehow, I know that he would. At the very least, it's not a risk worth taking.

"Totally," he says.

"I'm hanging up—"

"The Greystone Mansion," he says over me.

I close my eyes, the fear and fury that he didn't just stay out of this quelled by the selfish relief that floods my senses.

"Devi?" His voice is tentative. He's wondering if I'm going to hang up, or maybe wondering if I have already. I could do that, I realize. Just quietly close the phone and walk away. With luck, he'll still be safe. And maybe he'll realize that I was serious about not wanting his help.

I can't do it, though. Instead, I swallow to clear the dryness from my throat. "I looked at that," I said. "*Chinatown* wasn't filmed there."

"Doesn't matter," he says. I can hear the excitement in his voice. "It still fits."

"How?"

" 'A house not a home, though used for a fee,' " he quotes. "The big party scene in *Death Becomes Her* was filmed there. And the mansion charges. That's all it's used for these days."

"Yeah," I say. "I know." The Greystone Mansion covers over 40,000 square feet of Tudor-style ostentatiousness. But it's absolutely fabulous. Overwhelming and awe-inspiring at the same time, with beautifully landscaped grounds, now open to the public. "But again, it wasn't used in *Chinatown*. At least not that I can see."

"It's a clue, Devi. Not a literal translation. What, in general, is the first part of the message talking about?"

I bristle, irritated by his tone. "If you know the answer, Blake, then just tell me. In case you forgot, the clock is ticking. I don't have time for twenty questions."

"You remember *Chinatown,* right? You've seen it a dozen times," he continues, not letting me get a word in. "Where does Jack find the glasses?"

"In the koi pond," I say. And then it hits me. *"Oh."*

"That has to be it." Excitement laces his voice, and I can't help but share it. He's right. He has to be.

I hang up—but only after forcing him to promise that he won't go to the mansion. That he'll stay out of this now. I don't want him hurt, and I'm terrified that we've just painted a big red target on his chest.

I tell myself I can't think about that, though. I have to follow the clues. Save myself, and I'll be saving Blake, too.

I hurry downstairs to find Andy at my kitchen table again, drinking one of my Diet Cokes and tapping away at the keys on his Treo. He looks up, then gives me a wan smile. "It's like Nero fiddling while Rome is burning," he says.

"Huh?" I say, calling upon my razor-sharp verbal skills.

He holds up the phone. "Work. Answering e-mails. Doing normal life stuff." I start to say something, but he gets there before I can. "Listen, Devi," he says, his voice serious. "About earlier . . ."

"Oh, Andy," I say, wishing I'd thought more about what I

wanted to say. About how it was a mistake, and that I was sorry. And that I didn't want to lead him on. I take a deep breath and dive in, hoping the words will come. "We just—"

"I should never have done that," he says, and I close my mouth, not quite able to believe that he's saying it and not me. "We need to focus on the game right now. Keeping you safe is all that matters."

I swallow, because that's not exactly the message I want to get across to him. I want to put a complete kibosh on the whole thing. Andy, apparently, wants to postpone it. Still, he's right. One little kiss—even if it's coupled with his wild fantasies that something real sparked between us—is completely unimportant in the face of the horror of the game.

The talk can wait.

The clue, however, can't. "I think I might have an answer," I say. "About the clue, I mean."

"Really?" His brows lift and his focus shifts to the cordless phone still in my hand. "You didn't discuss this with—"

"*No.*" The lie comes easily to my lips. "We talked about to-morrow's scene. About the script. But something in our conver-sation reminded me, and I don't know, it just clicked."

"What clicked?"

"The Greystone Mansion," I say. "There's a koi pond on the property. The next clue is there."

"You're sure?"

"Yes," I say, as much to convince myself as Andy. I have to be right. Because if I'm wrong, then I'm all out of ideas.

Chapter

22

The computer sat on his desk, surrounded by the framed photographs of Devi, most cut from old magazines, each with her wondrous eyes looking right at him. He still couldn't grasp why she'd spurned him. Why she'd cleaved to other men instead of coming to him.

No matter.

In the end, she would be his, fully and completely. And the end, he knew, was coming soon.

He leaned back in his chair, his attention focused on the computer screen. The game had sent software, and when he'd installed it, he'd discovered a map of the city. That was all. But upon further investigation, he'd realized what it was—tracking software.

Soon after, his assumption was confirmed by an e-mail from the game. Once Devi solved the qualifying clue, the tracker would be activated. He couldn't simply follow the flashing red dot to her—that would take the sport out of it. But the software's intermittent display of her location (within a broad radius) would certainly help him find her.

Now, all he had to do was wait.

So far, the dot wasn't flashing.

No matter; he was a patient man, a fact that he had proved many times over.

He could wait as long as necessary.

He was just about to get up and change the DVD from one of Devi's old movies to candid footage he'd collected over the last ten years when the computer pinged, signaling an incoming e-mail.

With an eagerness he couldn't suppress, he rolled his chair forward, then clicked on the e-mail program. A single message from PSW—"You have a message in the Message Center."

Intrigued, he opened his Web browser and clicked over, his eyes widening as he read the message, which contained explicit instructions and directions. Several words seemed to scream out at him from the screen: *Rules broken. Consequences imposed. Repercussions.*

He read it once, then once again, just to be sure.

Then he leaned back, tilting his chair so that he could stare at the ceiling.

And then, Janus smiled.

Chapter

23

The Greystone Mansion happens to be one of my favorite places in all of Beverly Hills. I've been there dozens of times in the last few years, and even during my reclusive period, I couldn't resist the pull of the place. I would deck myself out in sweats and a gimme cap, then take a book and a bottle of water and enjoy the landscaped gardens that surround the property.

Because of my fascination with the place, I know a lot about it. I know the location of the koi pond (referred to by the staff as the Willow Pond). I know the mansion's history. I know that the entire property is surrounded by a fence. And that it's locked up tight at six p.m. during the summer.

In other words, I know that we aren't getting on the property any time soon. Not through the front gate, anyway.

"Are you saying you want to wait until morning?" Andy asks when I give him the scoop.

I do, of course. I mean, part of me wants to wait forever. But I know that I can't. That damn "toxin delivered" message still flashes in my mind. I can't completely believe it, but I'm not so foolish as to ignore it.

Most of all, in my gut, I know it's true.

I feel a little nauseous, and wonder if it's nerves or the drug. Either way, there's only one thing to be done. "We go tonight," I say.

Andy looks at me, his gaze appraising. Then he stands up. "Let's go."

We take my car. After all, I've driven the route so often that my Porsche probably knows the way even if I'm not behind the wheel. I've left it in front of the house, and now Andy's car is parked next to it. A Jaguar. And I'm embarrassed to say that I do a double take. I've always pictured Andy as the high school geek grown up. Couple that with the fact that I know he lived in New York, and I'm thinking a Honda Civic would be more his style.

Apparently, I'm not quite the astute character maven that I thought I was.

"Stock options," he says.

My cheeks heat, and I realize I'm staring. "Sorry. I didn't—"

He waves it off. "No one does." His grin is infectious. "What can I say? I like speed."

I nod toward my Porsche. "Me, too."

It's a nice, easy moment, and I actually laugh as we get in the car. As soon as I wave to Lucas and pull past the gate, though, my nerves return to their previous raw state. I shift in my seat, in control of nothing except the speed and route of my car. It's a humbling feeling, and I can't say that I much like it.

In the house, I'd fantasized about getting to the mansion, solving the riddle, and shutting this thing down. Now I have no choice but to face the truth: this nightmare is going to go on and on. Interpreting this clue isn't the end, it's just the beginning. And what's worse, as soon as I solve the damn thing, all bets are off. Right now, my assassin isn't waiting on a rooftop with an Uzi aimed in my direction. At least, I don't think he is. That would be against the rules, after all.

But as soon as I solve the qualifying clue, it's open season on Devi Taylor. Because once the target solves the first clue—all bets are off. Before that, it's like a handicap in sports: the target gets a head start. But solve the qualifying clue, and the game ramps up.

And the very thought makes my insides turn to liquid.

"Andy, I—"

"So tell me why you like the place so much," he says, cutting off my worried tirade before it can even begin.

I turn my head as I roll through a stop sign, but he just grins. "I really want to know," he insists. "If it's part of a clue, any little thing might be important."

I know he's only trying to distract me—and I appreciate that—but he's right, too. "My favorite thing is that it's not a movie star house," I begin. "Have you been before?"

He shakes his head. "This is the first time I've spent any length of time in Los Angeles. I'm still trying to figure out the cool places to go."

"Oh, well, stick with me. I'll either get you killed or give you a really good tour of the area."

"I'll take the tour," he says, deadpan. "If it's all the same to you."

"Mmm." I make a face, but I don't freak out. I consider that a good sign. What are those stages of grief? I've seen the movie *All That Jazz* so many times, you'd think I'd have them memorized. Anger—did that. Denial—did that. Bargaining—maybe. Acceptance—*Ah*. That's where I am now.

"At any rate," I say, determined not to dwell, "the mansion looks like a castle. And it has over fifty rooms, which makes Tom Cruise's house look like some piece of crap in Compton."

"You've seen his house?"

"Once. In his pre-Katie days. But I think it was a rental." I frown, because, really, who cares? "At any rate, the point is, the place is amazing. I mean, it cost four million to build, and that was back in the twenties."

Out of the corner of my eye, I can see him tapping his fingers against his thumb, as if he's doing mental math. I guess I'm right about that, because he says, "That's about forty-five million now, if you base the calculation on the consumer price index."

"You just know that? Off the top of your head?"

"What can I say? I'm a geek."

"You're a fucking genius. And I mean that in the best way possible."

"Then I accept your gracious compliment."

I smile and shake my head, realizing that I genuinely like Andy. Not in the boyfriend-girlfriend way that he probably wants. But in a friend way.

I also realize that I'm feeling a little guilty for my whine-fest with Lindy yesterday. I mean, this is the guy I was having second thoughts about inviting to my house. *This* guy. The one who's making me smile despite everything. The one assigned to protect me.

"So you can just tour the house?" he asks, sucking me back to reality.

I shake my head. "Nope. It's not open very often. But it's rented out a lot, mostly to movie companies."

"You ever filmed a movie there?"

"Actually, no. But Kirk Douglas got remarried here a few years ago, and I was invited. The wedding was great. The caterers were to die for. But it was the location that really convinced me to send in the RSVP card."

"A wedding." His mouth pulls down in the tiniest of frowns. "So is there a ballroom?"

"Oh, yeah," I say. "But who wants to be married inside, especially in Los Angeles? The grounds are the way to go."

"Pretty?"

"Amazing. The landscaping is absolutely awesome, and the property itself covers a gazillion acres. Well," I correct myself, "maybe just fifteen or sixteen, but this is prime real estate. The view of the city is astounding. I used to like to come sit here and just think, you know? Back when I—" I cut myself off, realizing I don't want to go there with this man. Blake, yes. He knows my secrets. But Andy is new territory, and I'm not quite ready to drop my shields. "When I wanted to get away from all the work pressures," I say, lamely covering.

"So is this where you're planning your own wedding?"

It's a rather invasive question, but I don't comment on it because I'm too busy blushing. I always have wanted to get married at the mansion, and a few months ago, I'd thought that I knew the man who'd be by my side. Now, though . . .

Well, now I'm walking a tightrope. Fall one way, and I'll land right back in Blake's arms. Fall another, and . . . honestly? I just don't know.

None of which I intend to share with Andy.

Fortunately, we arrive, and instead of getting down and dirty about my nonexistent wedding plans, I tap the brakes. A couple of cars pass us, but one slows, too, its headlights bright in my rearview mirror.

I frown, then adjust the mirror before waving toward the fence.

"That," I say, with suitable dramatic flair, "is our problem."

And then, because I don't have any ideas about how to get past that damn gate, I push down on the accelerator and start to circle the block, hoping to find a service entrance, a secret tunnel, or even a trampoline positioned just right to let me launch myself up and over.

A girl can dream, can't she?

Chapter 24

There.

He focused the binoculars on his quarry, then slid down in his seat. His bladder ached, but now that he saw her, his discomfort seemed trivial. She climbed out of her car, then rolled her neck, as if the weight of the world bore down on her shoulders.

He shifted the glasses, focusing on her face. She seemed close enough to touch, and oh so lovely. But then, he'd known she would be.

He watched her move along the side of the street, her face etched with concentration. Once she was closer to the house, that was when he would strike. Out of the way, under cover of the bushes.

She stopped, then turned sharply back toward her car. He frowned, wondering if she'd noticed him. Or, worse, wondering if someone else was inside her car.

Quickly, he shifted his binoculars to focus on the front seat. His perspective was from behind and several yards away, but he saw nothing.

Still, there could be someone . . .

He considered his options, then decided it didn't matter. His time was now. Before she got inside.

Deliberately, so that he would later remember each movement, he reached into the glove compartment, pulling out the hunting knife he'd kept safe for so many years. That was for her. Quick. Personal. And he would feel her blood as it ran from her and over his hands.

The gun he retrieved next, tucking it into the waistband at the back of his jeans. Cold and impersonal, it was only for her companion, if she had one. A means to an end.

A means to her.

He opened the door, the overhead light flashing on as he did so. He froze, a flash of anger at his stupidity ripping through him.

She looked up, and even from this distance, he could tell that she was looking at his car, searching her mind as she wondered if it—or he—looked familiar.

The car itself was nondescript. A Toyota Camry he'd rented for this occasion. Silver, so as to blend in. He blended, too. Dressed in basic khakis and a button-down, he looked like your average guy, just driving home from a late night at the office. Nothing odd, nothing untoward.

He told himself to keep moving. Don't let her get suspicious. With his knife hand still hidden by the door of the car, he stood up and waved. Just a casual passerby sort of wave. Nothing to make a woman on a dark street nervous.

And then, just as he'd anticipated, she waved back.

He tried to hide his glee, but wasn't sure he succeeded. His time had come, and it was everything he could do not to climb on top of his car and shout at the top of his lungs.

But no. He had more control than that.

That's why he'd been picked, wasn't it?

Chapter

25

"We are going to get in so much trouble," Andy says.

I try not to laugh, but it's hard. Despite the horror of the situation, there's something just too damn amusing about him straddling the wrought-iron fence that surrounds the property. He's a gangly man as it is. And perched up there like that, he resembles an overlarge monkey.

I press my lips together, but use my hands to motion for him to come on. When he doesn't, I swallow my laughter and urge him in a stage whisper. "Just swing your leg over and drop. It's easy." I indicate myself with my hands, proof of the feat's simplicity. "I mean, I'm a girl *and* I'm carrying my bag. And I didn't scratch me or the leather." That, actually, is a lie. I scratched my ankle *and* the leather. My ankle will heal—assuming the rest of me survives, anyway. The leather, though . . . well, I'm hoping Armen can work some magic.

I actually feel a little silly lugging my new Prada bag, but Andy insisted. And when I pressed him for a reason, he told me that we might have to run. Which means we might have to abandon the car. And if we do that, I'd want my belongings.

In other words, I never should have asked.

Andy, however, isn't impressed with the fact that I scaled the fence, Prada in tow.

"I don't like heights," he says.

"Then jump down," I say, which is convoluted logic, but the best I can do. I confess I don't have too much sympathy. I grew up on movie sets and on backlots. There's a lot of scaffolding, framed set pieces, cranes, and other miscellaneous dangerous and appealing things to keep a kid's interest. Back then, *I* was the monkey. And it had been no trick at all for me to scramble over the fence and drop into the soft grass on the other side.

Now that I'm safely inside the fence and he's still stuck up top, my empathy is waning. I mean, the damn fence wouldn't be an issue for Blake. Still, Andy is my protector, and he knows the game. So I tell myself to cut him some slack.

Through the shrubs that line the fence, I see the glow of headlights down the road. I have no idea who's in the car, but the last thing we need is some Good Samaritan calling the cops about people breaking into the Greystone Mansion. "Andy," I hiss, "jump. Jump *now*."

Thankfully, he does, and I release a slow breath as relief floods my body.

He lands hard, then grimaces and reaches down to rub his ankle. "Shit."

"You okay?"

He waves off the question. "Just sore." He looks up, squinting into the darkness. "Do you know how to get to the koi pond?"

"Sure. I just need to get my bearings. Come on." I head in, away from the fence. We'd circled the property, stealing in over a back gate most likely used as a service entrance. Dim lights line a narrow path, and we follow it a bit uphill before veering off onto another winding walkway that leads to one of many brick stairways.

The paths and ways seem to curve in on each other, and I'm not entirely sure we're going in the right direction. But at least we're not on that secluded service road anymore. That, I figure, would be a likely place for any guards who might be canvassing the property to go.

Of course, because I know all about securing a parcel of land, I also know that video surveillance could be an issue. Nothing we can do about that, though, except hope that all the videos are trained at the house itself. And if that turns out not to be the case—if a guard runs us to ground—I'll just have to play the wild and crazy celebrity with too much money and too much time.

I hope it doesn't come to that, though. I'll do what it takes to stay alive, of course, but an article about the return of my past wild days could set me back for years.

Even this far away from the mansion (not that I was certain how far we *were* from the mansion) the grounds reek of power, money, and taste. The whole area—all umpty acres of it—is landscaped. We've passed hidden courtyards, sculpted hedges, and lush landscaping. All around us, the grounds resemble a private forest, a princess's fairyland.

If it were day, I know we'd have an amazing view of the Los

Angeles vista, truly a stunning sight on any day without smog. Even at night, though, the place has a magical quality, and it's hard to believe that a location as beautiful as this has such an ugly past.

When I make that comment to Andy, though, he has no idea what I mean about the property's unpleasant past, and so I find myself whispering to him as we trudge along, telling him the tale of millionaire Edward L. Doheny.

"The house was a present," I say. "Edward Doheny had it built for his son, which is pretty much the coolest present ever, in my opinion. Except, in the end it didn't work out all that great."

"How so?" he asks, puffing a little because now we're climbing yet another set of steep stone stairs. Just one of dozens that litter the property.

"Some big political scandal," I say. "The Teapot Dome scandal?"

"I've heard of it," Andy says.

"Then you're better informed than me," I admit. "All I know is that it was a big deal, and dear old dad was somehow caught up in bribery allegations."

"And this affected the house how?"

"Well, I'm not sure of the details of how it came about, but the son ended up dying in a murder-suicide."

"Yikes."

"Pretty much. The widow lived here for a while, then left it to the city." I sweep my arm out, encompassing the place. "The rest, as they say, is history." Actually, it's pretty creepy history, now that I think about it. And I suppose the bloodshed and murder is apropos of our mission.

How glad I am that I thought of that. *Not.*

In order to take my mind off the really-not-comforting house history that I dredged up, I concentrate on walking and not falling on my face. The area we're in is planted with neat rows of trees lining the road and opening onto the forestlike surroundings. Despite the dark, I know that when we get closer to the house, exotic flowers will peek out at us, birds-of-paradise and other beauties vying for attention.

I'm thinking about the flowers and trying to get my bearings when the road shifts and rises. We climb, and as we crest the small hill, the mansion itself is spread out in front of us, illuminated by both the moon and the security lights.

It glows like something alive and welcoming, and despite the purpose of our mission, I can't help but smile. Beside me, Andy whistles.

"Wouldn't I like something like that . . ."

"Would you?" I tease. "All those rooms to clean."

"Who bothers to clean? With all the rooms in that place, you could just move to a new room. Do that once a month, and you've got—what?—five years before you'd have to hire a maid?"

I laugh, impressed by his mathematical prowess. "Works for me. Come on," I say, cocking my head.

The light reflects on the gray slate roof tiles from which the building acquired its name, and we move closer carefully, hoping that we're not too illuminated as well.

If I'm remembering right, the Willow Pond is in the garden at the rear of the house. The only trouble is, considering the roundabout way that we approached the house, I'm not entirely sure where the rear is. After all, this isn't exactly your typical front door/back door kind of place. Frustrated, I manage to lead us astray for a good five minutes. During that time, we see a flashlight bobbing in the distance. Andy yanks me back behind a tree, and we stand there, not breathing, until the flashlight bobs away.

"Guard?"

"Not sure," he says. "Better safe than sorry."

I take a deep breath as reality bears down on me. A reality filled with assassins and stalkers and odds that really don't skew in my favor.

The blackness starts to creep up again, that seductive place where I can get lost in my own head and not worry about the real world. I shove it away, because I know better. If I stop worrying about the real world, I'll find myself without any world at all. If that's not a motivation to stay sober, I don't know what is.

Determined, I step out behind the tree and continue on in the direction where I think the house lies. After a few minutes, I still haven't found the damn pond.

I stop, frustrated, and try to get my bearings. Andy stumbles to a halt behind me.

"Are we lost?"

"We're right here," I snap. "Everything else has just shifted."

It's a stupid thing to say, but I'm irritated. It's dark, and I'm tired and I'm scared. I'm also lost. Not that I'm going to admit that to Andy.

I turn this way and that, trying to spot something familiar in the dark. Nothing. Finally, I just pick a direction. "This way," I say.

"Wait."

I look back at him, confused. "What?" Was someone out there? Had he seen something?

"We're heading to the wrong place."

I shake my head. "No way. It all fits. The clues all fit."

"Except for the reflection part," he says. "What was the language? 'A reflection of grandeur, of good times once seen'?"

"Okay. So?"

"So that can't have been thrown into the overall clue for no reason. It must serve a purpose."

I swallow, because he's right. But we don't have time to follow rabbit trails, and I'm now pissed off at myself for leaping all over the koi pond thing. "Then what?" I ask. "Do you have any ideas?"

"You know the mansion," he says. "Is there some sort of reflecting pond?"

The sense of doom that had been settling over me vanishes with a puff. "Yes," I say triumphantly. "And I know right where it is."

Five minutes later, we've found the reflecting pond. A long, rectangular shallow pool cut into a stone patio. At one end, a majestic fountain sprays water into the air, creating a blur of ambient noise that will hide any approaching footsteps.

"What now?" I ask, frowning at the pond.

"We search for the clue," he says, slogging into the water, shoes and all. "You said Jack found something in the water, right? So the clue must be in here."

"Right," I say, shining the flashlight over the surface of the water. "In the movie, Jack Nicholson finds a pair of glasses. Is that what we're looking for? Glasses?" I have a sudden mental picture of me wearing the special decoder glasses, then flitting around the property like Batgirl or something. I shake my head to clear the idiotic thought. Clearly, I'm getting loopy.

"I doubt it," he says. "The game is never that literal. But I expect we'll find something."

As he tromps through the water, I move the light so that he can see what's near his feet. After a few minutes of this, the beam hits something shiny in the middle of the pond. The light glints off it, making the item shine and spark like a beacon sending out a little Morse code signal. *Look here! Look here!*

"Andy!"

"I see it," he says, and he's already bending over, his head tilted at an odd angle so as to not get wet while his arm is submerged up to his elbow. He looks cockeyed and off-balance and more than a little goofy. He's also grinning from ear to ear, clearly more than happy to be my white knight.

"My hero," I say with a laugh.

"If I'm a hero just for grabbing the thing, what am I going to be when I actually pull it out of the water?" he asks.

"Golden," I say.

He looks at me with a little too much intensity, and then he nods. "For now, that'll do."

I look away, because I can hear the undertone in his voice. I may want to put off the talk about the kiss, but I wonder if that's going to be possible. Still, compared to the poison in my body, Andy's lust is hardly a priority. As soon as we find the antidote—and I'm determined to think in terms of *when* and not *if*—I'll have the talk with him.

My rambling thoughts are interrupted when he stands up straight, triumphantly holding out a small metal disc.

"What is it?" I ask, reaching for it.

He slogs to the edge of the pond and hands it to me without looking at it, and I immediately start to scrape off the gunk.

"Anything?" he asks.

I squint at it, the silver emerging from the black ooze familiar. "It's a silver dollar," I say. "The old kind, like my grandpa used to keep in his coin box." An Eisenhower dollar to be exact, with the president's profile on one side and the Apollo 11 eagle insignia on the back. (Honestly, it's amazing I remember that, but Grandpa knew everything about his coins, and that little tidbit stuck.)

"Does it say anything?"

He holds out his hand for the dollar, but I ignore it, instead looking more closely and running my thumb over the image, looking for secret codes etched in the metal. "Nothing I see." I flip it over again and look one more time. Still nothing.

Discouraged, I pass it off to Andy.

He does the same routine, ultimately coming to the same conclusion. "It's a silver dollar."

"But it's the clue, right? I mean, something perfectly innocuous can be a clue. Isn't that how the game works?" My voice is rising, and I force myself to bring it down a notch. I might be screaming in terror inside, but the actress in me knows how to play the role of the calm, cool heroine.

"It must be," Andy says. "And the clue will tie in to the movies. We just need to find the connection."

I blanch. "But there could be a million possibilities."

He puts a calming hand on my arm. "Then we go through the million one by one. Come on, Devi. We can do this."

"Right," I say, gathering my courage and confidence. "Sure."

"So start naming some of those possibilities."

Naturally, my mind goes horribly blank. "Um." I'm floundering, a little fact that is particularly annoying since I was weaned both in and on the movies. My grandfather was a cameraman back in the day, and he worked on films now considered classics. I grew up watching films like *Arsenic and Old Lace* even while going to the premieres of movies starring me. A weird life maybe, but I liked it.

My grandmother, not to be outdone, read anything and everything about Hollywood itself. More than that, she wrote about it. That magazine, *Confidential*? She was one of the secret sources that fed the infamous rag all of its devilish dish.

In other words, if anyone knows movies and Hollywood trivia, it's me. But at the moment, my mind is a blank.

"Okay," I say, trying again. "It's an Eisenhower dollar. And there's a movie called *Why We Fight* that had a lot to do with Eisenhower. It was all about the war, after all. And if the war is the key, then there was a documentary in the forties called *The True Glory.*"

"But none of those are a place."

He has a point, and for a moment it takes the air out of my sails. Still, I'm not to be deterred. "Maybe it's not Eisenhower. Maybe the clue ties to *silver dollar.* Or just *dollar.* Or eagle. Or even Apollo."

"Apollo?"

I explain about the insignia on the back of the coin. "Could be a reference to the Apollo Theater. Except that it was demolished," I add. "But you get the idea."

"You're doing great," he says. "But we need to focus on places that still exist."

"Well," I say, racking my brain, "I know that Eisenhower gave a speech at the Hollywood Bowl in the fifties. Maybe we need to go to the Hollywood Bowl?" I toss the idea out there, almost lamely, but to my surprise, Andy jumps on it.

"Devi, you're brilliant. That has to be the answer."

"You think?" It certainly seems to fit, and I feel a swell of pride for coming up with the idea. "But *where* in the Bowl?"

"I don't know," he says. "We'll figure that out when we get there." He starts to walk back the way we came. "Come on."

I hurry to catch up, eager and excited. Maybe this nightmare will be over sooner than I anticipated. Maybe by morning, my life will be my own again.

Nearby, a bird squawks, its sleep interrupted by a rustle in the bushes.

I look at Andy, and see that his eyes are wide, too. And why wouldn't they be? After all, we're alone. So what the hell is moving in the bushes?

"Let's go," Andy whispers. "We have the clue. Let's get the hell out of here. Check the Hollywood Bowl. I think it's our best shot."

"*No.*" A deep voice rings out from among the bushes, and I scream, the shrill sound of my voice piercing the sky even as a black-clad figure emerges.

"Go!" Andy yells, and I do, almost falling into the reflecting pool as I race in the opposite direction.

"Wait!" the stranger calls. But it's not a stranger. I know that voice, and even as my terror subsides, a wave of anger washes over me.

"*Blake,*" I yell, skidding to a stop. "What the hell are you doing here?"

"Helping," he says, his voice perfectly calm. He nods toward the coin still clutched in my hand. "Are you sure you want to go to the Hollywood Bowl now?"

"What do you mean?" I ask. "Blake, I'm running out of time!"

"That's my point," he says. "What if you're wrong? What if the coin isn't the clue? What if the Hollywood Bowl isn't the answer? What if there's something else, and you end up right back here? You could be wasting hours. Hours you don't have."

My heart skips a beat, both from the information and from the way he's watching me. I'm livid that he's here after I specifically told him to stay away. And yet . . .

And yet my whole body tingles from the knowledge that, despite everything, he came.

Andy, however, isn't feeling the love. He's staring Blake down, his eyes as cold and as hard as if he believed that *Blake* were the one pulling our strings. "All right, Blake," he says. "You make a good point. But if the coin isn't the clue, then what is?"

"I don't know," Blake says.

"Dammit, Blake, are you trying to get her killed? Are you trying to get *yourself* killed? Because we've been through this before, and you're not supposed to be here."

"Well, I *am* here. And I'm staying. And until we're certain that Hollywood Bowl is where we go next, you both are staying, too."

Chapter 26

Blake stood firm, determined to stand his ground.

"Maybe he's right," Devi said. "Maybe we should be sure. The coin's pretty gunky, after all. What if it's not the clue at all? What if it's been in the water for months and months?"

It was a good argument, and Blake waited, watching Andy's face. He could tell the other man didn't like having his authority questioned—he was the one with all the experience in the game—but at the same time, what Devi said made sense. And after a few moments, Andy nodded. "All right. We look around some more and see if we find something else that might be a clue. But no more than half an hour. We can't afford to waste any of your time."

He said the last to Devi. She pressed her lips together and nodded agreement. Then Andy turned to Blake. "And I think you can leave now."

"Drop the argument, Andy," Blake said. "I'm not going anywhere, and if you keep beating that horse, you're just wasting more of the time she has to find the antidote."

"Blake . . ." That from Devi. "Please go. I don't like you here. What if—"

"I'm not terribly concerned with what you like and don't like," he said, reaching the end of his patience. "Because *I* like that pretty head on your shoulders. And for that matter, I'm rather fond of the rest of you." He allowed himself one quick glance over the rest of her, was rewarded with a quick brush of her teeth over her lower lip, a sure sign she knew exactly what he was thinking.

"I'm fond of all your various parts, too," she said, managing to make the statement sound matter-of-fact and not lascivious. "And that's why I want you the hell out of here."

"Too late. I'm already involved." He held his hands out to his sides. "I'm a lost cause."

"No." The word came out barely a whisper, and the tears he saw filling her eyes began to erode his stony determination. "Blake, please. You might still be safe. It's the middle of the night. Maybe no one knows you're here. *Please.* Please go."

The desperation in her voice cut through his heart, but he wasn't willing to back down. He had left her once; he wasn't doing it again.

She stared him down, then sighed. "Fine. Stay until we're sure about the clue. But after that, you have to leave. *Please,* Blake. For me."

It was the pain in her voice that finally got him, and he nodded. "All right," he said. But the truth was, he kept his fingers crossed. No way was he making that kind of promise. He might leave the area, but he damn sure wasn't leaving her.

He glanced at her, certain she knew what he was thinking, and thankful she didn't call him on it.

Andy looked at each of them in turn, his expression grave. "Come on, already. The clock is ticking, and for all we know some overeager security guard is going to find us here. A guard," he said, "or worse."

Blake scowled, then turned to inspect the entire area, taking in the cypress trees that lined the pond and the sculpted hedges in the distance. He turned to scour the house with his gaze, his attention drawn to the dark nooks and crevices, as well as the roof.

He saw no one, and for a moment he let himself relax. He'd remain vigilant, of course, but his impression was that they were safe.

Devi, he saw, was peering again at the coin. Andy was circling the reflecting pond, his flashlight beam scouring the bottom of the reflecting pond. "I don't see anything else on the bottom of the pool."

"And I don't know where else this coin could lead," Devi said, her voice cracking as she moved toward Blake.

He put his arms around her, noticing Andy's scowl as he did so. But Blake wasn't in the mood to coddle the feelings of a crew member harboring a crush on the star, and as he held her, he shifted them, turning so that his back was to Andy and his full attention was on Devi.

"Hey, hey," he said. "We're going to figure this out."

"I'm losing it," she whispered. "Don't let me lose it in front of Andy."

"You're not," he said, working to keep his voice firm. "I'm not going to let you lose it."

"It's happening all over again. Except it's not. It's as if I survived one nightmare just to walk into another one."

"Listen to me," he said, turning her face up so that she had no choice but to look at him. "You're strong. You did survive. You beat the drugs. You resuscitated your career. You are not the victim here."

"No? Then what the hell am I?"

"The winner," he said. "I don't care if I have to push you every step of the way, I'm going to make sure you win this damned game."

That actually earned him a smile, but it wasn't long-lived, the corners of her mouth turning down as the spark in her eyes faded. "You can't stay, Blake. I want you to—dear God, how I want you to—but I couldn't stand it if you got hurt."

"Then you understand exactly how I feel."

"Blake—"

He silenced her protest with a soft finger to her lips. He wanted no more protests. No more fear. He just wanted her to have herself back, and he hated the fact that he couldn't give her that.

Gently, he brushed the pad of his thumb over her lower lip, wanting desperately to kiss her, but knowing he shouldn't. Not with Andy somewhere behind him staring daggers at his back.

He heard Andy moving behind them, the sound reminding Blake that the time for comfort was over. There would be time for that once they kept Devi alive.

"The coin," he said, reaching for it. "Maybe I'll see something you don't."

"You won't see anything," Andy said. "You won't, because you were right. The coin isn't the clue."

Blake turned to find Andy staring at the house. When he turned to face them, a slow grin spread across his face. "We've been looking in the wrong place," Andy said.

"It's not the reflecting pond?" Devi asked. "But it has to be."

"A reflection of grandeur, of good times *once seen*," Andy said. "It's not in the reflecting pond. It's somewhere that you go to *see* the pond."

Blake couldn't fault the logic there, and they all started to turn, finally zeroing in on a lone black bench next to a short wall, just a few feet away from one end of the pond.

"Looks like a bench," she said as soon as they reached it. She dropped down, then bounced a little on it. "Feels like one, too." She looked up at them. "Either of you see anything unusual?"

"Not at first glance," Blake said. "Hang on." He got down on the concrete, then scooted up under the bench.

"See anything?" Devi asked.

"Too damn dark."

"Hang on," Andy said, then bent down with the tiny flashlight.

Slowly, Blake ran the light over every inch of the bench's underside, his heart pounding at the thrill of what he saw. "This is it."

"And?"

"It's backward. Flipped and backward." He slid out enough to show his head. "Got a mirror?"

Devi rummaged in the black bag that Blake had noticed earlier in her kitchen. "Voilà," she said, producing a compact.

He took it, then slid back under the bench.

"Okay. It's a Web site: www.canyousurvivethegame.com."

"That's it?"

He slid back out. "That's it."

"Andy?" Devi asked.

"Already on it."

Andy tapped away at the tiny keypad on his phone. After a few seconds, he sucked in a breath, then held the device out, the screen positioned for both Blake and Devi to see.

> *The world turns on its axis*
> *And then it's all done*
> *Dressed for the red carpet*
> *But it's the end of your fun*
> *And though the truth cuts like a knife*
> *Find the antidote, or it's a wrap of your life*

Blake's stomach twisted as he considered the garbled message. On the whole, it meant nothing to him. Nothing, that is, other than the basic sentiment of *bad*. He reached out, searching for Devi's hand, and his heart lifted in both sadness and joy when he realized she was reaching for him as well.

"Am I right about what this means?" she asked, her fingers tight in Blake's hand and her gaze fixed just as firmly on Andy. "Twenty-four hours? One turn of the axis? Is that how long I have to live?"

"I think so," Andy said. "Devi, I'm sorry, but this doesn't change anything."

"The hell it doesn't."

"Toxin delivered, remember? We already knew you'd been poisoned."

"He's right," Blake said. "This isn't confirmation, it's just a timeline."

She tilted her head back, looking at the sky as she took a deep breath. When she looked back at them, she tried a small smile, but mostly failed. And the tears glistening in her eyes threatened to undo Blake. "I just . . . I guess I just hoped I was right."

"Right?"

"It's stupid, but I thought that maybe—you know—since I'm hard to get close to . . . I guess I just hoped that it was a mistake."

"Devi," Andy said gently. "The game doesn't make those kinds of mistakes."

She nodded, but the sadness coming off her was palpable. As was the fear.

"How long exactly?" Blake asked, determined to get down to business. There wasn't a damn thing he could do about Devi's fear. Nothing, that is, except find the assassin and stop the game. "Twenty-four hours from when?"

"That's the question of the hour," Andy said.

"Another fucking riddle," Devi put in.

"We'll figure it out," Blake said. They had to. "Start with the red-carpet reference. What does that mean?"

"That I was infected on the red carpet? Maybe something in the air at a premiere?"

"Have you been to a premiere lately?" he asked.

She shook her head. "Not in a couple of months."

"And they wouldn't release something in the air anyway," Andy added. "Too much risk of other people getting infected. And that's not the point of the game."

"Slipped something in my drink at some sort of red-carpet function?"

"You haven't been to one," Blake reminded her.

"It says dressed for the red carpet," Andy said, staring intently at his screen. "Maybe it just means you're dressed like you would be. If you were going to a red carpet premiere kind of thing."

"Maybe," she said, sounding dubious.

"Have you done that recently?" Blake pressed. "Gone to a formal function?" The truth was, he knew the answer to that. When they were together, they hadn't gone anywhere formal for over five weeks. After the breakup, he'd heard through the grapevine that Devi had pretty much stayed tucked away.

Sure enough, she shook her head. "Nothing recent."

"Okay, let's look at this from another angle. How do you dress for the red carpet? Have you gone shopping lately?"

She lifted an eyebrow, and he laughed.

"Okay, have you bought any Prada formal wear lately?"

"No. Just this bag and a few other odds and ends." She held up her new bag. "And I didn't even buy it. It was a gift." Her eyes widened. "Oh! What about the dress I wore to the Oscars last year?"

They both looked at Andy, who shrugged. "What about it?"

"I have no idea," she admitted. "I borrowed it, anyway. It's back at Versace."

"But that's a good point. You dress formally for a red carpet affair, right? So maybe the point is that we're talking about something formal."

"Like . . ." She twirled her hand, urging him on.

"I've got nothing," he admitted. "I still can't figure out how I'm supposed to dress for these things."

"A tux," she said, teasingly. "And not rented from a dry

cleaner." She laughed, obviously enjoying the memory. Not that it was his fault he was so clueless on their first date. He'd never had occasion to wear a tux before.

He was about to defend his past tux-renting fiasco when her laughter abruptly stops.

"Dear God. That's it."

"What?" Blake and Andy asked, both at the same time.

"The chocolate. The strawberry. Don't you remember? It was wearing a little tux."

"Hell," he said. "You're right." And it had tasted bitter. Suddenly, the confection he'd swiped weighed way heavy in his stomach.

"Oh, Blake," she said, reaching out for him. "Blake—"

"I know," he said. "You're not the one poisoned. I am."

"Shit," Andy whispered, as Devi took and squeezed Blake's hand, her eyes wide with horror and apology.

"I guess there's a tiny bit of good news for me in the mix," Blake said, trying hard to keep himself together.

"Are you crazy?"

"Maybe a little," he said, pulling her close. "But there's no way you're getting rid of me now. At least not until we find the damned antidote."

Chapter 27

No way you're getting rid of me now . . .

The words play out in my head, a sense of joy coupled with deep grief and fear. I'm so afraid for Blake, and yet I'm so grateful that I've lost all my excuses to send him away. I *want* him with me, and the force of that need hits me so unexpectedly it sends me reeling.

I take his hand, then silently squeeze it. "I'm so sorry."

He pulls me close, then kisses the top of my head. "It's not your fault," he says. Which is true. But it doesn't change the oppressive guilt that I feel. Because while I would never in a million years wish Blake harm, I have to admit—even if only to myself—that I'm relieved that it's him and not me who's been poisoned.

I shiver, pulling free of his embrace to wrap my arms around myself. I can't even believe I'm thinking that, and yet it's so true, and there's nothing I can do to erase the thoughts.

"Devi," he says, as firmly as if he's reading my mind. "It's okay."

It's not okay, of course, but I'm not going to argue. Instead, I focus, just like we all need to be doing. "We need to get to work."

"We damn sure do," Blake says, and I reach out to brush his fingers with mine.

"But we don't know where to go next," I say. "So we must be missing something."

"Maybe something in the first clue?" Blake says.

Andy shakes his head. "That would be odd. The game's pretty linear. One clue to another clue to another clue. Sometimes when the clues get harder they feed on each other, but this early on all the first clue does is lead you to the qualifying clue."

Blake and I lock eyes. *The qualifying clue.* "It's one thing to say the game's linear," Blake says, his voice sharp with tension and, I'm sure, fear. "But what the hell is it linear from? I need to find the damn antidote. We need to—"

"Wait!" I look up sharply, surprised by my own sudden insight. "You guys . . . this can't be right."

"Devi . . ." Blake's voice trails off. "Denial isn't the way to go here."

"No, no." I wave off his comments. "I'm not in denial. I'm thinking."

"What?" Andy says, and since he's clearly more receptive, I turn to him.

"The strawberry came from Tobias," I say. "There's no way it was poisoned."

"That's true," Blake says, and I hear the hope in his voice.

And since he's now backing me up, I shift a little to bring him more into my line of sight.

"Devi, don't assume things. That's how people end up dead."

"It's not an assumption," I insist. "I know the man. It probably sat on Marcia's desk all day until Tobias got around to writing that note and—oh, shit. *The note.*"

Both look at me. "What note?" Andy asks.

"There was a note with the strawberry. A Web page. I thought it was from Tobias, but now that we know about the strawberry—"

"Someone either doctored Tobias's gift, or set it up all together," Andy finishes, his tone all business. "So what did the note say?"

"It was a Web site. That's all. I thought Tobias was being funny. You know, since he's so computer-illiterate and the movie is all about computers."

"Do you remember the site?" he asks, his Treo pulled out and ready.

I rack my brain, but I can't remember. "I could get Lucas to go inside and find the note," I say, pulling out my phone even as I'm suggesting it. Before I can do anything, though, the thing vibrates in my hand.

I jump, startled, my life flashing before my eyes. My mini-movie ends in seconds, though, once I realize it's just a call coming in. And when I see the caller ID, I hurry to answer.

"Tobias!" But that's as far as I get. Because Tobias is breathing hard, his voice both edgy and sad.

"Mac's dead," he says, without preamble. "Devi, I'm so sorry to tell you, but Mackenzie is dead."

Chapter 28

This can't be real. This can absolutely *not* be real.

That thought, and nothing more, goes through my head as Blake pulls his car up near the throng of people gathered outside Mac's house. A police officer signals for him to stop, and he does, then rolls down the window to explain who we are. The officer's expression changes from professional to sympathetic, and he waves us farther in, telling us to park just in front of the crime scene tape.

Crime scene.

Oh, dear God.

I can't do this, I think, even as Blake strokes my cheek and murmurs, "You can do this. You'll be okay."

Even through his own horror, he's thinking of me, and I can't help but realize that he still cares for me. Maybe even loves me.

I can't think about that now, though, and so I work up my

courage and open the door. Andy's already out, and I follow him to the tape, where we join the rest of the gawkers.

"What happened?" Andy asks a nearby woman, standing there in jogging shorts and a tank top.

"I'm not entirely sure," the woman says. "But I think it was a mugging."

"Mackenzie . . ." Her name leaves my lips before I can draw it back, and I fight the tears that I know will follow.

The woman turns compassionate eyes on me. "Oh, gosh. You're a friend. Honey, I'm so sorry."

I nod, my throat too dry to even thank her.

Blake has been talking to the police, and now he comes over, his face serious but his eyes soft. He holds out his arms, and I fall gratefully into them. "Shhh," he says, along with other comforting noises, as he steers me away from the crowd to a grassy area near the house across the street. We're in Burbank, and the little stucco houses are close together. There's not much privacy, but no one is paying attention to us. All eyes are on the murder scene across the road.

"Do you think this has to do with . . ." I trail off, unable to even give voice to the thought.

"How could it?" he says. "She doesn't have anything to do with the game."

I nod, but I still feel uneasy. I look around for Andy and find him a few yards away, head to head with Tobias, both their expressions serious. I close my eyes and remind myself to breathe. The truth is, horror fills the world every day. Random violence can take us out in the blink of an eye. Caught like I am in the game, I think I'd forgotten that. I'd focused on how much I was the victim, entirely forgetting the world outside mine.

Tonight, Mac is the victim. And, unlike me, she didn't even see it coming.

I wipe away a tear and see that Tobias is looking at me. He says something to Andy, then they both head my way. "How are you doing?"

I want to snap that I'll be doing a lot better if everyone quits asking me that, but I don't. His concern is genuine, and my pain is very real.

"I'm not sure," I finally say, giving the only honest answer I know.

He releases a noisy breath. "Well, they think it's random."

There's nothing in his words to put me on alert, but I hear something in his tone, and immediately pounce on it. "But?"

He hesitates, but dives in. "It doesn't look like your typical mugging."

I look to Andy for confirmation or explanation, but he doesn't meet my eyes. A cold wariness fills me, and I hold tighter to Blake. "What do you mean?"

"Her throat was slit," Tobias says, speaking matter-of-factly, as if that will make the words hurt less. It doesn't, of course, and it's as if I can feel that very same knife slam into my heart, and then twist.

Blake must understand, because he steps behind me, gathering me close in his arms. "What are the police thinking?"

Tobias shifts his focus from me to Blake, and I can almost feel his relief that he doesn't have to look me in the eye anymore. He clears his throat. "They . . . well, they just don't know. It could be random. But the knife had a serrated edge, and considering who Mac looks like . . ."

He doesn't have to say any more. I've already broken free of

Blake and am squatting at the side of the road, my arms tight around my stomach to keep me from puking my guts up.

Blake immediately crouches down beside me, Tobias and Andy right there with him.

"We don't know anything for certain, babe," Blake says. "Not a goddamn thing."

"We know you need to be careful," Tobias says. "I want someone with you all the time. Just a precaution until the police can do a little more investigation. Maybe she broke it off with a psycho boyfriend." He pulls out his phone and starts to dial.

I reach up, trying to take the phone from his hand. "Don't."

"Devi, you need protection."

"I've got it," I say. And I do. I have Andy, my official protector. And Blake, who's promised not to leave my side. One thing I don't need is another person being dragged into this mess.

Tobias hesitates, then looks to Blake. "Does she?"

"You know the boys in her guardhouse. They'll pull together whatever's necessary." It's a nice lie, and I'm impressed with how quickly it comes to his tongue.

Satisfied, Tobias slips his phone back in his pocket. "I want you two keeping a low profile the next few days, you understand?"

"I thought you wanted the PR machine to crank," Blake says. "Happy couple and all that."

"Time for that later. Right now, just lay low. Shouldn't be too hard since you're on hiatus for the near future."

"We're— Wait, what?" I have no idea what he's talking about.

"Bonding company requirements," he says. "And we have to find you a new stunt double. Damn insurance bullshit, but it's for the best. Your head won't be in the right place if you show up on the set tomorrow."

He's got that right.

"So, we just wait for your call?"

"That's about it. I'm going to fly to New York. Use this downtime to get things ready for the location shots next month. Okay?"

Now, his eyes are fully on me, and I recognize the man who for years I've thought of as a father. "Sure." The idea of having a set call time didn't sit well with me, anyway. It would be too much like shooting ducks in a barrel.

"Come here," he says, holding out his arms.

I go, breathing in the scent of his cigarettes. A very gauche habit in uber-healthy L.A., but Tobias hasn't ever been one to care about what the masses are doing. He captures me in a bear hug, then releases me, hooking an arm around my shoulder as he steers me a few feet from Andy and Blake.

"I haven't read your notes yet," I say, which is my way of trying to pry out the truth. "I guess now I can wait a while."

I desperately hope that he will brush off my comment and tell me to go to the Web site in the note some other time. That there's no rush at all. Instead he just looks confused, confirming what I already knew in my heart—Tobias didn't send the strawberry or the note.

"What notes?" he asks.

I force out a laugh. And then—before he can latch on in that oh-so-Tobias way of his—I wave my hand, dissipating the dust of the entire conversation. "I'm such an idiot," I say. "Someone sent candy and a note. And even though Blake said something about giving me a treat, I just assumed the note was from you. You know. Story notes. That kind of thing."

"No need for notes," he says. "You did great."

"Thanks."

"As for Blake, though. The man really is sweet on you," Tobias says. "Are things . . . ?"

I shrug, because I'm not entirely sure how things are.

"I'm glad you're with him. He's a good guy, Devi."

I know that, but at the same time, I'm tired of everyone telling me so.

He waits a moment for me to respond, and when I don't, he shakes his head. "Well, anyway, tomorrow is off. And even though I said I want you to keep a low profile, I want you laying low *together*. This movie has enough scandal without your breakup heating up in the news again."

"Right. Sure. Whatever you want, Toby."

"I want you to be careful," he says, then kisses my forehead.

"I will," I promise, which is quite the understatement.

"I'll be back in about a week. We'll probably start up again then."

"Right," I say, then watch as he walks back toward the huddle of policemen by Mac's fence line. I hug myself, even though I know that I can take a few steps backward and lose myself in the warmth of Blake's arms.

One week before Tobias wants me back on the job. One short week. I think of the strawberry note that leads to a Web site I didn't bother checking, and I wonder what it says there.

One week.

I only hope I'll still be alive by then.

Chapter 29

I kept it together in Burbank, but lost it during the drive back to Beverly Hills. I'd simply broken down and cried. A rush of tears for Mac, and all she'd lost. And, yes, tears for me and my fears that I would soon be joining her. I don't know if that's selfish or not, but I honestly don't care. I just needed to get it out, and in the backseat, curled up against Andy, who patted my back and said soft things, turned out to be the place to do it.

We're turning onto my street when I finally feel in control enough to get down to business. Or, rather, I'm ready to fake it. Actress, remember? And the show must go on.

"Tell me the truth," I say. "Was she killed because of this?"

"You asked that earlier," Blake says.

"And now I'm asking it without the police and half of Burbank standing nearby."

"No," he said. "That would be against the rules. Why would she get pulled in?"

It's a rhetorical question, so I don't answer it. But I do look at Andy. "Well?"

"Hell yes it's related," he says. "It's too damn coincidental not to be." He shoots Blake a look that makes it clear that Andy thinks that Blake is just one step above being an idiot. I fight the urge to send them to separate corners.

"But *how*?" I say instead. "How could Mac get pulled in? I didn't call her for help."

"It's all part of the rules," Andy says. "You pull in outside help, and there's a risk."

"Yes, but to just anyone? And what outside help?"

Andy doesn't bother answering that one; he just stares at the back of Blake's head.

"You really think that whoever is running the game knew that Blake was around? That he called? That he helped?"

"Yeah," Andy says flatly. "I really believe that. You're not understanding the breadth of the game here. It's been going on for years in the real world, and no one's been able to run it to ground. The FBI's been involved, and Mel has more resources than you can imagine. It just keeps going. Information, clues, facts. It's astounding and impressive and terrifying all at the same time. Most of all, whoever is running the show has access and information. You need to remember that, Devi. You need to burn it into your brain."

I shudder, but I nod, feeling more than a little chastised. "I still don't understand, though. Why kill Mac? I broke the rules by talking to Blake, right? So why kill Mac? Why not—" But I choke on the question, unable to give it voice.

"Why not kill Blake?" Andy asks, not nearly as squeamish.

"He couldn't kill me," Blake says from the front seat.

I manage a halfhearted smile despite the overpowering guilt I'm feeling from getting him involved. "You're invincible? How convenient for me."

"I'm your motivation, remember? I'm the one who ate the chocolate. Without me, you can just poke along, or not try to solve the clues at all."

He's right, of course. But still, something is off. I roll it around in my still-addled head until it bumps up against a question. "But how does our assassin know that?"

"I already told you," Andy says. "The game told him."

"Eyes everywhere," I say, but mostly to myself.

I want to pull out my cell phone and call Susie. She's the one who delivered the strawberry to me. Where did she get it? Maybe a messenger brought it by, just saying that it was from Tobias. If she could describe the messenger . . .

Overall, I can't help think that there's some bigger connection to the movie. After all, it's not easy getting access to a studio backlot, or to the development offices. And yet whoever is pulling our strings seems to be everywhere and nowhere all at the same time.

Most of all, it all circles back to the movie. A movie about a game I'm now playing in real life.

I shudder, hating the game. And, for the moment, hating the movie, too.

We've arrived at my house now, and Lucas lets us in through the gate. Blake maneuvers down my long driveway, and all the while, I'm trying to remember where I put the note with the Web site.

"It must be in my old purse," I say as soon as we're out of the car. Once in the house, I rush upstairs to my purse closet, Blake right on my heels. We arrive together, me breathless, and him as cool as always.

"Good lord, Devi," he says, looking into the room. I realize then that he's never actually seen my purse closet. I suppose it is a bit overwhelming. I turned one of the spare bedrooms into the closet, then filled it with freestanding shelves for all of my bags. Since I keep each in a cloth sack, I have a picture of each purse taped on the shelf to identify what's in the sack. A large table sits by the door, a resting place for purses in transition. Finally, there's a bureau in the back of the room to hold my collection of wallets, cell phone cases, and the like.

All in all, the room seems perfectly reasonable to me. Blake, however, clearly thinks I'm a loon.

"I like purses," I say.

"I guess so." He rolls his eyes and makes a show of looking around the room. "So. Where do we start?"

I smack him, because now he's just being a pain. "That one," I say, pointing to the teal blue Prada bag I was carrying yesterday. I look around, suddenly realizing we're missing someone. "Where's Andy?"

"I really don't know." And it's obvious he doesn't care. Instead, he's focused on inspecting my bag. Since I'd only transferred the essentials—and not all the little bits of detritus that gather in a purse over time—he manages to pull out quite a bit of stuff. He lays it all on the table, and we start to pick through it.

"You don't like him," I say. It's a statement, not a question, but I pause, waiting for him to deny it. Because that's what people do. They take the polite, nonconfrontational route.

I should have known Blake had to be different.

"No," he says. "I don't."

"Why?"

"I don't like the way he looks at you."

I feel myself blush. Not because of Andy, but because of the way *Blake* is looking at me. "He's just a fan," I say. "He's got a crush thing going on."

"That doesn't mean I have to like it," Blake says.

"I'm not so sure you're entitled to an opinion," I say, even though the mere fact that he is jealous makes my heart beat a little faster. Girlie and immature, but there you have it.

"No?" He moves around the little table until he's right there beside me. "I don't think entitlement matters." He's so close I can breathe in the scent of him, and it's all I can do not to reach out, grab his shirt, and pull him toward me. I want him badly, desperately. I want his arms and his comfort and his humor. I want his love.

I want everything I lost, and I have no idea if we can get it back. But as I look in his eyes, I know I want to try. At the same time, though, I'm terrified of getting hurt again.

He reaches out and strokes my cheek. "I don't like the way he looks at you. Like he has a piece of you. Like there's a connection."

My cheeks heat even more.

"Come on, Devi. What aren't you telling me?"

"Nothing," I lie.

"Mmmm."

"What's that supposed to mean?"

"There's a look."

"A look?" I ask.

"Yeah," he says, his voice defensive. "There's a look between the two of you."

"There's no look," I say firmly.

"Maybe. Maybe not. Why don't you just tell me?"

"Dammit, Blake. There's nothing to tell." Since that's a blatant lie, I back off a little. But I don't want to tell him about Andy's stolen kiss. That would be too much like gossiping on Andy.

He curls a strand of my hair around his finger. "There was a time when you'd tell me anything."

I look away and lift a shoulder. But whereas before I would have been angry, now I'm only sad.

"Devi," he says, pulling me into his arms. "I'm so sorry. I know I've said it before, but I'm going to keep saying it until you believe me."

"Sorry is just a word, Blake."

"Do you really believe I don't care about you?"

I shake my head, forced to admit the truth. "No." I press my face against his shirt, breathing deep of his scent. "I've missed you."

"I'm right here," he says, and then his mouth closes over mine, the kiss hard and possessive, and yet at the same time sweet and sensual. I open my mouth to him, tasting him, pulling him in.

Our bodies are pressed together, and there's a desperation in our touches, in our kisses. As if we both know we might not live to see tomorrow, and we have to fight for this one moment of intense pleasure.

His hands stroke me, sending chills racing through me. I want him—I want him so desperately—and yet this is hardly the time or the place. And the fact is, we do have company downstairs.

"We can't," I murmur.

"I know," he says, but his body tells a different tale, his lips demanding, and his low moan of pleasure almost undoing my resolve.

"Blake . . ."

"I know, I know." And this time he really does pull away. We look at each other, speaking without words, and then he presses his finger to his lips, and then mine. "Believe me, I know better than anyone. It's time to get back to work."

The way he says that makes my heart break, and I reach out to stroke his cheek. "I'm so sorry I got you into this. I'm so sorry you're—" I can't finish the thought.

"I'm not going to die," he says, holding firm to my wrist. He smiles at me, the expression warming me right down to my toes. Honestly, I wouldn't have been surprised to see anger in those eyes. After all, he's in this mess—literally—because of me. But I don't see anything there but love.

I can't help but feel a little humbled.

"We'll find the antidote," he promises. "And you didn't get me into this. That honor goes to the bastard who's yanking our chain."

"Maybe," I say. "But I'm not doing a very good job getting you out of it. I can't even remember where I put the damn note." And then I look at him and thwack the heel of my hand against my forehead. "Duh! The script. I stuck it inside the script."

We race back downstairs to find Andy hunched over his Treo, busily typing. "What are you doing?" Blake demands.

"Covering all bases," he says. "Sometimes information about the game comes into a player's message center."

"Like the note that said the toxin was delivered," I say.

"I half hoped I'd have a message giving us some idea what to do next."

"Any luck?" I ask, hopefully.

"Not a single message." He looks at me. "You?"

"The note's in the script," I say. I have it now, and rifle through the pages, finally holding it up in triumph. "Although you raise a good point. Should I check my messages, too?"

"Absolutely," Andy says. "Check your messages. Go to that Web page. Do everything and anything we can to get the game moving along with as much information as we can collect."

I nod, then sit down in front of my computer, oddly invigorated. But we have a plan now, with at least two steps before we're stymied again. It may not be a good sign, but at least it's something.

The Web site on the card is www.YourGivenchyCode-MovieNotes.com, and I try there first. But my browser is slow, and nothing much seems to be happening. I figure the Web page is probably huge, filled with slow-loading graphics and the like. Either that, or my Internet connection is just slow.

I open up another browser box, letting the YourGivenchy-CodeMovieNotes page load in the background. In the new address bar I type the URL for Play.Survive.Win, then navigate to the message center as soon as the page loads.

"I was right," Andy says, tapping the screen. "You have a message."

I shift in my chair and give him and Blake a quick look.

Andy is looking at the screen, but Blake is watching me, and now he puts a hand on my shoulder for strength.

I hold my breath, and click on the icon to take me to the messages. As soon as I open it, the sender alone sends shock waves of terror through my body—*Janus.*

I must have whimpered, because immediately Blake's arms are around me, and he's whispering curses as he reads over my shoulder.

I just sit there, numb, the world closing in like a tunnel around me, as Blake scrolls down, revealing the full text of the waiting message:

>>>http://www.playsurvivewin.com<<<

PLAY.SURVIVE.WIN

PLEASE LOGIN

PLAYER USER NAME: *LuvPrada*

PLAYER PASSWORD: ********

. . . *please wait*

. . . *please wait*

. . . *please wait*

Password approved

>>>Read New Messages<<<   >>>Create New Message<<<

. . . *please wait*

WELCOME TO MESSAGE CENTER

You have one new message.

New Message:
To: LuvPrada
From: Janus
Subject: My Darling Devi

You broke the rules.

Next time, solve the clues without help.

Chapter

30

Everything is black. I mean everything. The world around me. My thoughts. My fears.

All colored black. And slow. As if I'm moving through tar. *This can't be happening! This can't be real!*

But it is real. Even through the pitch, I know that it's real. It's real, it's dangerous, and I need to come back.

But there's comfort and warmth here in the dark, and if I can just crawl further into it—if I can just lose myself—I know that I'll be safe.

"Devi."

A whispered voice. Blake's. So near, and so compelling. I want to go to it, but at the same time, I don't want to leave this place. Don't want to face the truth. Don't want to face *him.*

Dear God, can it really be him?

"*Devi.*"

This time, I have no choice. The voice insists, cutting down through the layers of fear until I have to come out. Soft hands caress me, and I breath in the familiar scent of safety, of Blake.

"Devi, honey, are you in there?"

The blackness starts to shift, to melt away, and as I look, the world comes back into focus. There's Blake's face, right in front of mine, his eyes full of concern.

"I'm here," I whisper. "Is it really true?"

"Maybe it's not the same Janus," Blake says. "Maybe our assassin just picked that name, knowing it would scare you."

"I doubt it," Andy says, and Blake shoots him a look that could kill. Andy cringes, but doesn't back down. "We have to face reality here. And the truth is that Janus must have been the user name of this guy for a while. At least before the game started. I'm guessing whoever's behind the game did what the police couldn't."

"What do you mean?" I ask.

"They figured out who Janus is. And then they offered him another chance at you."

"Oh, God." I'm pretty sure I'm going to be sick.

"Devi." Blake squeezes my hand.

"I'm okay." I suck air into my lungs, then squeeze back. "I can handle this."

"Yes," he says. "You can. We both can."

I nod, because I know him well. He's not going to say more than that, but he's terrified, too. Both for me and for him. He's in as much danger as I am. And we both need to get moving if we want to survive. And I *have* to survive. "I want to see that bastard dead," I say, with a sudden burst of fury. "For what he did to me. And for what he did to Mac."

Revenge. That was my fragile link to sanity. Under the circumstances, though, I was happy to take whatever I could get.

"The page is up," Andy says.

I look over and see that he's closed the screen with the message from Janus, leaving the YourGivenchyCodeMovieNotes page that had been loading.

And although I'd expected it to be overflowing with graphics, in fact, it's simply a blank page with a pink background and a clue in the middle:

> *Trap a parent, be a brother*
> *You just need one place or another*
> *Where the Loire meets the Angels*
> *Where Led rides to be seen*
> *Where Bogie plays with a thumb so green*
> *The service is stunning, it's sure to wow*
> *So find the message—for the girl you are now.*

Chapter

31

"**D**amn this *fucking* game," Devi said, slamming her palm so hard against the laptop screen that Blake was afraid the thing would break. "So here we are with another fucking dumb-ass clue. What does it mean?"

"It means we're one step closer to finding my antidote. And after we do that, we can find a safe place to hole up for a nap. I don't know about you guys, but that's pretty damn motivating."

"Yeah," she said. "It is." It was after two a.m., and he'd been up since seven. Devi, he knew, had a five a.m. call, so she'd been up even longer. At the moment, they both had to be operating on adrenaline.

She tapped the screen. "Any ideas?"

"You're the movie buff," Andy said, which earned him a frown from Devi. A little fact that didn't bother Blake in the least. She might have said there was nothing going on between them—and she might have even meant it, too—but he still couldn't stop the little green thoughts in his head. He wasn't proud of them, but that didn't mean he could stop them.

"So let's take this one step at a time," Devi said. " 'Trap a parent, be a brother.' What can that possibly mean?"

"Boys getting their parents back together again?" Andy asked.

"Maybe," Devi said.

"Even if it is, so what?" Blake asked.

"We're just trying to work through it," Devi said reasonably. Blake nodded, but he wasn't feeling particularly reasonable at the moment. Not with the hours ticking away, and the chance of finding the antidote right along with them.

He stood up, pushing the fear out of his mind. The same technique he used for fighting was coming in handy at the moment. Though in a way, he supposed it was apropos. He was fighting, after all. Fighting an unknown toxin and an unknown assailant.

Fighting to stay alive.

"What about the next line?" he said. " 'One place or another'?"

"No idea," Devi said. "But I think it's too vague. I bet it's not a clue. I mean, it's part of the riddle and means we have to go someplace, but I'm betting that's all it means."

"Andy?"

"I think she's right." He reached out and squeezed her shoulder. "Good job."

Her smile lit the room, and she turned eagerly back toward the screen. "Okay, this next one, though. 'Where the Loire meets the Angels.' Any brilliant ideas?"

"Something French that's here in Los Angeles?" Blake said.

"Oh!" Devi held up her hand. "That's got to be it. L.A. is the City of Angels, right?"

"Progress," Andy said with a grin. "Hallelujah."

"So, what would be French?" Devi asked, more to herself than to him and Andy.

"Wine," Blake offered, because it was the only thing he could think of.

"Fashion," Devi said.

"There you go. So who are some French designers?"

"Ah, um. Prada is Italian," she finally offered. "Honestly, I mostly just buy what I like. I know who has stores in Paris, but I don't know if that's home base."

"Right," he said. "Fair enough."

"So maybe we should get on the Internet and figure it out?" Andy suggested.

"Go for it," Blake said. "We'll work our way through the rest of these clues." At least, he hoped they would.

While Andy got settled in at the computer, Blake and Devi sat across the table from him, studying the cryptic message they'd copied onto notepaper.

"The only Led I know of is Led Zeppelin," Devi said.

" 'Stairway to Heaven,' " he said. "Anyplace in L.A. fit that description?"

"Nothing I can think of. Besides, what's the 'ride' reference?"

"What are *any* of the references?" he countered, frustration coloring his voice. Time was ticking away, and they weren't getting anywhere. "Like this reference to Bogie. That's got to be Humphrey Bogart, but in what? A movie? There are dozens and dozens to choose from."

Frustrated, he pushed back from the table and started pacing, determined to keep the fear at bay. And equally determined
not to look at the clock.

"Maybe it's someplace that Bogart and Led Zeppelin have in
common," he said, forcing himself to get with the program.

"Okay, but what? This is insane!"

"Babe, I completely agree. Not exactly number one on my
list of ways to pass the time. Especially since time *is* passing."

"I'm sorry," she said, immediately contrite. "I'm tired. I'm
not thinking clearly. And I'm scared to death."

"I know." He reached out and stroked the back of her neck,
wishing he could transfer all the tenseness he felt there from her
body to his. He looked up at Andy. "Have you figured out anything on the France-L.A. angle?"

"Not a thing," Andy said. "You want to give it a go?"

"I do," said Devi. She moved around to the computer, and
Blake heard her tapping on the keys. After a second, she started
tapping faster. And then, after she'd practically typed out a
novel, she looked up, a wide grin on her face.

He held his breath, not quite able to believe there was good
news after all the crap that had been thrown at them so far.

But then she spoke, lighting a tiny spark of hope.

"Come on, boys," she said. "I know where we're going."

Chapter 32

He kept the engine off, just in case. The computer, however, he kept powered up, and the bluish glow from the screen illuminated the interior of the car, making him slightly visible to anyone who might be looking.

So far, no one seemed interested.

The tracking software had yet to kick in, but he was a patient man. And now he was patiently waiting outside her house, almost half a block from the gated entrance and just around a curve in the road.

Amazing, really, that the game knew an address that he'd been trying to track down for years.

He thought of all the time he'd missed watching her coming and going. . . .

Such a loss.

Soon, though, the past would be forgotten, and they'd be together for an eternity.

It was almost too much to believe, too much to hope for. And yet he knew that it would come true.

Once more, he glanced at the computer, still notoriously silent, refusing to give up its secrets. He knew that she had already solved the qualifying clue—the computer had revealed that much. He wished the tracking software would cooperate, but he was willing to be patient. All that mattered was that the game had commenced . . . and she was now fair prey.

Minutes passed, seemingly as long as hours. Cars eased by, but only a few. The hour, after all, was late. When he saw the lights approaching, he gently closed the laptop, dimming its light.

No one questioned him.

He was simply there. Part of the scenery. All of which confirmed his belief that he belonged there. Belonged with *her*. Why else would it be so easy?

His thigh muscles were beginning to ache, and he shifted uncomfortably, weighing his choices. He was just about to open the door when the gate in front of her house eased open, and a long convertible rolled out. He couldn't see the driver, but he knew without a doubt that Devi was in that car.

With a smile in his heart, he turned the key, the engine revving to life, mirroring the power that now pulsed through his veins.

The hunt was on.

Chapter

33

The Chateau Marmont.

As we race through the night, I ponder our destination, because once I started thinking along the right lines, interpreting the clue really had been simple.

It was the reference to trapping a parent that helped me figure it out, and I hoped like hell I was right. I thought I was, though, and the guys agreed with me, especially after I ran through my reasoning.

Once it clicked in my head, actually, it was pretty obvious. I'd started by putting *trap* and *parent* and *Hollywood* into Google. The first hit was *The Parent Trap*, which was an awesome movie, both in its original Hayley Mills incarnation and its Lindsay Lohan remake.

It was Lindsay, though, that caught my memory. Because not too long ago there'd been a whole big to-do when she was called on the carpet by a producer who thought she was partying too much. (Sounds like me back in my wild days, although I never missed a call.) The letter was all over the trades (and the tabloids . . . and the Internet) and was addressed to Lindsay care of the Chateau Marmont, where she happened to be living at the time.

Okay, that was my starting point. And honestly, I just got lucky. Because the Chateau is one of my all-time favorite places in the world, and the whole Lindsay fiasco made me think of it. And since the famous hotel looks like a castle, I knew I had to be on the right track.

After that, it wasn't too hard. The all-powerful Google confirmed that the Chateau was modeled after a Loire Valley castle. And the Chateau's own Web site said that Bogie and Led Zeppelin had stayed there (and the rockers had ridden their bikes through the lobby). Even the reference to John became clear. John Belushi. One of the Chateau's sadder claims to fame.

I let the guys know where we were going as we hurried out the door, tote bag with laptop in tow. The rationale, I filled in on the way as we sped out the gate and onto the deserted streets of Beverly Hills.

Now, as we turn onto Sunset, the wind whips through my hair, and I'm glad Blake left the top down on Blue, his 1960-something Buick. I was with him when he bought her, after trading in the late-model sports car convertible that had twice as many problems and not nearly as much character.

The thing is, a big honking boat of a car like this really is Blake. He's not pretentious. He just *is*. And that was what I'd loved the most in him. That boy-next-door outlook on the world coupled with looks that will soon have every other woman in American drooling.

Unlike me, Blake didn't grow up in the spotlight. He wasn't used to the pressures of coming up with a quotable comeback on the spur of the moment. He hadn't taken media training in lieu of kindergarten.

Is it any wonder he completely blew it on *Letterman*? Because assuming he really did—and does—love me, then that's all that happened. Letterman caught him by surprise (not so unusual, that), and he blurted out something that to his un-PR-educated brain sounded like the right thing. After all, the PR devil would have been sitting on one shoulder telling him to look sexy, act hot and available. Make millions of women wish they were in his bed. And the honesty angel would be urging him to just say what he felt.

So he did both. He told America we were together, but there were no plans for marriage in our future.

A technically true statement, even if it had scared me and angered me. Because if I could give my heart to him and he could so casually toss it aside . . .

The truth? I still think I had a right to be scared and angry. But I do know where he was coming from. I've learned a bit about stress and pressure in the last few hours, with Andy being a case in point. And I think it's fair to say that we don't always say or do what we should. Or even what we feel.

"Shit," Blake says, his stern tone interrupting my reverie. "Hold on."

And then, before I can ask what's up, he jams down on the accelerator. I heave back against the seat, breathless. "Blake!"

"What the hell is going on?" Andy leans forward from the backseat, his head and shoulders between me and Blake.

"We have a tail," Blake says.

I turn around and see a car in the distance, its headlights moving as we move. "Are you sure?"

"Pretty sure," he says.

"Well, don't go to the Chateau," I say. "If it's the assassin, we can't let him know where we're going." On the whole, I feel very calm. Maybe it's the unreality of the situation. Maybe it's because I'm with Blake and Andy.

Or maybe I'm just in denial.

All I know is that my mind is whirring, but it's not freaking out. Thank goodness for small favors.

"Can you lose him?" Andy asks from the backseat.

"Gonna try," Blake says. We're on Sunset now, and he hits the accelerator, sending us screaming through a red light.

"Yikes!" I screech as a clunker swerves out of our way, the driver yelling curses.

"Are we even sure that's our assassin?" Andy asks, but when the other car runs the red light, too, that pretty much answers the question.

"Lose him," I say, reaching over to grip Blake's leg.

"That's my plan." But we're foiled pretty quickly by the traffic on Sunset in front of the various restaurants and nightclubs.

I might have enjoyed it at first, but now I am seriously regretting leaving the top down on the car, especially as Blake orders me to get down, just in case the assassin has a gun.

I don't waste any time, but even as I scoot down, I see and hear people on the sidewalks calling our names. A flurry of camera flashes follow, and I know damn well I'll be reading about this tomorrow.

"Go!" Andy said.

From my perspective, I can see only that the light has

changed, but the car in front of us must have moved, because Blake guns it, then shifts to the left. I shift, too, and as I lean sideways, I'm looking almost straight up at a huge billboard hanging from the side of one of the office buildings on Sunset. "The Givenchy Code," it says, along with the cool logo the studio's art department came up with. "Coming this Christmas." And there's my name and Blake's right at the top, larger than life.

I close my eyes and say a silent prayer. Because if we don't survive this game, somebody else is going to be in my movie.

And that would wreak havoc with my comeback.

"You okay?" Blake asks, reaching down to hold me in place as he makes a sharp turn onto Laurel Canyon.

"Yeah. Just a little hysterical."

"Understand that."

"We need a gun," I say.

"No argument from me," Blake admits.

I risk a peek over the seat and find myself staring at the back of Andy's head. "Where is he?"

"A few cars back," Andy says. "I'm surprised this car's got it in her."

"She's got a few tricks," Blake says.

"We'll need them. He's gaining."

I'm still thinking about the gun. I have sudden visions of me hanging out of the back of the car in typical action-movie style, a pistol in one hand and an Uzi strapped across my back. Instead, I'm cowering on the floorboards.

"I don't see him," Blake says, his eyes on the mirror. He turns sharply onto Mulholland, and we careen along the famous street, the lights of the city far below us.

"Headlights," Andy yells.

"Turn! Turn!" I scream.

Blake turns, and now we're barreling down Coldwater Canyon. Blake turns off as soon as he can, heading into the neighborhoods and following the winding streets until we're pretty sure we've lost the guy.

We weave around a while longer, just to be sure, but after twenty or so minutes with no sign, we're all breathing a little easier.

"How did he find us?" Blake asks.

"He was near my house," I say. "Oh, God. He must know where I live." Memories of the last time Janus was at my house start to overwhelm me, and I take deep breaths, reminding myself that this time it's different. This time, the nightmare has rules.

"Or he's got a tracking device," Andy says. "We're at the point in the game where it must have turned on."

"Of course," I say. I know from my research and the script that the assassin usually has access to some sort of tracking device, provided by the game. The yuck part is that whoever's running the show got close enough to me to tag me with something for the device to cue off of.

I look around the car, trying to think where something could be hidden. Once again, though, I go back to the basic point that I'm hard to get near. So how could something have been planted on me?

"Phones," Andy says, when I voice the comment. "Phones have GPS built in now."

"Give me your phones." I hold out my hand, and both men comply right away. I toss our three phones into various yards as we tool down the mountain.

We've reached the bottom of the hill, and Blake maneuvers his way over to Ventura, then turns right toward Laurel Canyon so that we can head back over the hill.

This time, we make the journey at a much more relaxed pace, and by the time we hook a right onto Sunset, I'm feeling almost normal. I see the simple brown sign that marks the entrance to the Chateau Marmont, and I have to smile.

Score one for the home team.

Just in case, though, we ask the valet to park the car out of sight.

"We made it," Blake says, as we climb out of the car. "I hope it's worth it."

"It will be," I say. "The clue's here."

What I don't mention, of course, is that I have no idea where.

Chapter 34

The Chateau is one of the most happening places in Los Angeles. At all hours of the night, you can find movie stars, billionaires, power players, rock stars. Folks gather in the bar, the lobby, and the little bungalows that dot the property. People come and go. It is, in all honesty, a free-for-all.

Just walking into the place I see four people I know, including last year's Best Actor winner. He gives me a kiss, then pats Blake on the back, congratulating him on the movie and on getting back together with me. I guess the fact that I'm clinging to his arm in both fear and exhaustion telegraphs the renewal of our relationship.

Andy, thank God, is all business. He aims us through the crowd to the concierge desk, fully manned even at three a.m.

A woman about my age with a blond ponytail and an expression way too perky for the hour greets him with, "How can I help you, sir?"

Andy looks at me.

"Ah, right. Are there any messages here for me?"

"Just a moment." She taps at her computer, then shakes her head. "I'm sorry, Ms. Taylor. Nothing."

See, that's another reason I love the Chateau. Even though she's delivering horrible news, she's doing it in a nice way. I mean, she knows who I am despite the fact that I haven't stayed here for over a year and don't exactly look my best at the moment.

The bad news, though, is that there is no message. Which leaves us in a bit of a quandary.

"What now?" Andy said.

"I have no idea," I admit. I'd been so certain that the 'find the message' reference in the clue was literal. Now, I'm at a complete loss.

"Now we get a room," Blake says.

"Blake, no—"

"Yes." He cuts me off gently but firmly. "We're all dead on our feet. We need a place to huddle down and figure this out, or that will be more than just a metaphor." Tension lines his face, and I can tell he's worried about the time ticking away.

"Fair enough," I say. "And you're right. We know the clue centers around the Chateau. It just makes sense to stay here."

The concierge—who must have been puzzled by whatever snippets of our conversation she overheard—immediately waves over a bellman, who escorts us to one of the poolside bungalows. No check-in. No discussion over what type of room I need or want.

This is the nice part of being a celebrity. These folks just know.

Honestly, I think part of their job is to study the trades. I can almost imagine them at staff meetings, taking pop quizzes on the likes and dislikes of up-and-coming celebs.

I shake my head, realizing I'm drifting into that zone of exhaustion where everything is amusing.

The bungalow is just as charming as I remember it. We enter through the front door into an airy living room decorated with modern, comfortable furniture. It's two bedrooms, too, and I head inside, then make a left turn into the kitchen, leaving Andy and Blake behind to work out their sleeping arrangements between themselves.

I hear them tip the bellman, who obviously has decided that we don't need to be shown the lay of the land. After a few minutes of low conversation, Blake comes in. I'm standing in front of the red-and-black-tiled sink, the faucet running. I lean forward and splash my face, then look up at Blake as I pat my skin dry.

"I told Andy to go upstairs and get some sleep. I finally convinced him he's not any use to us if he can't think. He agreed to a one-hour nap."

"Good," I said. "He's smart. He'll be smarter if he's sharp."

"I told him I'd sleep on the couch."

I lick my lips, not certain what to say to that. But then again, Andy is upstairs. So I nod. "Right. Of course. Although . . ."

"What?" I hear the hint of interest in his voice.

"Well, maybe you should have the bed."

"Because this may be my last night *in* a bed?"

"No, no," I protest. "I didn't mean that." Except I did. Just a little. Because I'm so afraid we're going to fail him and not find the antidote in time. I feel horrible even thinking that, though. And I feel all the more horrible since it's because of me that he got sucked into this damn game in the first place.

"Yes," I say. "You definitely should have the bed."

"Only if you join me in it."

"Blake . . ." I lace my voice with warning, and glance upward to where Andy is probably now sleeping.

"Well, that's progress at least," Blake says.

"Huh?" I say, completely confused.

"You didn't tell me to go to hell," he clarifies. He tilts his head back, looking at the ceiling. "In fact, if Andy weren't here, I think you'd take me up on my offer."

As if to illustrate the point, he moves forward, hooking his arms around me so that his palms cup my rear. I press up against him, hooking my arms around his neck and lift my face for the kiss I know is coming.

He doesn't disappoint, and the demand and need in his kiss make my entire body tingle. I want this so badly, and I lose myself deep in the kiss for just a little while.

My knees seem to lose their ability to hold me up, but it doesn't matter. He's got me. And I let that knowledge fill me, heart and soul.

At the same time, I can't help the niggles of doubt that fill my head. Regretfully, I pull away, breaking our kiss and meeting his eyes. "Blake, we shouldn't."

"I think we should."

"You walked out on me," I say, having to choke my words out. "You left a hole in my heart."

"I didn't walk, sweetheart. You did."

He's right, and yet at the same time, he isn't. "I wasn't going to be a victim again."

"So you left me before I could leave you. That was your way of fighting."

"Yes," I whisper, as a tear slides down the side of my nose.

"Like you're fighting now. Like you're fighting in this game?"

"Yes."

"Like you're fighting for me. For finding the antidote."

"*Yes.* What are you—"

He silences me with a firm finger. "Well, I'm fighting for you. And I'm not going to give up."

Tears seem to knot in my throat, and I know that I'm going to be undone. If not by his words, then by the expression in his eyes. "Don't do this to me, Blake."

"Do what?"

"Don't make me fall in love with you again," I whisper, this time looking at the floor.

He cups my face, forcing me to look at him. "You never stopped loving me."

"No," I say, my voice choked. "I didn't. But if you leave again, I don't think I can survive."

"Babe," he says, pulling me close for a kiss, "I'm not going anywhere." To prove it, he pulls me in even tighter, sealing the promise with a deep kiss.

I melt against him. All my doubts, all my fears, melting from the heat we're generating.

I press myself against him, my body wanting more and my mind going along with the program. A small voice in my head justifies that this might be his last night. But that's not the real reason. The real reason is that I want him.

I love him.

And right then, I think I'll die without his touch . . . to hell with what happens in the game.

"Devi?" he whispers, the question in his voice asking so much.

"Yes," I say. "Oh, please, yes."

Chapter

35

wake up to the harsh jangle of my cell phone. Then I remember. I don't have my cell phone. I sit up, confused, then realize that it's not my cell that's ringing but the bungalow phone on the bedside table.

I scoot across the bed, over the still-warm spot where Blake slept next to me last night, at least to the extent we got any sleep. I check the clock. Seven a.m. I managed two hours of sleep. Gee, I should be bright as a rose.

The phone rings again, and I allow myself one slow, satisfied stretch, and then I snatch up the phone.

"Hello?" I say, expecting to hear from the front desk. Instead, I hear Lindy.

"What the hell are you up to?"

Since that is about as loaded as a question can get, I sit up and run my fingers through my very tousled hair. "Um. What?" My brain kicks in, I remember the game, and I suddenly feel small, vulnerable, and very exposed. "How did you find me here?"

"I tried your cell," she says. "I keep getting voice mail. What did you do? Toss it in the trash?"

Since that's just a little to close to the mark, I sit up straighter. "I'm serious. How did you know I was here?"

"Okay, okay. Calm down. About five different blogs have your picture front and center today. I guess you went there with *two* men? Honestly, Devi, I didn't think you had it in you."

She's teasing me, of course, but the odds are good the blogs are spewing forth all sorts of tripe about how the wild Devi is back, and this time she's got two men in tow.

Great. Somehow I don't think that kind of publicity is going to make my PR team happy. Or Tobias.

Honestly, it doesn't do much for my endorphin levels either.

"It's a long story. Movie-related. Very boring. I promise I'll tell you all about it, but I've got to go—"

"Wait!"

"Lindy, I really—"

"I just want to know. Are you and Blake back together? Just throw me that little tidbit and I'll leave you alone."

I laugh, then I hum a little, my heart lifting a bit since she just zeroed in on the one bright spot in all the horror.

"I *knew* it," she shrieks. "Thank heaven!"

"Lindy," I say, but I'm mostly laughing.

"All right, I want *all* the details," she says. "But later. I know you must have an early call." She pauses for a second. "Actually, why aren't you on the set? Isn't today the big scene?"

Obviously, she hasn't heard about Mac. And I'm not going to tell her. Not now.

"Tobias had to go to New York, so the schedule's all turned around. Like I said, a big boring mess. I'll see you soon, though, and update you."

"I want all the details about you and Blake."

I think about our wild time between the sheets last night, and decide that *all* the details is an elastic term. "Sure," I say.

"Promise?"

"Absolutely." And despite Janus and this stupid game, that's a promise I intend to keep.

In fact, it's time to get busy again. I'm rested, my body is still humming from last night, and I'm feeling pretty much invincible.

At least until I remember the blogs that Lindy mentioned. If she could find me, so could Janus, and I hurry a bit as I climb back into my clothes and rush into the main area of the bungalow.

I find Blake in the kitchen, staring down a pot of coffee, as if watching it will make it brew faster.

"We need to get out of here," I say, then explain about the blogs. "If Lindy can find us, so can Janus."

"Agreed," he said.

I look around. "Where's Andy?"

"Said he was heading to the business center. He thought maybe the message was hidden on one of the hotel computers." He sighs and runs a hand through his hair. "I hope to hell he's right, because I sure don't have a better idea. And the clock's ticking down. We need to figure this out and find the damn antidote."

"We're going to find it," I say, moving closer and hooking my arms around his waist. "I promise."

He strokes my hair. "Look at you," he says. "Trying to make me feel better when you're just as deep in this shit as I am."

I manage a smile, but he can probably tell it's fake. "You're the one with a countdown. Me, I just have to deal with an assassin." I lick my lips, trying on false bravado to hide my fears. "I survived Janus once before, after all. I can do it again."

"I know you can," he says. "We'll both survive, and then we'll get back to our life. Back to the movie. Back to . . ."

He trails off, but the message is clear. *Back to us.*

I hear it, but I can't focus on it. Not right now. Because it's the other thing that he said that has caught my attention. "The movie," I say, then plant a quick kiss on his lips. "Blake, sweetheart, you're brilliant!"

Blake wasn't sure that he was brilliant, but he appreciated the compliment nonetheless. More, he appreciated her easiness with him now. The way she touched him and looked at him. The fact that she wasn't shy at all with him after their time together last night.

He'd been so afraid that she'd opened her arms to him simply out of fear or pity or both. Fear of the game. Pity that he might not have another night left. Or maybe just in the hope that when they were alone in bed, the horror would evaporate.

It had. For just a few hours, there had been only the two of them. She'd been so soft in his arms, and yet so intense. And he'd known that—at least right then—she needed him as much as he needed her.

Now, he saw that it hadn't only been about sex, and that one simple fact fueled his courage and gave him hope.

"So why am I so brilliant?" he asked, but she just smiled and dove for the phone.

"Um, hi. Devi Taylor again. Listen, do you have a message for Melanie Prescott?"

She put her hand over the receiver. "He's checking." And then, "Yes, yes. It's for me. It's the character I'm playing. Long story. Right. No, thanks. I'll run in and get it. Great. And, listen, can you do me one more favor? I need to get three cell phones with Web access and a laptop. Yeah, right. As fast as you can. And some clothes, too." She gave the concierge her size and Blake's, then described Andy and asked the guy to guess. Then she hung up and smiled at him. "We're set."

"Tracking device?" he said, with a significant look at her laptop.

"Can't be too careful. I'll give mine to housekeeping. In the meantime, let's go. The message is waiting at the front desk."

"And the concierge is just going to find us phones and clothes? No explanation necessary?"

She just laughed and took his hand. "Doting on celebrity whims is the earmark of a good hotel. As is no-questions-asked." She gave him a quick hug, then a kiss on the nose. "You have a lot to learn about being a bad-boy celebrity, Blake Atwood. Don't worry. I'll teach you."

She tugged him toward the door then, and he realized he was actually laughing, his mind far from the horror in which they'd been living for these last hours. A nice break, and undoubtedly his head's way of keeping him from totally losing it under the pressure of the game. He hated the thought that soon they'd be on the run again. At least, he hoped they would be on the run again. It was, of course, a double-edged sword. He didn't want to play the game. He had to play the game.

Devi, he realized, had been playing a game of How to Think Like a Celebrity her entire life. The concierge was a case in point. The life she knew wasn't real . . . and yet it was, for her. Just like the damn game they were playing wasn't real . . . and yet if they lost, the consequences were very real indeed.

She reached out and grabbed his hand as they moved from the private patio into the open pool area. "You have a look. Are you doing okay?"

"A look?"

"Yeah." She squeezed his hand. "We're going to figure this out."

She smiled up at him then, and he breathed it in, the sparkle in her eyes almost enough to cure him of whatever poison was running through his veins.

Almost, but not quite.

"I know we will," he said. "Come on."

He'd only been to the Chateau once before, when he'd been dating an up-and-coming television action star. He'd worked with her on all her martial arts sequences, and she'd worked on him until she got him in her bed. Not long after that she'd started to lose interest in him. Fortunately, it was mutual. But she was quite the party girl, and before they split up, she'd taken him to more L.A. hot spots than he could ever have imagined.

Most weren't his style, but he had to admit he'd been impressed with the Chateau Marmont. It truly did resemble a castle perched high above Sunset Boulevard. And, of course, the place was both famous and notorious, having been the home away from home of many a movie star, and the site of many a tragedy.

He'd only seen the main lobby and the bar before, and this early-morning view of the pool was enough to take his breath away, and *almost* enough to make him forget about the game. The pool itself wasn't huge. But it was the presentation—not the size—that made it so remarkable. An oval oasis, surrounded by bungalows, all hidden by thick foliage and privacy fencing.

They walked along the edge of the pool, passing the few people lounging on the carefully aligned chaise longes. They followed the path, then entered the lobby, the foyer of which had an open feel, with painted white brick walls and furniture that seemed vaguely Moroccan.

They made their way over to the front desk, and Blake was impressed that the girl already knew they were coming. "Someone will be right here with the envelope," she said.

As they waited for that someone to track down the message, Devi leaned on the counter, then gave him an appraising look.

"What?"

"I'm really . . . I don't know . . . freaked out about who could be behind this."

"Babe, I think the situation is freakish enough. Do we need to waste time pondering who's pulling our strings?"

"Not even if it helps us end this thing?"

"What? You're thinking of doing an end run around the game? Figure out our ultimate bad guy and stop the game in its tracks?"

Her chin lifted a little. "Well, yeah. That's exactly what I was thinking."

She looked so confident and stubborn that he couldn't help

but smile. And wasn't that just like Devi? Why take the cir-cuitous route when you can go straight to the source? Unfortu-nately, there were serious flaws in her plan. Like the fact that it was already almost nine a.m.

If their calculation was right, he had eleven hours before any antidote would be useless. In theory, he'd love to find the asshole behind the game.

In reality, he just needed to solve the next clue. And fast.

Chapter 37

Patience.

He had such patience. And that, he knew, would be his reward.

They may have lost him in the foothills, but now he knew where they'd gone.

The Chateau Marmont.

He parked nearby, with a view of the driveway leading up to the famous hotel. He'd considered going inside, looking for them. But the tracking device that the game had blessed him with lacked specificity.

Better to wait. To watch.

Sooner or later, they'd have to come out.

And he'd be right there, waiting for them.

Chapter

38

This time the clue is actually printed on a piece of paper. I consider that good karma. I'm a paper-and-pencil kind of girl, converted to the wonderful world of Macintosh and the like only because I had to. A paper clue will surely be easier to interpret. Paper has life. It has a vibe.

It can tell you its secrets.

Unfortunately, this piece of paper is determined to stay remarkably quiet.

Not terribly surprising, I suppose, considering the nonsense printed on the page. As we're walking back to the bungalow, I hold tight to it, my eyes dipping down to soak in this new riddle:

> *You can do-si-do*
> *And then do more*

You can pull horsetails from the floor
By the ocean, by the sea
From an age long past, but still here to see.
Don't talk, don't speak, you can't, you're full
All it will take is a little pull.

I mean, honestly! Who was thinking this shit up?

"Anything?" I ask Blake.

"Not a damn thing." He looks at his watch, his expression grave.

I reach over, cupping my hand over his wrist and hiding the watch. "We *will* figure this out in time. We've started something again, and I'll be damned if you're getting out of working on a relationship just because you've got some stupid poison in your veins."

"Started something, huh?" he says, looking at me with dark, inquisitive eyes.

I feel my cheeks heat. "Didn't we?"

"Oh, yeah."

I want to say more, but we're back at the bungalow. As we come inside, Andy stands up, his face a mask of fury. "Where the *hell* were you? I've been going nuts!"

I take a step backward, surprised by the vitriol. "We went to the lobby. Looking for the message, just like you."

"Dammit, Devi, I'm your protector. You can't just fucking leave."

I stand up a little straighter and open my mouth, prepared to let him have it. But then I deflate. Because you know what? He's right.

I might feel safe at the Chateau, but I'm not. Until this game is over, I'm not safe anywhere. And, yes, I was with Blake. A little fact that makes me feel all the more guilty for leaving, because the truth is, I feel safer with Blake. Not unreasonable, really, considering Blake's training. But Andy *is* my protector. In my heart, though, that job belongs to Blake. So, for that matter, does my heart.

"Well?" He's staring me down, clearly irritated, and clearly waiting for me to say something.

I say the only thing I can. "I'm sorry. I was stupid. I won't be stupid again."

I think my contrition surprises him, because he gapes at me for a second, and then nods. "I didn't find a damn thing in the business center. You?"

My grin stretches so wide it's almost painful, and I pass him the paper without comment.

"Wow," he says after reading it. "Have you got any leads on interpreting this thing?"

"Not a clue," Blake admits.

"Me either," Andy says. He looks between the two of us. "So how did you find it?"

"The girl I am now," I explain. "I'm playing Mel. So I asked if there was a message for her—"

"And there was." He nods approvingly. "Good job."

I can't help the little rush of pleasure. I may have been freaking when this damn game started, but now I'm at least holding my own. That's good, I think, since the consequences of playing poorly are more than a little severe.

I shudder, thinking about the man against whom we're playing. *Janus.* A man I've imagined around so many corners, but never once seen. And now here he is again, holding my life in his hand.

I give myself a quick shake, determined not to sink back into that quagmire of fear. I'm no good to anyone in that place, least of all myself.

I tap the note still in Andy's hand, forcing my voice to sound calm. "So where do we begin?"

"The first line," he says with a sigh. "What the hell is a do-si-do?"

At that, I manage a genuine laugh, because Andy really is a computer geek if he's never heard of a do-si-do. "It's a square-dance move," I say. I look at Blake for confirmation, because I've never square-danced in my life. "Isn't it?"

"Pretty sure it's the part where you circle your partner," he says. "But square dancing isn't exactly all the rage in L.A., so what are we supposed to do with that information?"

"It will key in somehow," Andy says. "That's the way these clues always work."

There's a tap at the door, and both men move closer to me, their stances protective. "Guys," I say, "I don't think the killer is going to knock first."

Just in case I'm wrong, though, I call out before opening. It's the bellman, who has a new laptop for us, courtesy of the hotel and a local computer store. Our phones and clothes should arrive within the hour. I tip the guy a huge amount, give him the old laptop to pass off to housekeeping, then hand the new computer to our resident computer geek. He immediately gets it up and running, and we spend the next few minutes searching for information on movies and horses, ultimately learning that there were a lot of movies about horses made in Los Angeles. Some took place by the ocean (but not many) and some of the stars (in this case, many) lived near the beach.

Too bad we haven't the faintest idea what to do with that information.

"Maybe we're coming at this the wrong way," Andy suggests. "After all, Devi could just as easily be getting L.A.-themed clues as movie-themed."

"That's true," Blake says.

"But where does that get us?" I ask.

"Lets think about where in the area we'd find horses by the beach," Blake says.

"Malibu," I say right away. "And Santa Barbara. Didn't Kevin Costner buy an equestrian ranch up there?"

"Santa Barbara's probably too far away," Blake says. "Unless you have a connection to it? Ever live there? Own a house? Shoot a movie?"

"None of the above," I say, and we cross Kevin's ranch off our list of possibilities.

"There must be some horses in Malibu," I say, and Andy types *Malibu Horse Rentals* into Google and ends up with a gazillion sites, none of which are screaming *Pick me! Pick me!*

"What about the do-si-do thing?" Blake asks.

"What about it?" I ask, too sharply, but I'm feeling surly.

He holds up his hands in a classic self-defense maneuver, and I immediately feel contrite. He's the one at immediate risk here.

Well, I am, too, but at least I don't have some poison in my blood.

"How do horses and square dances mix?" Blake asks, apparently forgiving my bitchiness.

"Hay rides, barn dances. Horses would be all over that kind of thing," I say.

"Any barn-type dance halls around here?" Andy asks.

"Umm." Honestly, I have no clue. I nod at the computer. "Give it a shot."

Blake starts pacing as Andy tries this new search. "If we could just latch on to one part of the clue—"

"Horses," I say, hoping to spark a flash of insight. "Near the ocean. And they're old horses."

"But still around," Blake says, pointing a finger at me.

"Right . . ." I hold my breath. I know that look in his eye.

"Okay, this is a long shot, but what about the Santa Monica Pier?"

Andy's head pops up. "How do you get that?"

"The carousel," Blake explains. "Old horses. From a past age."

"Hmm." Andy frowns, clearly considering. "I think you may be on to something."

"What about the square dancing?" I ask. "I've been to the pier hundreds of times, and trust me when I say that square dancing would not fit in."

"Not square dancing," Andy says. "Do-si-do."

He stands up. I guess we're ready.

I don't move. "Explain, please."

"That's the circle-your-partner part, remember? That's what he said," he adds, pointing to Blake.

"Damn, Andy," Blake says. "Good call."

"Hang on, boys. I haven't jumped on the do-si-do band-wagon yet."

"The carousel moves in a circle," Andy explains.

"Oh, man." I reach down and grab my Prada bag, then tuck the computer and phone inside. "Let's book."

Chapter

39

The Santa Monica Pier is a bustling, loud, boisterous, touristy hangout.

And I love it.

It's like stepping into a carnival atmosphere, with street vendors lining one side of the wide wooden pier, and an actual amusement park on the other side, complete with roller coaster and Ferris wheel.

Blake and I had come here on our very first date, and I'd dragged him around to look at all the things I'd loved so much as a kid.

Today, we'd come under much less auspicious circumstances.

We'd left the Chateau via the concierge desk, and were lucky enough to arrive just as our phones and clothes did. We used the lobby restrooms to change, then raced to get the car and head toward the beach.

Blake parked Blue on the street, and this time I'd transferred the new phone to my back pocket and left my bag and laptop in Blake's trunk. I'd already scratched it once; I didn't intend to do that again. We'd backtracked down the street, then turned toward the ocean and walked down the paved roadway that leads to the entrance of the pier.

Now we stand there, looking up at the arched sign at the entrance announcing that we've reached "Santa Monica. Yacht Harbor. Sport Fishing. Boating. Cafés."

Ya gotta love it.

"Which way?" Andy asks.

"That's the carousel house," I say, pointing to the yellowish building in which is a real, honest-to-gosh old-fashioned carousel. Someone told me it's one of the few surviving all-wooden carousels in the world, and it dates back to the early 1900s. It's romantic, a shadow of a past age, and I never come to the pier without visiting it.

Fortunately, it's not very far out on the pier, either. The whole place bustles, but the amusement park part is near the beginning, before the pier turns into what you'd traditionally think of as a pier—wood planks extending over the water. Down at that end is a restaurant, sightseers, and fishermen. The vendors are mostly down with us, where we're still over sand and parking lot.

The place is a crush, and as we move, I'm jostled from all sides. Blake takes my arm, and we ease through the crowd, aiming for the horses. I'm searching the crowd, looking for anyone who seems suspicious, but there are just too many faces. I'm about to tell Blake to hurry when I overhear a kid talking.

"No way that's a real gun."

"Dude! Hit the deck."

I spin around, terrified. And through the crowd I see a face I haven't seen for years—*Janus*.

I can't help it. I freeze. And then I scream.

Chapter 40

"**D**ammit, Blake, you're running out of time. *Go.*"

We're racing through the pedestrians, both men beside me like bookends. Andy pulled me into a throng of tourists even as my scream hung in the air, and now the place is chaos.

"Devi!" Blake yells.

"*Go!*" I screech, even as we start shoving our way through the crowd. Janus is behind us, so we head down the pier, hoping to lose him in the crowd. "Just go. I'll be fine."

I'm not actually so sure that I will, but if Blake doesn't get that antidote, I *know* he won't. And Janus isn't going to follow him to the carousel. That man is all about killing me.

The thought puts an extra little zip in my step.

"Do what she says," Andy yells, keeping a tight grip on my arm. "I've got her."

Even as Andy speaks, he's pushing through the crowd,

roughly shoving pedestrians into our wake, and trying to trip up the kids on Rollerblades and skateboards. People are screaming and cursing, but there's no stopping us.

I chance a look back over my shoulder, terrified, but hoping that we've lost Janus.

No such luck, and I can see him raising a pistol, heedless of the innocent bystanders between us and him.

Screams erupt, and the crowd mostly drops to the ground. We can't, though. We have to run.

And we do, racing pell-mell down the pier, zigzagging in the hope that Janus won't be able to get a clean shot.

All around us, tourists are either on the ground or scurrying out of our way. Street performers are backed up against the edge of the pier. In the distance, I hear the welcome scream of a police siren.

Welcome, but not nearly close enough.

To our right, a mime with a trunk full of balls and other props looks like he's seen better days. Andy grabs my wrist and pulls me that way, then dumps the trunk over, sending a dozen or so small balls rolling over the wooden planks of the pier.

Doesn't even slow the son of a bitch down, and I cry out as a bullet screams past my ear to lodge in the wooden barrier lining the edge of the pier.

"Jump!" Andy yells.

We've zigged to the other side, moving as far away from that bullet as possible, and although I want to keep moving, I can't help but stop and gape at him. *"What?"*

He indicates the side, and the water below. We're almost to the restaurant at the end of the pier, so we're pretty far out, and in my gut I know the water must be deep. Still . . .

"Dammit, Devi, *now!*"

I swing my legs over, take a deep breath, and jump.

The Pacific is not a warm ocean, even in the summer, and the chilly water stabs at me like so many little icicles. I go completely under, the weight of my jeans and shoes pulling me down. It's midday, but all I can see is a greenish blur. The water is murky, pollution and sand mixing to completely bar my view.

I'm trying to get my bearings—knowing I need to get under the pier if I want to be safe—when there is a splash and flailing beside me. My fears spike again as someone grabs my wrist, and I'm being tugged up. We break the surface, and I open my mouth to scream, but a hand is there.

Andy.

He meets my eyes and nods in question. I nod back, still on edge but with the program.

I chance a look above us and see bystanders peering over the railing, calling down and snapping pictures.

What I don't see is Janus. *Thank God.*

"Is he gone?" I hazard the question as soon as we're safely under the solid wooden pier, fighting the current even as we hang on to the barnacle-covered posts.

"I'm guessing he is," Andy says. "That siren was coming fast, and if he's still around—"

"The cops," I say. "Andy, there are rules. What are we going to tell the cops?"

"We're not going to tell them a thing," he says. "Can you swim over there?" he asks, pointing to the far side of the pier. Out in the sun, we see some guys boogie-boarding.

"Sure," I say, because it's not that far.

"Be careful. The current will be stronger than you think, and with our clothes on . . ."

He's right, of course, and I'm tempted to strip down to my undies. The only reason I don't is because it's just as hard getting out of wet jeans as it is swimming in them.

Well, that and the fact that as soon as I peel off my clothes, some reporter from the *Enquirer* will magically appear and snap a photo.

I almost ask Andy what his plan is, but then I decide not to bother. He obviously has one, and as we swim out the other side of the pier, it becomes obvious enough. Above us, a few people are looking down, but nothing like the throng that had been gathered on the south side. I see one girl wave behind her—presumably to the cop whose car is on the pier, if the sound of the siren is any indication.

"Andy . . ." I say, managing to swallow half the ocean at the same time.

As I choke and spit, he grabs me and tugs me toward the shore.

Now, the crowd on the north side of the pier has increased, and I hear "Please stop!" coming from the cop's megaphone. That overly polite official "request" that most people are trained to follow.

I'm not most people, though, and neither is Andy. We've reached the beach now, and Andy takes my hand. "Run!" he says.

And I do.

Blake's heart hadn't stopped pounding since he'd heard Devi scream. She and Andy both had yelled for him to go into the carousel house even as they raced farther down the pier.

He hadn't wanted to leave her alone, but in that split second he'd had to make a decision, he knew that he had to. Time was running out, and he was no use to her dead.

But that didn't mean he couldn't put a few kinks in Janus's plans even as the bastard tried to get a bead on Devi.

So as she turned back to the west and started racing down the pier, he'd looked for ways to make Janus's life miserable. He'd caught a break when he'd seen Janus not ten feet away, the bastard raising his gun for another shot.

Fuck that.

He'd grabbed a small helium tank from a balloon vendor, then tossed the thing. It made contact right as Janus was firing, sending the shot wild. At the same time, Blake raced toward him, so that when Janus turned to aim the pistol at him, he was ready.

A nicely placed round kick had knocked that gun right out of the bastard's hands, but in the confused mass of people, Janus had torn off in the opposite direction before Blake could cross the distance between them.

He'd retrieved the gun, hoping like hell it was the only one Janus had, but not really believing it. He jammed it in the back of his jeans, then cut sideways behind the arcade buildings so he could circle back to the carousel house. He told himself that Devi was safe, and he kept repeating that as a mantra as he slowed to a fast trot and tried to blend into the crowd.

He was amazed that no one had tried to stop him when he'd snagged the gun. Maybe they recognized him and thought this was some sort of movie stunt. Or maybe they were just plain scared. This was Los Angeles, after all, and gangs were prevalent enough that people knew to mind their own business if they wanted to stay alive.

A few more yards, and he was back almost to the start of the pier. The door to the carousel house faced the foot traffic down the wooden pier, and now he moved in that direction, keeping his attention sharp, looking for any sign of Janus—or of Devi.

He saw nothing, though. The crowd had moved back in on itself, like water diverted in a stream. He thought there might be some sort of commotion down at the far end of the pier where it actually extended over the water, but he couldn't get a good enough look. Behind him, though, on the paved street that ran directly up to the pier, he heard a police car, the siren blaring. *Good.*

Surely the approach of the police would scare Janus off Andy and Devi's trail. He only hoped that Andy and Devi could blend into the crowd before the police latched on to them.

He noticed one other thing, too, that filled him with hope: the police car was alone. No ambulance racing to catch up. No more sirens rushing through Santa Monica toward the pier.

He couldn't see them, so he couldn't be sure. But he believed they were safe. And he intended to cling tenaciously to that belief until Devi was in his arms again.

The entrance to the carousel house was only yards away. He stepped inside and entered a past era, the lights and brightly painted carousel and horses reflecting a Byzantine age, when grandeur was of as much importance as the ride itself.

He'd been here once with Devi, but not having grown up in Los Angeles, he was hardly a regular at the pier. Now, he almost wondered why, because this place was surely magical. Even more so, he was certain, at night.

He didn't have until night, though, and so his acquaintance with each of the ponies had to start now.

Fortunately, the carousel wasn't running, which meant that he could step onto the platform with the horses and walk around, looking at each, trying to find the antidote that he would pull out of one of the horse's mouths.

There were a few other people in the structure. Tourist types, there with their kids, either not realizing the carousel wasn't on at this time of day during the week, or simply taking the only opportunity they could to see the famous landmark. He did his best to ignore them, but as he went from horse to horse to horse, sticking his fingers into the open mouths of the ones that had been molded that way, he could feel their curious eyes on him.

A few months ago, he would have felt compelled to explain himself. Now—after living in the celebrity spotlight—he was comfortable enough to just go about his business. One tourist did snap a picture when he was face-to-face with a horse, and he had to wonder if he'd see that picture in an upcoming issue of *Entertainment Weekly*. He looked up to see if he'd been tagged by the paparazzi and found himself looking at a skinny man with graying temples wearing an I ™ Santa Monica T-shirt and too-baggy Bermuda-style shorts.

Not paparazzi—*tourist*.

Thank God for small favors.

"So whatcha doing there, buddy?" the man asked in a thick southern accent.

"Scavenger hunt," Blake said.

"Right . . ." The guy cocked his head, obviously trying to decide if Blake was bullshitting him or not. "So, something's supposed to be hidden in one of them horse's mouth's? And then what?"

"Hopefully I find the prize."

"Prize, huh? Want some help?"

"No thanks."

The man squinted at him. "Not the sharing kind, huh?"

Blake closed his eyes and prayed for patience. "I don't mean to be rude, but—"

"Yeah, yeah." The guy shot him an angry look and then grabbed up his shopping bags and stormed out.

Blake shook his head in exasperation and moved on to the next horse.

Once again, nothing.

And nothing in the next horse, or the next, or the next.

A mom standing with her small son watched him curiously. He gave them a sheepish grin, then walked the perimeter of the building's interior, reciting the clue in his head, then pulling it out of his pocket to double-check.

They had to be right. The carousel horses fit the clue perfectly.

So where the hell was his damned antidote?

He spent another useless hour inspecting the building—looking in every nook and cranny, searching every horse thoroughly.

Not a goddamn thing.

An unwelcome wave of fear crested over him, and he looked at his watch. Already past two. Just six hours left.

God.

He pressed down on the fear, determined not to let it control him. As much as he hated to admit it, they must have been wrong about the carousel. He was searching in the wrong place, and he needed Devi's help if he was going to figure out where he should be looking.

Devi's help, and, yes, Andy's, too.

He pulled out his phone and dialed her new number, but only got her voice mail. That's when he remembered that she'd left her purse with the computer in his trunk. She probably forgot to move her phone to a pocket, too.

No matter. He dialed Andy's number. Voice mail as well.

Damn.

He left a message, but wasn't confident they'd get it. For all he knew, Andy had tossed his phone at Janus, hoping to give the assailant a concussion.

Which means he was shit out of luck, all alone in Santa Monica and without any idea where to go next.

He needed to find them. But where?

Frustrated, he moved out of the carousel house and looked up and down the pier, hoping for a miracle. Because his luck wasn't running toward good these days, of course no miracle occurred.

Think, dammit, think.

Devi would be looking for him, too. She'd want to hook back up, not only to get the next clue, but to make sure he'd found the antidote. She'd be trying to think of a location that Blake would know to go to. But where?

He thought back to their first date. They'd come to Santa Monica, walked along the beach, played tourist along the pier, and then they'd ended the evening with a stroll along the Third Street Promenade and dinner at one of her favorite restaurants.

He cocked his head, certain that had to be it.

Because if she wasn't at the restaurant, he was fresh out of ideas. And almost out of time, as well.

>>>http://www.playsurvivewin.com<<<

PLAY.SURVIVE.WIN.

PLEASE LOGIN

PLAYER USER NAME: *Janus*

PLAYER PASSWORD: * * * * * * * *

. . . *please wait*

. . . *please wait*

. . . *please wait*

>>>Password approved<<<

>>Read New Messages<<   **>>>Continue To Game<<<**

. . . *please wait*

>>>WELCOME TO GAMING CENTER<<<

>>Retrieve Assignment<<   **>>>Report to Headquarters<<<**

>>>WELCOME TO REPORTING CENTER<<<

>>Enter Journal Entry<<   >>>Submit Viewable Report<<<
PLAYER REPORT:
REPORT NO. A-0002
Filed By: Janus
Subject: Failed Attempt—Lost Tracking Device
Report: Target located at Santa Monica Pier. Attempt
failed due to interference by protector, nature of crowd, and arrival of police.

Tracking device still functioning, but noting location opposite from the direction target ran. Assumption: Target separated herself from tracker.

Will attempt to relocate target.

The hunt continues.

>>>End Report<<
Send Report to Opponent?   >>Yes<<   >>No<<

I'm dunking bread into the herb-and-spice oil at Gaucho Grill, my absolutely favorite restaurant in Santa Monica. I'm not enjoying being there today, though. Heck, I can barely taste the bread. I'm too worried that something has happened to Blake.

It's a reasonable fear. We barely got away ourselves, and ended up slogging across the beach in our wet clothes until we could steal new ones from someone foolish enough to leave shorts and tank tops just sitting there on empty beach towels.

"Why don't we go look for him?" Andy says.

I'm tempted, but I shake my head. "No. It's not even been an hour since we split. Give him a few more minutes." I've spent the last half hour kicking myself for not having a plan for if we got separated, but there was nothing we could do about that now. I just have to hope that Blake has the same idea I do about where to come.

"We can't stay here forever," Andy says. "We need to keep moving. Janus could be out there right now."

I nod, because he's right. But we're in the back, near the exit. And we have a view of the inside of the restaurant, plus the foot traffic along the promenade. For the moment, we're safe.

"Devi?" Andy prompts.

"Without the next clue, where would we go?" I ask.

"Hole up in a hotel," Andy says. "We've already talked about this. The tracker doesn't pinpoint an exact location. If we check into a huge fancy hotel, he'll never figure out what room we're in."

"What if the tracker in this game is better?" Certainly it was well hidden. Because although we'd tossed our phones, Janus had still found us. Which meant we'd ditched our phones for nothing. And the location of the damn tracking device was still a mystery.

"It's not better," he says, with such surety that I blink. He must see my confusion, because he explains. "He obviously tailed us from the Chateau, right? But he didn't come *in* the Chateau. He waited for us to leave. Why? Because he didn't know exactly where we were."

"Thirty more minutes," I say. "We'll be safe that long, and we have a good view."

"I'm not willing to risk your life for his," Andy says, his voice harsh.

I close my hand on his. "I am," I say, even as the truth of that statement hits home. Because it's true. I've never felt that way about anyone before—never thought that I could willingly sacrifice for someone else. Now, I know I could. And if it came down to it, I would.

Not that I want it to come down to it.

Andy, however, doesn't seem too keen on my revelation. "I lost one target," he says. "I'm not going to lose another because you've got survivor's guilt." He stands up, tugging at my arm as he does. "Now come on."

"Dammit, Andy, *no*. I want—"

The words die on my tongue as I see Blake walk into the restaurant, his eyes taking in every face as he works his way toward the back.

I stand up, waving, and watch as he sees me from the front of the restaurant and smiles.

He rushes over, pulling me into his arms even as Andy looks on, his face passive.

"I was terrified something happened to you," Blake confesses. "I couldn't get you on the phone, I couldn't—" He stops, plucking at the blue tank top and baggy shorts I'm wearing, a huge departure from my usual Prada attire.

"Long story," I say.

"So long as you're safe."

"We are. You?"

"Did you find the antidote?" Andy asks.

Blake's expression tightens. "I scoured the place. It's not there."

"It has to be there," I say, fear welling. "It's almost three o'clock. It *has* to be there."

"Believe me," he says. "I know exactly what time it is. And I searched that place from top to bottom. It's not there. We must have got the clue wrong."

"We can't have," Andy says. "It fits perfectly. Maybe we should go back. All look together."

I look at Blake. "He's right. What else could the clue mean?"

"I've been thinking about that all the way over here," he admits. "I don't have an idea."

There's something so dejected about the tone of his voice that I reach out and squeeze his hand. "Don't you dare give up, Blake Atwood. We still have plenty of time."

The smile he gives me is clearly forced, but at least it's there. For the moment, that's enough. He pulled me out of a black funk earlier; there's no way I'm going to let him slip into one. Not when we still have time left to save him.

Andy stands up. "Well, I'm going back to the carousel. We're not doing any good sitting here." He nods at me. "And I'm not letting you out of my sight. So come on."

"No."

"Devi . . ." A tone of warning laces his voice.

"Blake said he searched, and I believe him. We interpreted something wrong. There's no other explanation."

"The explanation is that he missed it," Andy says.

"No, I didn't," Blake counters.

Since I'm really not in the mood, I look to Blake. "Do you still have the note?"

"Right here."

He opens it flat on the table, and I scoot closer for a good look. I'm certain Andy is seething, but I don't care. The man might be sweet, but I know Blake. And there's never been a more thorough man. If he says the clue's not in the carousel house, I believe him.

I examine the text again, frowning as I read the nonsensical message:

You can do-si-do
And then do more
You can pull horsetails from the floor
By the ocean, by the sea
From an age long past, but still here to see.
Don't talk, don't speak, you can't, you're full
All it will take is a little pull.

Unfortunately, the carousel house seems to be exactly where the cryptic riddle leads.

I shove that thought from my head. The carousel is wrong. Which means we're looking at the clue wrong. We just need a change of perspective, and it will all fall into place. That, at least, is what I tell myself.

"I still think we have to pull the clue physically from something," I begin. "We thought it was a horse's mouth, but maybe it's just *like* a mouth. A box? Like a post office box or something?"

"What about a radio? Full of something that's not supposed to be there so that it doesn't work?"

I think Blake's suggestion is a good one, but Andy just rolls his eyes. "Then *you* come up with something," I say, irritably.

"All right," he says, clearly upset that I'm upset. "The ocean and sea reference. That one seems clear enough. Maybe the aquarium? Sea horses?"

Since that's such a good suggestion, I feel guilty for my snippiness. "That's brilliant," I say.

He stands up. "Let's go."

"Wait," Blake says. "That's only part of the clue. I'd rather be certain than waste time on another wild goose chase."

"What else can it be?" Andy asks.

"I don't know," Blake admits. "But we said that about the carousel, and we were wrong."

Andy sits. "Fine, but I think this fits. Even the reference to a past age. Aren't sea horses supposed to be sort of leftover prehistoric creatures?"

"I think so," I say. "They sure look like it."

"But what about the reference to horsetails? Or the floor?" Blake asks. "I'm thinking that's where we went wrong last time. And, yes, I did check the horse's tails on the carousel. You should have seen the looks I got from a three-year-old."

"How many things can horsetails refer to?" I ask.

"No idea," he admits.

"Let's find out." I signal to the waitress, who rushes right over.

"Listen," I say. "Have you got the Internet on your register computers?"

"Sure," she says.

"Could I use one for just a second?"

She licks her lips. "I'm not supposed to . . ." She trails off, and I'm just about to switch to begging mode when she adds, "But maybe for an autograph?"

"Sure," I say with a laugh. "I didn't realize you recognized me."

She shrugs. "We're not supposed to gawk, you know? And considering what you're wearing, I figured you're trying to keep a low profile."

Ouch. I recover nicely, though. "I am, actually. In fact, you guys have logo gimme caps, right? Can you add one to our bill?"

She agrees, and leads me to the computer, leaving me there

with Andy hovering behind me while she runs off to get my cap. Blake stays at the table, just a few feet away, afraid that if we all gather round we'll be calling way too much attention to ourselves.

I pull up Google, then immediately type in *Horsetails Santa Monica*. My finger is aiming for the enter key as Andy pipes up with, "We don't know it's Santa Monica. You should put in *ocean* or *sea*."

"Dammit," I say. "You're right." But it's too late. Google's doing its thing, and I'm already mousing back to the search box, preparing to revise the search, when I see the results and realize I don't have to. Because the answer is right there in front of us: *Dinosaurs*.

Chapter

44

"I can't believe we missed that," Blake says as we rush south down the Third Street Promenade. Now that we know the answer, I have to agree with him. It's completely obvious. And yet, if we hadn't made it to Santa Monica—if I hadn't blown that first search by not typing "ocean"—it might have taken us several more hours to figure out.

Hours that Blake didn't have.

This time we're certain that we're right. The Santa Monica dinosaurs are topiary dinosaurs, which means they're formed from wire upon which a creeper-type plant grows. The dinosaurs are life-size (well, I think they are—they're big, anyway). And they're flanked by a plant called a horsetail.

Hallelujah.

According to the Web site we found, "horsetails" are a reedlike plant that actually survived from prehistoric times, so it's fitting that it's there with the dinosaurs.

And if that weren't enough to make us certain, the "do-si-do and do more" part of the clue really sealed the deal. Because a promenade is part of a square dance, too—the "more" referred to in the clue. Since the dinosaurs are on the Third Street Promenade—a shopping/walking street in Santa Monica that is closed to vehicular traffic for several blocks—we knew we had to be right.

Our only real problem was which dinosaur to go to, because there is one guarding each entrance of the promenade. For no particular reason, we decided to go first to the south entrance. It's by far the busier. And I think, from the way the road and beach curve, that it's technically a tiny bit closer to the ocean.

If we're wrong, we can always backtrack.

It doesn't take us long to get there, and now we're standing under Dino, trying to decide what to do.

"I think we were right about the horses," Blake says.

"Are you nuts?" I counter. "It has to be one of the dinosaurs."

"Not about that," he says. "I mean about the clue being in their mouths."

I gape at him. I know he's right, but still. "How are we supposed to get up there?" I say, even though I know the answer.

"We climb."

"You mean *I* climb. That thing can't possibly support your weight." Hopefully it can support my hundred and seven pounds. I mean, these dinosaurs were built to be permanent, right? So surely they didn't use chicken wire.

But it's not the thought of collapsing in a heap that has me hesitating. It's the crowd. I look around us at the throngs of moms with strollers, tourists with shopping bags, street vendors with their wares. It's not yet five, so the walk isn't as busy as it will be in the evening or on a weekend, but it's still plenty bustling.

At the moment, no one is paying attention to me. But I know damn well that if I haul off and start scaling a dinosaur, all eyes are going to be on me. And someone will undoubtedly recognize me.

And what do you bet somebody will have a camera?

Five minutes later, I realize that it's even worse than I thought. I'm halfway up the dinosaur (which, honestly, isn't that hard to climb), and people are not only snapping pictures of me, they're shouting out to passersby that I'm up there, and tossing questions at me as I climb.

"Hey, Devi!"

"That's Devi Taylor." (Flash of cameras.)

"The actress? What's she doing on a dinosaur?"

"Publicity." *That* from Blake. "It's just a PR stunt. I'm Blake Atwood, Devi's costar. Autographs, anyone?"

I keep climbing, sure I'm either going to laugh or cry. So much for keeping a low profile, but since I hardly want to field dozens of questions about what the heck I'm doing on a dinosaur, I have to admit Blake's jumped in with the right approach.

"So this is for *Givenchy*?" someone yells up.

"What else?" I answer, because—hey—in a way it is.

By the time I've reached the dinosaur's head, we've gathered quite the crowd. My fear, of course, is that Janus is out there. That he'll see the cluster of fans, see me on Dino, and take aim.

Just the thought makes me work a bit faster, and I hook one arm around the dinosaur and shove the other one down his throat.

Nothing.

I bristle, fighting tears, because I really don't want to repeat this whole process on the other end of the street with a different dinosaur. But I'm afraid that's exactly what I'm going to have to do.

No, my brain screams in denial, and I decide to listen. I shift my position so that I can shove my arm farther in, then I do just that.

I feel bits of vines and the raw edges of wire as they scrape my arm, but I shove in all the way up to my shoulder. I'm in the throat now, and I feel around, wishing I could see inside, but this time of year the topiary is too damn thick to even pick aside.

My fingers curve up, down, and then—*yes!*

Something small and plastic, stuck to the back of the wires. I grab on tight and tug, then feel the thing pull loose from what is probably strong tape. I bring my arm out slowly, terrified of letting go and having the package drop down into Dino's tummy.

Below me, fans are still screaming, but I'm too lost in happiness to hear them. I look down and give Blake a thumbs-up sign. When I look up again, I see him.

Janus.

And right then, I know that he's seen me, too.

"**B**lake! Catch!"

Blake looked up, expecting to catch a package, and then found himself holding his arms out to catch Devi instead. He managed it with an *ooph* as the crowd around them applauded.

"*Run,*" Devi hissed, pointing north.

Blake didn't know if she'd found his antidote or not, but he wasn't about to waste any time. "Thanks for watching our stunt," he called out. "Now you get to see how it ends."

With Devi's hand tight in his and Andy following on their heels, he sprinted up the street. He didn't know exactly what she'd seen, but he could only assume it was Janus. And from the commotion he heard behind them, he assumed he was right.

"This way," Andy said, urging them over to the right and the crowded sidewalk. An arcade was there, with a fast-food place opening onto the sidewalk, and games and stores inside along an open sidewalk.

They barreled inside, ignoring the people who shouted obscenities in protest.

"Are you sure about this?" Devi asked.

"There's a door in the back," Andy explained. "Opens onto an alley."

Sure enough, just seconds later they found the back door. They raced through, then turned to the left, trotting up the alley until they reached the back of the huge Barnes & Noble.

"In here," Devi said, turning down the street toward the front of the store.

"Devi, wait!" Blake shouted. "He could be there."

She slowed to a trot, then waited for him to catch up. When he did, she held up the bag, which contained a single CD. "No antidote," she said as his gut twisted. "Just another clue."

"Shit." Since that summed up the situation nicely, he didn't say anything else. Just a few hours left until he was toast. And right now, the odds weren't stacking in their favor.

"They have listening stations in there," Devi said, pointing toward the building. "We have to find out where to go next. And the car's parked too far away to be any use to us." They'd left the car in a parking lot on the south side of the pier, quite a trek from the promenade. Which meant they couldn't use the CD player in Blue, or the laptop she had left in the trunk.

Blake knew she was right; they didn't have time to go back to the car, and they needed to maneuver back down the promenade to get to the bookstore. And at that moment, the extent of what she was willing to do for him truly hit home. The killer was *right there,* with a gun aimed at her. And still she climbed the damn dinosaur. And now she was willing to go back into the battle zone, all because he needed the antidote—and he needed it now.

"Blake—" She took his hand. "I'll be fine," she said, apparently reading his mind. "But if we don't hurry, you won't. Now come on."

"Devi," Andy said. "I'm not sure this is such a—"

"*I'm* sure," she said, and this time it was in that tone of hers. The one that said she'd been getting her way since she was four years old and didn't intend to stop now.

They all went.

They were careful rounding the corner, of course, but once they were actually there, peeking around the building to see if Janus was there, it looked like the coast was clear.

"I think we lost him," Devi said, and Blake hoped she was right.

"In," he urged. "And move fast."

They ran into the entrance, ducking through the doors and heading for the stairwell in the middle of the store with lightning speed.

"Where to?" Andy asked.

"Up," Devi said. "That's where the CDs are."

The floor was mostly deserted when they arrived, and that was good, especially once Blake realized what Devi intended to do. "There," she said, pointing to one of the listening stations. "We need to get the case open and change CDs."

"You've got to be kidding," Blake said. "How?"

Andy shoved past him, obviously thrilled to be coming to

the rescue. "I'll get it," he said, which for some unknown reason really ticked Blake off. He bit back on the emotion, though, once again reminding himself that he didn't have to like the guy to work with him. Not if Devi's life was at stake.

True to his word, Andy got the locked section of the CD display case open. While he worked, Blake and Devi puttered about, mostly trying to block him from view of anyone who might be coming to that section of the store. And, of course, keeping an eye out for Janus.

"Got it," Andy said.

They turned around to find him wearing the headset and frowning. A small door in the CD rack was open, revealing a CD player hooked to several sets of earphones. Andy pushed a few buttons and kept on frowning.

"What?"

"Hang on." He opened the case and pulled the CD out. "Dammit."

"What?" Devi asked again.

"It's not playing."

"Shit," Blake said. "I bet it's a data CD. We need a computer," he added, irritated with himself that they hadn't thought of that possibility before. They were down to the wire, here. They didn't have time to be wrong.

Devi gave Andy a shove. "You're our computer guru!"

Andy held up his hands. "Hey, I'm stressed out, too, you know."

She made an unhappy noise, but didn't smack him again. "Fine. Let's just find a computer."

"The Apple Store," Blake said. "There's one just down the street. And it's closer than the car."

Since that seemed their best option, they headed out of the bookstore and trotted the short distance to the computer store. Dozens of people milled around, buying computers, iPods, and all sorts of gizmos. The sales clerks were so busy they barely took notice, at least not until Blake elbowed a teenager out of the way so that he could get to one of the demo laptops.

"Hey!"

"Sorry. Emergency."

"Jerk," the kid sneered, then skulked away. Blake felt a tinge of guilt and then shoved it away. The kid could shop for the rest of his life. At the moment, though, the rest of Blake's life might consist of only a few hours. Desperate times and desperate measures.

"Okay," he said, sliding the CD into the drive. "Here we go."

Nothing happened, so Devi scooted over, then moused down until she found a directory. "Just click on Finder," she said, "and . . . *there.*"

Sure enough, the little box showed two files. She clicked on the first one, and a new program immediately opened. After a few seconds of whirring, the screen went black.

"What happened?" Blake asked.

"I don't know," Devi said, staring at the machine in astonishment.

"Andy?"

But Andy just shook his head and held up a finger. "Just wait."

"To hell with that." Blake was just about to turn and get

someone from the staff to help them when the screen filled up with a man's face. Then the face faded, replaced by a woman. And again and again. Six faces on a constant loop.

"Who—" Andy began, but Devi cut him off, her finger tapping the screen.

"Bud Abbott . . . Marlene Dietrich . . . Lou Costello . . . Mae West . . . W. C. Fields . . . Jimmy Stewart . . . and Bud again." She looked up at Blake. "I don't get it."

"Me either," Blake admitted. "Maybe the other document?"

As soon as he suggested it, she clicked over, then opened the document:

> *Oh, Marnie, send me no flowers. I'd rather be*
> *rich than face a kitten with a whip. But a bullet for a*
> *badman? Ah, such bliss. As soothing as the island of the*
> *blue dolphins.*

"That's supposed to make sense?" Blake said. Once again, he wanted to lash out and hit something. There was a poison in his veins. He didn't have time for inscrutable puzzles.

Then he got a look at Devi's face, and her smile told him everything he needed to know.

"You've got it," he said.

Her grin widened. "Not all of it," she admitted. "But I do know where to go."

"Where?" Andy asked, as she pressed the button to eject the DVD.

"Universal Studios," she announced. *Kitten with a Whip. Send Me No Flowers. I'd Rather Be Rich. Marnie. Island of the*

Blue Dolphins. Bullet for a Badman. They're all Universal movies."

"And you just know that off the top of your head?" Blake knew she always won Scene It? and the movie editions of Trivial Pursuit. But this was especially impressive.

"Of course she does," Andy says, with more than a little pride in his voice. "She's been in movies all her life."

"He's right," Devi said. "But these I know because of my grandpa. He worked for Universal for a while. He told stories. Lots of stories. And I remember all of these titles from some of the tales he used to tell." As she spoke, she tapped the key in the upper right hand of the machine.

"What?"

"The disk isn't ejecting."

"Maybe we should—" He cut off the thought, though, because a sales clerk was coming toward them, the teenager he'd edged out of the way right beside him. And looking more than a little pissed.

"We know the clue," he said. "Keep your head down so he doesn't recognize us, and let's go."

She hesitated for a moment. "What if we need the disk? Let's just buy the computer and take it with us. You've got your wallet, right?"

"Yeah," Blake said. And since that wasn't a bad idea, he started to pull it out. Then stopped when a police officer stepped into the store, then crossed over to a nearby salesman and started talking earnestly with him.

"Shit. Change of plans." He nodded toward the uniformed officer. "If he knows what happened at the pier . . ."

"Right," Devi said. "We don't have time to deal with questions."

The three of them race-walked for the door, heads down, then pushed out onto the promenade without looking back.

"I hope this is okay," she said. "We can go to Universal, but what if we can't figure out *where* to go once we get there?"

"We will," Blake said. Because about that, they had no choice.

Chapter

46

They'd lost him in the crowd, and Janus was finding it hard to keep hold of his famous patience.

He told himself it would all work out. It had to. She was, after all, his destiny. Never mind the way she looked at Atwood. He'd be taken care of soon enough.

She'd be punished soon enough.

He stood in the middle of the promenade, his gaze skimming over the area, looking for any sign of the three of them.

Nothing.

He took a deep breath and told himself it would be fine. Soon, he'd pick up her scent again.

And then—as if to prove that she really did belong to him and no one else—he heard the sweet, sweet words.

"Honest to God. It was Devi Taylor and that guy who's starring in that movie with her."

"Bullshit," said yellow-haired teenager, carrying a skate board.

"No, man. It's solid." That from the first speaker. A dark-haired boy with a black T-shirt.

"You're really not shitting me?"

"No way. Here." He pulled out a disk. "This was what they'd shoved in the computer I was working on. The clerk got it out after they left."

"He just gave it to you?"

"I lied. Told him it was mine. He was a little po'd, but what was he gonna do? Keep it?"

"So what's on it?"

"Don't know. Haven't looked yet."

"Well, come on, man. Let's go back to your place and look. Maybe it's sex stuff like Paris Hilton or that Pamela Anderson tape."

"Whoa. You think?"

"We can hope, right?"

As the two boys walked toward the parking garage, Janus followed, fingering the gun hidden in his jacket. He wouldn't fire it if he didn't have to. That wouldn't be sporting.

But if he needed it to persuade?

That he was prepared to do.

Chapter

47

Even though I grew up on movie sets, I've always had a special affinity for the Universal Studios theme park. That is, in fact, one of the reasons we had the cab drop us off there rather than at the black tower that makes up Universal Studios' corporate offices. The game's about me, we figured. And I have more knowledge of the park than the offices.

Plus—on a more practical note—we had to assume that whoever was leaving these clues around Los Angeles would have had easier access to the park, too.

As always, the Citywalk and the area in front of Universal is loud and vibrant, filled with the buzz of locals and tourists, not to mention the honeybees, lured there by the many tourists who've lugged soda-pop cans with labels promising a few dollars off the ticket price. I stand there, shifting my weight from one foot to another, as we wait in line near the giant Universal globe, a fountain with a cloud of fog emerging from below.

The line moves at a snail's pace, and I'm sure Janus is going to walk up behind us and blow my head off. I'm considering using my celebrity status to get us in—so much for low profile—when Andy spots the Fast Tickets line for those of us willing to pay full price with a credit card.

We're willing, and we're inside the park in no time at all. Being inside, however, doesn't answer the question of where to go next, and we shift off to the side away from the incoming crowd as we try to figure that one out.

"What do you think?" Blake asks, looking around the plaza area with the kitschy shops, the hacienda-style furniture, and the bronze sculptures of various folks shooting a movie.

"Honestly," I say, "I don't have a clue."

"Is there an Abbot and Costello exhibit in the park?" Andy asks. "A tribute to Mae West or Jimmy Stewart?"

Since I don't know the answer to that, I can only frown and look down at the map of the park we'd been handed along with our ticket. I'm about to announce that I don't see anything along those lines when I hear someone screech my name, and all of a sudden chaos erupts.

For half a second, I'm terrified. And then I realize what's going on. *Fans.*

Dozens and dozens of teenage girls and boys (and a few adults, too) are standing around me, pads of paper, maps, hands, and anything else you can write on thrust at me. I'm not really sure what to do, since we need to get out of there, and I sign a few as I try to explain that we're in a hurry and need to get a move on.

I'm not making a dent, though, so Blake gives it a shot. That, of course, only leads to more squealing when the girls clue in to who he is. (They do shift away from me, though, giving me some breathing space. Which is good . . . except for the fact that it does little for my ego.)

The problem has only been exacerbated, though, because now we're both surrounded, and only Andy is there to break the crowd up, and although he's trying, he doesn't really seem to be making a dent.

That's when I hear someone call his name, and it sounds familiar. I cock my head, as I hear it again.

"Andy? Andrew Garrison?"

Lindy!?

"Hey! I thought that was you," she adds. "I'm Devi's friend Lindy. We met once during rehearsals when I was visiting the set. What are you doing—"

"Lindy!"

She turns, her eyes wide as she sees me. Fortunately, she knows me well enough to know that I'm not interested in being mugged for autographs. And she's also enough of a take-charge woman to do something about that.

"Okay, folks. That's enough for now. Ms. Taylor and Mr. Atwood have important meetings to get to. Check the schedule later to find out when they'll be doing an appearance for more autographings."

I raise an eyebrow at that last bit, but it seems to work, and the crowd scatters. "What are you doing here?" she asks, as the last person disappears into one of the nearby shops. The question is asked with quick, sharp glances at both Blake and Andy. Lord only knows what she's thinking.

"Long story," I say, which really doesn't cover it, but it's all I *can* say. "You?"

"Jenna's in town," she says, referring to her fifteen-year-old niece. "I'm being the good aunt and taking her through the park."

I turn and look in the direction she's facing, and sure enough, there's Jenna loitering by the exit.

"We were on our way out when I saw you. I did right rescuing you?"

"Totally," I say. "I was beginning to feel claustrophobic."

"Yeah, well, I wouldn't have bothered if you were still working for Universal. But since you're not currently on our payroll, I decided to cut you a break." She says it with a smile, but the effect on me is hardly funny, and it's all I can do to withhold my excitement as she begs off from spending any time with us. "I've promised Jenna dinner," she says.

"No worries," I say, much too eagerly, practically shooing her away.

Thankfully, she doesn't notice my hyperness (or else figures I'm just being me). As soon as she's gone, I pull Blake and Andy off to one side. "Employees," I say. And then, because they're looking so blank, I add, "All those actors were contract players for Universal at one time or another."

"Brilliant," Andy says.

"No kidding," Blake says. "But what do we do with that tidbit?"

"I have no idea," I admit. "But we've got to be getting close."

A guy wearing a name tag walks by, and Blake calls him over. "Is there someplace the employees go to change clothes? Especially you guys who have to wear costumes?"

The guy stares at Blake, and then me, and for a second I think we're going to have another fan on our hands. Then I guess his don't-annoy-the-celebrities training kicks in, because he nods and says, "Yes, sir," and points vaguely into the park. "Down the Star Way," he says, referring to the giant, multilevel escalator that leads down into the lower level of the park.

We thank him, then head on, passing restaurants like the Frank 'N Stein and strolling characters like Groucho Marx and Doc Brown from *Back to the Future*. Finally we reach the Star Way, and as we begin our slow descent, a canned voice tells us about the attractions and urges us to enjoy our day. Even under the circumstances, I have to admit I feel a tingle of nostalgic excitement. The park is kitschy, but I do love it. And I dearly wish that instead of going on some life-or-death scavenger hunt, Blake and I had come here alone to ride the silly rides and then take the tram through the backlot. We'd hold hands and listen as the guide told us stories about the movies and television shows filmed on the lot, like *Psycho* and *Back to the Future* and *Desperate Housewives*.

Since we're stuck on the escalator behind a family of five, I allow myself a minute or two to feel sorry for myself. But the second we step onto the pavement of the lower level, I force myself to turn it off. I'm stuck playing this game, whether I want to or not. No sense moaning about what I can't change.

As soon as we reach the end of the escalator, we're accosted by the roar of the Jurassic Park Splash Ride. We get our bearings and find an employee over by the Revenge of the Mummy Coaster. A few minutes later, we're heading toward the *Backdraft* show and the employee area tucked just behind.

We've obviously arrived during a shift, because the place is essentially empty. One teenage girl looks at us curiously as we enter, but doesn't say anything, and after a minute or two, she leaves through a back exit.

As soon as she does, I slip down the aisle, checking to see if anyone else is around. No one.

"What now?" I ask, a little frantically since we're so close to running out of time and I'm completely out of ideas.

"The clue has to be somewhere permanent, right?" Blake says. "And with so many people coming and going, it can't just be on a shelf. What if the gizmo gets lost? Or the cleaning crew sweeps it up?"

"Makes sense," I say.

"And we're pretty sure we're dealing with employees, so I figure it must be in a locker."

"Brilliant," I say, looking around us. "That has to be it."

"So we just need to start opening all the lockers?" Andy asks. "That's going to take some doing. Especially since most of them look to be locked."

He has a point.

"We need to figure out which locker," Blake admits. "That part I haven't managed yet."

"No worries," I say. "We've come this far."

He *is* worrying, though. He has to be. Because it took us over an hour to get here from Santa Monica. Traffic in L.A. is bad at the best of times, but during rush hour it's insane. We'd left the pier around four. It's now already past six. If we're remembering right, Blake ate the strawberry around eight. But we could be off half an hour—and if he ate the thing at seven-thirty, we're really pushing it timewise. Especially since we don't even know for certain that this is the last clue.

"The movies," I say. "The clue has to tie to them. The weird message listed, what, six movies? And there were six faces on the slide show."

"Six it is," Blake says, already moving to that far end of the building. "Shit," he says upon arriving. "It's locked."

"Can you break in?" Andy asks.

"I damn well better be able to." He gives the lock a tug, and when it doesn't budge, he turns to the side, bends in a move I've seen him do during many a workout, then thrusts his leg out. He hits the locker dead center, making the metal crumple in and one of the nicely fitted corners stick out. "A lever," he says, and Andy and I both scurry around, looking for something that will work.

The only thing I find is a metal folding chair, but Blake puts it to good use, jamming the back into the opening and using the leverage he's created to force the door off.

I hold my breath . . . and then let it out when I see the contents: Three copies of *Seventeen*. Lip gloss. And some shoes that obviously don't comply with company policy.

"Maybe locker sixty-six?" Andy suggests.

Blake just looks at him, then exhales. "That better be it. I'm in fighting shape, but not for taking down a metal locker."

We head that way, not nearly as optimistic as we were two minutes ago. This locker's closed up tight, too, and just as Blake is about to whack it good, I have a thought. "Wait!"

Both men turn to look at me. I look only at Blake. "Do you still have your phone?" Mine and Andy's were destroyed in the ocean. But if Blake has his . . .

He does, and he hands it to me. I immediately try to get a Web browser, and realize I can't.

"Hang on," I say. I run to the door, opening it and standing half in and half out as I look at the signal bar on the phone. I shift around until, finally, a signal.

Then I go to the Internet Movie Database. I type in *Kitten with a Whip*, then *I'd Rather Be Rich*. So far, so good. Just to make sure I'm right, I type in *Marnie* and *Island of the Blue Dolphins*.

I don't remember any of the other movies, but I don't need to. I'm completely confident that the answer is the year these movies were released, and I race back inside. "Locker 1964," I say. "Try locker 1964."

We're in enough of a hurry that neither man asks me how I came by that. Instead, Blake just does his Hot Martial Arts Dude shtick again and gets the locker open.

I can't see the contents from where I'm standing, but I can tell from Blake's words that we've hit the jackpot.

"Oh, baby," he says. "I think we've got it."

When he steps into my sight, he's holding one of those fake Oscar statues. I can see that something's printed along the base, and I point to it. "What's it say?"

"Hollywoodland," Blake says. "Holy crap, is that another clue?"

"It can't be," I say. "This has to be the end. We don't have time to go anywhere else."

I can hear the hysteria in my voice, but that makes sense, because I *am* hysterical.

"What we don't have time for," Andy says, "is dawdling. So let's figure out what Oscar and Hollywoodland mean and get there." He looks at his wrist. "And fast."

"He's right," I say to Blake. "Let's go."

I turn back toward the door, just in time to see a shadow. I have no idea who's out there, but even so, my heart leaps in my chest, terror suddenly gripping me, and I turn around, running back toward Blake.

He sees my wild eyes, and then I see his widen as he looks past me. "Get down!" he yells, pushing me to the ground, the statue tumbling down with me.

I'm falling, and it's like slow motion. I notice every little thing—Janus, brandishing a gun on the other side of the room. The statue, shattering on the floor and releasing a small ziplock baggie containing two pink pills from the hollow space inside. And Blake, reaching into the back waistband of his jeans and pulling out a gun.

Where the heck did he get a gun?

He fires before Janus manages to, and then I watch as he squeezes the trigger again, this time releasing nothing but a click. Frustrated—or maybe as a defensive maneuver—he hurls the gun at Janus. I have no idea if it hits my assassin or not; I'm too busy racing for the back door, the little baggie of pills clutched tight in my hand.

Chapter
48

Thank God he'd kept the gun, Blake thought, as they slammed through the back door and found themselves in a nonpublic area. He would have liked another round, but at least the one he'd gotten off had slowed the bastard down.

And smashing him in the face with the pistol had felt damn good, too. More important, it had bought them a few minutes.

Now he looked around, realizing that they were in some sort of service alley that ran behind the locker room and a few of the buildings that housed exhibits. A tall wooden fence faced them, and for a brief second, he considered climbing it. It was too high to jump to the top, though, and without a place to get a toehold, there was no way they'd make it over the top before Janus joined them.

All that went through his head in a split second, and with

barely a pause, he cut to the left, Devi's hand tight in his, and raced down the alley.

"Where are we going?"

"No idea," he admitted. "Just away." Once they were free of Janus, he'd figure out where to go next. The clue, or a hospital. And considering an Oscar statue with "Hollywoodland" printed on the base was hardly the best of clues, he was thinking that checking himself into Cedar Sinai might be the best course after all.

He heard Andy puffing right behind them, then heard the slam of the metal door. He risked one glance over his shoulder and saw Janus emerge, the gun aimed at their backs.

"Here!" he called, tugging them sideways and into a cutoff from the alley into the space between two buildings. It dead-ended in front of them, but several doors lined each side of the narrow corridor. He decided on one, found it locked, and then tried the next. And even though it was marked with a red Danger! Authorized Personnel Only! sign, it was thankfully unlocked. He hesitated only a second; as far as he was concerned, the man chasing them with the gun was authorization enough.

The three of them rushed inside, and as soon as Andy cleared the threshold, Blake slammed the door shut, then looked for a way to bolt it. An old-fashioned bar lock—made out of serious-looking steel—ran across the door. He turned the lever, forcing the lock into place, all the while having the feeling that they'd truly lucked out. Most likely this door was supposed to be permanently shut, and one of the kids who works on the lot forgot.

No problem. Blake was more than happy to take advantage of their mistake.

"What now?" Devi whispered.

"We keep moving. We need to get out of here before he figures out where we went."

He started to move toward the left, but Devi grabbed the back of his jeans, pulling him to a halt. He turned, looking at her quizzically, barely able to see her in the dim light of the red exit sign.

"Here." She pressed something into his hand, and when he looked down, he saw a tiny baggie with two pills. "Inside Oscar," she said, before he had time to ask.

His chest welled, relief flooding his body. "Oh, babe," he said. "I love you."

Her smile was small and teasing. "I know. Now take the damn pills."

Since he wasn't about to argue with that, he popped the pills into his mouth, hesitating only briefly over the fact that he had no idea what he was taking. He took comfort in the fact that the antidote had worked for Mel. Surely the rules of the game hadn't changed in that regard.

Devi watched him curiously, as if she was certain he was going to turn all different shades of purple. Andy watched him, too, but his face was more impassive, and Blake had the uncomfortable urge to apologize for not dying. Like, *Sorry, chum. She's mine, and I'm not leaving.*

He brushed that off, feeling like an ass for being even the tiniest bit jealous. Andy had been nothing but helpful, and he was doing his damnedest to protect Devi even though it had to be clear to the man that his crush wasn't reciprocated.

"Are you okay?" Devi asked, her hand on his arm.

"I'm still breathing," he said. "I guess we'll know in a few hours if it worked."

"It worked," she said, with more conviction than he felt.

"She's right," Andy said. "You're fine now."

Blake turned to him quizzically, but the other man just shrugged. "That's the way the game works," Andy says. "It's not a game if the rules can change on a dime."

Tell that to Mac, Blake thought, but he kept it to himself. Instead, he pointed into the interior of the building. "I might be safe, but Devi isn't. We need to keep moving."

He veered off to the left, Devi right behind him. "Watch your step," he called back in a low whisper. "We must be inside the engineering for one of the shows."

They crawled through a maze of metal pipes and tubing, finally ending up in an open section, low-ceilinged with thin pipes running in parallel lines above them. An odd room, to be sure, but on the far side, he saw a door, marked with yet another red Exit sign.

"I feel like Alice," Devi said, probably referring to the fact that the low ceiling made them feel like giants.

"Crouch down so you don't hit your head on the pipes," Andy said as they started forward.

"What's that smell?" Devi asked.

"I don't sme—" But then he did. Something almost sweet, but still sickly, like—

Shit.

"Hit the ground!" he said, just as the flames erupted above them, from the natural gas flowing out of the pipes above their head.

Devi screamed, and Blake shoved her to the ground. The three of them shimmied forward, holding their breath, their hands burning on the tiled floor. Asbestos, Blake realized. Where the fuck were they?

They reached the exit door, and he thrust himself against it. It didn't budge, and he felt a ball of panic building. But there was no way in hell he went through all of that bullshit to get the antidote only to get fried in the engineering components of some show.

He gave it another shove, this time with Andy at his side. The door burst open, and they tumbled out onto a carpeted walkway filled with people.

A little boy standing by them screamed, and they jumped to their feet, flustered, and then kicked the door closed again.

A guide was leading the group, and she stared at them, her mouth hanging open.

"Right," Blake said. "Sorry." He started to shove through the crowd, moving against the traffic toward what he was sure was the show's entrance. And all the while, he was thanking God they'd survived. Because he'd gotten a good look at the room.

They were right in the middle of the *Backdraft* show. The one about the firefighters battling the killer flames.

Which put a whole new spin on that saying: Out of the frying pan, and into the fire.

Chapter

49

Ten minutes later, I still feel hot. And I still can't believe we survived. Janus *or* the fire. But we did. And Blake had the antidote. And as far as I could tell, we'd lost Janus.

For the time being, anyway.

Except for being a little sooty and a lot shook up, we're doing okay. We're crouched in a corner, sucking down water and soda that feels *so* good on our charred throats.

This bit of respite, though, is just an illusion, because the game is still in full force. Yes, we've found the antidote—thank God—but the toxin in Blake's blood was just the kill switch; just an incentive to get me to play the game. A horrible game where I'm trying to follow the clues to stay one step ahead of an assassin who's stepped right out of my nightmares.

Solve the clues, win the game. But even if I manage to elude Janus all the way to the last clue—even if, like Mel, I see that wonderful computer message reading "Game Over"—I don't think I'll really believe it. How can I, unless Janus is dead?

And oh, how I want him dead.

Right now, though, I have to focus on the game. I have to push my fears aside. Win the game. *Survive.* And worry about the rest later.

The only trouble is that we don't have the next clue. I'd left the smashed Oscar statue on the floor of the employee locker room. At the time, I'd been thinking only of grabbing the two pills and getting out of there. Now, I can't believe I ran off without it.

"We go back," Blake says, as soon as I voice my concern.

"Are you sure it's safe?"

"No," he says. "But the only way to keep *you* safe is to get that clue."

"Let's get some clean clothes first," Andy says. "For one thing, we stink. For another, Janus is probably still out there, keeping a lookout for us."

He has a point. The place is completely crawling with tourists, so it was easy enough to get lost in the crowd. But at the moment we're far too recognizable. So we take Andy up on his suggestion and end up buying oversize Universal Studios T-shirts and black caps. I'd wanted some sweatpants, too, but there were none to be found. So instead I look like a little girl, with my extra-large shirt and the baggy shorts I'd stolen from the beach.

If Miuccia Prada could see me now . . .

We have a short heart-attack moment when we realize that Oscar isn't on the floor in front of locker 1964 anymore, but then Andy has the brilliant idea of checking the trash can. Sure enough, that's where he is.

With the base stuck in my pocket and the body stuck in Andy's, we head back out to the plaza area, this time forgoing the escalator for the very long set of stairs—just in case we have to make a run for it.

We huff up to the top level, carefully checking faces as we walk, but there's no sign of Janus.

"So now we leave?" I ask, pausing to catch my breath at the top.

"Not yet," Andy says. "The only way out is through the main gate. If he's waiting just outside the turnstiles, it would be like shooting fish in a barrel."

I'm not crazy about the metaphor, but I can't disagree. "So what are we going to do?"

"Waste time," Blake says. "And then leave carefully."

And since neither Andy nor I have a better suggestion, that's exactly what we do. Which means that I get my tram ride after all.

Since that's the longest feature in the park, we stand in line for it, feeling a bit antsy until we're actually seated and can see that Janus isn't seated anywhere near us. I'd half considered playing the celebrity card and getting moved to the front of the line, but the word of the day was low-profile, and that just didn't fit the bill.

Soon, we're being guided through the backlot, hearing stories about old movies, seeing the discarded set pieces and building facades, and getting caught up in the kitschy stuff like the pretend earthquake in the subway. We see Six Points Texas, Little Europe, Amity Island from *Jaws,* and much more.

Sitting there so close to Blake, our bodies pressed together and our hands held tight, feels right. *Romantic.* And as we enter one of the tunnels and the world turns dark, Blake sneaks a kiss that's even hotter than the flames we've just escaped. I know it's only the calm before the storm, but the moment is precious to me, and I eagerly soak it up, knowing full well what awaits me when the tram stops and we return to the real world—and the game.

The ride is over all too soon, and we get off the tram. Andy's expression is guarded, and I feel a little guilty, so I reach out, grabbing his hand with my right, so that I'm holding on to the two men in my life who are taking such good care of me. He turns to look at me, and the corner of his mouth lifts. I smile in return, and the little band of guilt around my heart eases a bit.

"Now?" I ask.

"One at a time," Blake says. "Let's each try to blend in with a group or a family."

Blake goes up first, boldly going up to a group of teenage boys who are about to leave and asking them if they can show him where something on the Citywalk is. They try to give directions, he plays stupid, and they end up exiting the park with him.

There's no gunfire or screams when he reaches the Universal globe fountain, so I figure it's my turn. I see a mom with a baby stroller—always a pain to get past those turnstiles—so I trot over and offer to help her out.

She agrees, and we chat about babies and the park and the California weather as we pass through the exit. I try to look engaged by the conversation even as I'm keeping an eye out for Janus.

We get through without any hassle, and I'm starting to feel pretty confident.

That feeling increases as Andy comes up while I'm saying good-bye to my new friend, just as safe and sound as Blake and I.

"Did he just give up?" I ask, not really believing it.

"My guess is that he's relying on the tracker," Blake says.

It takes me a second to figure out the ramifications of that, but then I get it. "So you're saying he still has the tracker aimed at us, and he figures he can just bide his time and wait until we turn up again. Hopefully someplace less crowded next time."

"Exactly."

"So we can do the hotel thing, right?" I direct this at Andy, who'd suggested it earlier, reminding me that the tracker wasn't specific enough to pinpoint where we were in a hotel. Just like, apparently, it couldn't pinpoint us in a theme park.

"Absolutely," he says. "What's nearby?"

"Let's go downtown," I say. "Someplace like the Radisson. It's huge and tall. That's gotta confuse a tracking device."

"And while we're there, we'll inspect everything," Blake said. "If we can find the damn thing, we can hide it on the subway. *That* should keep the bastard entertained."

I have to laugh at that, not only because the image is so amusing, but because as a native Angelino, it still amazes me that we have a real, true subway. Considering it's been around for well over a decade, you'd think I'd be used to it, but I'm not. And I get a kick every time I step on the thing.

We're walking as we make our plans, and by the time we're in agreement about where to go, we're midway down the Citywalk. We'd walked down the Citywalk on our way into Universal, but at the time my attention had hardly been focused on the place. Now I take a better look, because it has been years since I'd been here, and it's changed. It's full of even more stores. More lights.

More color. More noise. There are kiosks everywhere, some open for business, some shut down and waiting for the weekend. People flow in and out of restaurants, and in front of us, water squirts up from a fountain in the ground that has attracted a group of kids. All in all, loud, campy, and fun.

Best of all, though, are the shops. Lots of them, ranging from clothes to toys and right back to clothes.

"You have that look," Blake says.

"What look?"

"That I-want-to-go-shopping look."

"I do not," I say, but not very enthusiastically since, of course, he's totally busted me. "Okay, maybe a little, but only because there are some fun stores here, and I really could use a pair of jeans." I'd seen a particularly cute pair in a window, and now I take his hand to tug him with me to the right.

That's when the pain rips through me, sharp and hot, and so intense that I'm not even sure where it's coming from.

"Fuck!" Blake yells, even as I realize that I'm clutching my shoulder, and that blood is spreading like water under my fingers.

I open my mouth to speak—to scream—but nothing comes out. Instead, my knees go weak, and I collapse down on the hard stone of the Universal Citywalk.

Chapter 50

Blake watched in horror as Devi collapsed to the ground. He could hear the blood pounding in his ears, fury building as he dropped beside her, desperate for a sign that she was okay.

Her chest rose and fell under his hand, and as he listened, he heard her steady breathing, then watched as she shifted and tried to push herself up. *Thank God.*

"Stay still," he ordered as he inspected the wound in her shoulder. "It's not as bad as it feels. I promise."

All around him, a crowd had gathered, but through the throng of people, he saw Janus positioning himself to get off the kill shot.

No way. No fucking way.

He was on his feet in seconds, his body on alert and fueled by rage. He stormed forward, not thinking, just letting his training take over.

Janus saw him coming, and his eyes went wide even as he raised the gun. "She's mine!" he screamed. "We're destined to spend an eternity together!"

"You can spend eternity in hell," Blake shot back, even as he lashed out against the man, his solid kick to the gut knocking the wind out of him, and the upward thrust snapping the gun right out of Janus's hand even before it smashed his chin up, knocking his head back with a sharp snapping noise.

In the brief second it took for Blake to get his balance, he saw a flash of black, then realized that Andy had jumped the man. He and Janus tumbled to the ground, rolling over and over, a tangle of arms and legs, until they ended up behind one of the many festively decorated merchant kiosks.

Blake was after them in a second, but he was already too late. He heard the scream. A wailing *aiiiiiiiieeee*—the painful keening sound of a man in deep and mortal pain.

Chapter

51

It is the scream that gets me moving again. A horrible, high noise that—somehow—I know is coming from Andy.

From Andy, the man who stepped in to keep me safe even when it was Blake I really wanted, and Blake I trusted.

Andy, the man who'd just tackled my assailant.

I'm light-headed and operating solely on adrenaline, and my left arm hangs limp at my side. I hardly feel the pain anymore, but I know that it's there, and that it's going to come back with a vengeance soon enough.

Now, though, I cherish the brief respite.

Blake is already racing toward the kiosk, and I start to follow when I see the gun. I snatch it up, then stagger forward. In the distance I hear the sound of sirens, but it seems far away, hidden behind the rush of swirling sound within my head.

A few people move toward me, as if they want to help me. I

wave the gun wildly, though, and they ease back. I don't want help. Not now.

All I want is revenge.

I get to the merchant cart, and then with one shift to the left, I can see the horror behind it. Andy is prone on the ground, a knife protruding from his gut and blood staining the concrete around him. Blake is holding him, keeping pressure on the wound, and Andy makes a small sound. He's alive, and that gives me hope, and I cling to it like a life raft.

Beside them, Janus is on his back, clearly stunned, as if Andy had got in one good blow to the head before succumbing. Or maybe Blake nailed him as he rounded the corner. I don't know. It's all happening too fast, and my head is too fuzzy.

"Devi," he whispers, and bile rises in my throat merely from the sound of my name on his lips.

"Bastard." I take the gun and point at him.

"No." He puts one hand on the ground, then starts to push himself up. I keep my eye on those hands, terrified that he has a weapon.

"Stay down," I say.

"I love you," he says. "Why didn't you ever know that? You're mine. Mine, and you always will be."

"No."

"Devi," Blake says. "It's okay. The cops are coming."

"We die together," Janus says, and suddenly he's reaching under his jacket, and I know there must be another gun under there.

I don't hesitate. I pull the trigger, then watch as the red star-burst blooms on his forehead.

He's dead.

And I'm glad.

"They shouldn't have given me morphine," I say, through my fuzzy, happy head. "What if I like it too much again?"

"You won't," Blake says, holding my hand. "You're stronger now."

He's right, and I smile, although I'm pretty sure it's a goofy smile. I've only been awake a minute or so, and I'm still getting my bearings.

"Andy?" I ask.

"He's fine. Amazing, actually. The knife missed everything important. The doc sewed him up and they checked him in for observation, but he's fine. The surgeon said it couldn't have been a cleaner wound if it had been planned."

"That's good," I say. "He's a sweet guy."

"He's head-over-heels for you."

"Yeah? Well, who can blame him?" I tease. "I mean, so are you, right?"

He laughs. "You have a point."

"And I'm okay?" They rolled me into surgery the second we got to the hospital, so Blake knows more about me than I do.

"You're perfect," he says, and with such conviction that I have to laugh. But the sound dies in my throat. "And Janus?"

"Dead," Blake says. "Good job."

"The police?"

"Tons of questions," he says. "They'll talk to you, too. But there are about eight thousand lawyers on the case already, and it looks like the police part will be wrapped up quickly."

"He was about to kill me."

Blake's eyes shift just a little. Something that probably wouldn't even be noticeable to most people. I, however, notice.

"Blake? What is it?"

"He didn't have a gun. We don't know what he was going for, but it wasn't a gun."

I take a second to process that information, trying to decide how I feel about it. I've heard so many stories of people who have shot a gun and killed someone. So many stories of regret. Of fear. Of overpowering guilt.

I don't feel any of that. Even knowing that my shot wasn't really fired in self-defense, I don't regret it for a second. He tormented me. Not once, but twice. With deliberation and intent. He wanted to kill me. He wanted to take himself with me, as far as I could tell.

I wasn't about to mourn his death. Hell, if I thought my legs could hold me, I'd stand up and dance in celebration.

From Blake's expression, I can tell that he understands. He

leans over and strokes my forehead. "You won," he says. "You're not a victim anymore."

"I'm sorry," I say, and tears spill out of my eyes. I've clearly confused him, as I don't think tears are the response he's expecting. I manage a smile. "For what I did. For how I pushed you away. I had to do it first. Before you could. And I was so afraid that you would. That everyone would just look at me with pity again, and that I'd be in the victim's chair all over again."

The words spill out, and I'm not even sure if I'm making sense. But I mean it. Every word. I may not have understood what I was doing before, when I told him to get the hell out of my life. But I understand now. Mostly, I understand what I almost lost.

In a way, I guess the game was good for me. It forced me to the dark edge of the abyss. Forced me to look into it again.

Most important, it forced me to survive.

And I did survive.

"I'm sorry, too," he says. "I knew the way your head worked. I just got so damn mad at you for overreacting that I let go of the most important part."

"What part?"

"That I love you. That I needed to fight for you."

"You fought for me these last couple of days," I say, holding tight to his hand.

"Yeah, well, I'd say we fought for each other."

Since I can't argue with that, I smile, then sink back farther against the foam hospital pillow. "Is it over now?" I ask.

"The assassin's dead. That's about as over as it gets."

I nod, because I like the sound of that.

"Of course, we still have to deal with the fallout."

I'm immediately on alert. "Fallout?"

"The press," he says. "We're the hot news of the day."

I have to laugh. Because for the first time in years, I really don't mind.

Chapter 53

"I'm your best friend," Lindy says, one eye on me and the other on Lucy, who's determined to steal one of the tortilla chips I'd dumped in a big ceramic bowl. "You should have told me."

I snuggle up against Blake, completely content. "I already told you I couldn't. No way was I putting you at risk, too."

"So it's really all over?" she asks.

"Yes," Blake says firmly. From the other side of the patio, Mel echoes the sentiment. Like she's been telling me ever since she flew out, one assassin, one target, one protector. That's the game. And once the assassin's out of the picture, there's nothing left of the chase. Of course, *her* chase is still going strong, and she and Andy have been working together for the last few days, trying to figure out who's the ultimate bad guy behind this thing.

Andy doesn't say anything now, but he's leaning against the deck railing, watching me and Blake. I can see a hint of jealousy in his eyes, but he's been good about it. And I'm even considering fixing him up with Susie once we start filming again. Until then, I'm taking a much-needed rest.

Although I haven't been getting *that* much rest. Not with Blake staying in my house. And in my bed.

"I still can't believe your Prada bag was bugged," Lindy adds.

"Not bugged," I correct. "They stuck a GPS-type gizmo in it. So Janus could tell where we were." I'd found *that* out when I'd taken the bag in to Prada to see if they could fix the scratch in the leather. All in all, a nasty surprise . . . not to mention a curiosity. Because it boosted my theory that whoever was ultimately behind this thing had something to do with the movie. Who, though, I still didn't know.

"Have the police found out anything else?" she asks.

"Not much," Mel answers. She's been working with them, sharing information she's gathered over the years. "Although they did track down Janus's apartment." She glances at me when she says that, and I shudder. The police had already told me about the place. One room completely filled with me. Honestly, it was creepy as hell.

"*Lucy!*" Lindy leaps out of her seat and manages to snag her daughter's finger before she can shove it into the hot sauce. "You would *not* like that."

She rolls her eyes at me. "Trouble," she says.

I laugh, because I wish trouble were that easy.

"I should run," Mel says, which is pretty much the cue for everyone else to leave, too. I can't say I'm too unhappy about that. After all, I've been sitting wrapped in Blake's arms for a good twenty minutes, and I'd be lying if I didn't say I was getting a little turned on.

Okay, a lot turned on. And as soon as everyone's out the door, I press myself against him. "You know what? I think I could use a shower."

"Really?" he says, pulling me close. "What a coincidence. I could use one, too."

Chapter 54

Water sluices over me, steam billowing up. I like the way it feels. Like the misty, romantic quality. Most of all, I like the way it keeps my secrets.

He's right outside that door, the man I want more than anything. And just thinking about his touch makes my nipples peak. Makes that sweet spot between my legs quiver. It's so tempting to pull down the handheld showerhead and get the satisfaction I need. But I don't want it that way. I want it only from him.

Why isn't he coming?

Frustrated, I turn off the water. I reach outside the shower until my fingers close on a fluffy white towel. I wrap it around myself, then step out, my body still damp.

I press my palm against the closed door, ignoring the bright lights that cut through the steam. He's over there, and yet he's not coming in. Can't he tell that I want him to come in?

I waver, unsure if I should make the first move. And then—working up my courage—I do just that. I pull open the door, and find him standing right there.

He's wearing no shirt, just jeans, slung low on his hips. His chest and abs are firm and perfect, and as he pulls me close, the heat from his body seeps through the towel and into my blood.

I don't have any time to think as he opens his mouth, drawing me in. I lift my arms, wrapping them around his neck, and between us, the towel falls away. I don't care. All I want is this man. All I want is this moment.

I can stay like this forever . . .

"Cut!"

Tobias's sharp cue cuts through my addled brain. Since it's a semi-nude scene, most of the crew is off the set, and a female PA brings me a robe. I peel myself off Blake and slide my arms into it. I can feel myself blushing, and wonder if anyone else can tell just how aroused I really am.

Blake, I'm sure, can tell. A little fact that's proven true when he leans down to whisper in my ear. "Tonight. We'll finish this tonight."

Oh, yes. We most definitely will.

"Now *that* is what I'm talking about," Tobias says, coming over and swinging an arm around each of us. "What a fabulous first day back. Che-mis-try. You two got it. Everybody wants it." He kisses each of us on the forehead. "Glad to have you back. Hate the circumstances, but that crazy fuck sure managed to kick up some damn fine publicity. Kids, we are going to make a mint."

He's rattling the words off a mile a minute, even as he's leading Blake aside to discuss the next scene. I smile. After all, I understand his enthusiasm. The press is going nuts. Was someone really trying to kill Devi Taylor? Or was this just some big publicity stunt dreamed up by her PR team?

That, my friends, is the question of the hour.

It's also a question I've refused to answer. After all, Mac is dead. So is Janus. And Blake, Andy, and I barely escaped with our lives. To me, that's proof enough it was real. Let the damn tabloids print whatever they want. I know the truth.

And the truth is, it's over.

I'm standing there in my robe when Mel comes over. She's heading back to D.C. in the morning, but wanted to see at least one day of shooting.

"That was great," she says. "And it's spooky the way Blake looks so much like Stryker."

"Tell him hi for me," I say. "I know you must miss him. Was it worthwhile? Did you and Andy get any leads at all?"

"Nothing specific. But I've got notes. I'm going to poke around once I get back home."

I nod. The office located on her property could give the NSA a run for its money. And since she now works for the NSA, she's pretty much got all bases covered.

"Elliot," I say, still figuring there must be a movie connection. "He hates me. And Marcia, even though I don't really believe it."

"And Tobias," she says. "I know you don't want to believe it, but—"

"I know. I know." And I do. He had access. And he maybe even had motive. After all, he needs a hit as badly as I do.

"I'm following another lead, too," she says.

"Yeah?"

"The thing is, Grimaldi's body was never found."

"You think Archibald Grimaldi is the one behind all of this?"

"It makes sense," she says. "He's rich enough to have pulled it off and then had plastic surgery to make sure no one recognized him. And he sure knows the ins and outs of the program. And every game that's been played in the real world has somehow filtered through the online system."

True enough, but since we are totally out of my league now, I just nod. *Wow.* A fake death. How freaky would that be?

"Listen," she says, switching gears. "I've got to run. I'm meeting some friends from the L.A. FBI field office, and then I have to finish packing. My plane leaves first thing in the morning."

"I'll miss you," I say. "But I'll see you at the premiere."

She laughs. "I wouldn't miss it. Oh, and that reminds me. I have a few friends who are begging me for signed photos of you. Would you mind—"

I cut her off with a laugh. "I've got some head shots at home. E-mail me their addresses, and I'll do it tonight."

"You're the best," she says.

We're finishing up the conversation when I notice that Andy is loitering nearby, waiting to talk to me. I realize that the full crew is back on the set, and I'm still wearing the robe, with nothing on underneath except my bikini bottom. Great.

"Hey," Andy says as Mel heads off the set. "Any interest in getting a coffee after you're done for the day?"

"Oh, Andy, I can't. I've got a ton of errands."

That, actually, is true. Even if it weren't, though, I'd still

say no. I'm just too afraid that saying yes would be leading
him on.

His face falls. "Maybe later this week?"

I open my mouth, planning another brush-off. Then I realize
I have to just get it over with. We'll have coffee. I'll explain that
I'm back with Blake. And that, hopefully, will be that. "Sure," I
say. "Later in the week will be just fine."

Chapter
55

I spend way too long shopping, and I'm running late by the time I turn into my driveway. Lucas opens the gate, and I give him a quick wave, but don't stop to talk. I want to get the house ready. It's exactly one year since Blake and I first started dating, and I'm planning quite the anniversary party.

An hour later, I'm showered and scented, and dressed in a filmy thing that reveals way more than it should. I've put candles all around, filled the tub with hot water and rose petals, and scattered more petals on the bed.

I had my housekeeper set me up with snacks, so the kitchen is well stocked with all sorts of yummy tidbits. And, of course, I have a bottle of red wine for Blake and Evian for me.

I pour myself a glass, then wander through the house making sure everything is perfect. It is. In fact, the only thing missing is Blake.

Unfortunately, half an hour later, he's still the only thing missing. *And* he's late.

I pace a bit, telling myself not to be the clingy female and call to harass him. He had scenes scheduled later than me today, plus an interview for some men's magazine. So he could easily be running behind.

Still . . .

I manage to hold it in check for another twenty minutes, then I can't stand it anymore. I pick up the phone and call, then hang up when I get his voice mail. *Damn.*

Okay. Fine.

I pace a bit more, then decide that I need a distraction.

My laptop is on the breakfast bar, and I fire it up. I'd planned to mail the head shots to Mel's friends earlier and got side-tracked by my preparations. But I'd promised her I'd do it tonight, so I suppose now is as good a time as any.

It's not Mel's e-mail that I see, though. Because right there at the top of my in-box is a message from Play.Survive.Win.

Oh, God, no. Please, not again.

The blackness threatens to pull me in, but I beat it back, my hands so tight on the edge of the bar that the tendons hurt. I kept myself together throughout this whole ordeal—there is no way in hell I'm losing it now.

I take deep breaths, slowly and carefully, until I'm sure that I'm back to myself. Then I stare at the computer, wishing I could just toss the whole thing in the trash compactor.

I know what I have to do, but I don't want to. Even so, I use my finger to move the cursor over the e-mail. Two taps, and it opens, revealing a message containing only a hyper-link. I click on the link and wait for the Web page to open.

When it does, it takes everything I have in me to hold in the scream.

CONGRATULATIONS ON YOUR WIN
BUT NOW IT'S ROUND TWO.
SO BE QUICK, QUICK, QUICK AS A FOX
AND TYPE THE ANSWER INTO THE BOX.
THE LAST CLUE YOU FOUND,
THE KEY'S WHAT IT SAID
TYPE IT IN HERE BEFORE YOUR
BOYFRIEND'S DEAD.

Same rules as before: No police. No help.
Let the games begin.

will hold it together. I will. I will. I will.

My instinct is to call Mel or Andy, but the warning on the message is too much to ignore. As for Blake, I hope the threat is some vague warning of something horrible that will happen in the future, but I don't really believe it.

Blake's too late for our date. And in my heart, I know he's in trouble.

I stare at the little box, waiting for me to type in an answer. Some sort of code that will tell me how to save the man I love.

Focus, Devi. Think and focus.

Right. I can do that. Because I don't have a choice. Screw this one up, and it's Blake that pays. And that's not something I can live with.

The last clue you found, the key's what it said.

Okay, fine. I can figure this out. After all, it's not like I don't have practice.

I think back to our adventure. The last clue was the note and the CD. So I type *Universal* into the text box on the Web page and get . . . nothing.

Frustrated, I try it again, this time in lowercase.

Still nothing.

I try *Universal Pictures, Universal Studios,* and each of the movies and stars listed on the clue.

Not a damn thing.

I'm just about to lose it when I remember: Oscar.

The last clue didn't send us to Universal. The last clue held the antidote. We just didn't have to follow it because we took Janus down.

I frown at the thought, because we *did* take Janus down. More specifically, I did.

So who's now playing the game?

It's not a question I'm going to ponder too long, though, because the answer doesn't matter. Not at the moment. All that matters is typing the clue into that box.

My fingers fly over the keys as I type in Oscar, and then I scream in frustration when nothing happens.

I'm about to try it in uppercase, when I remember the imprint on the base of the statue. I hold my breath, because if this isn't the answer, I've run out of ideas.

Hollywoodland, I type. And sure enough, the screen hums with life, linking finally to an image of the Hollywood sign.

Hollywoodland Realty, I think. Because years ago, they're the folks who placed the famous sign. The "land" has been lost, but "Hollywood" has stayed a landmark. A protected landmark, too.

It's not like it's a public park that you can walk around in. I was given a tour once, and the security is insanely tight. The only access is via a small service road, and the place is watched over by L.A. Park Rangers and guarded tighter than the White House, with dozens of security cameras watching over it 24/7.

So what exactly am I supposed to do?

Actually, the thought of the security cameras reminds me, and I click over to Google and do a quick search. I remember a Web site that ties in to the security cameras so tourist-geeks can see what's going on at the sign any time they want to. (This is, quite literally, like watching grass grow.)

Not a damn thing going on up there. The sign. A news helicopter in the distance. The sign. Another view of the sign. Yet another view of the sign.

I'm just about to give up and assume that I misinterpreted the clue when I see the news helicopter again. *Exactly* where I'd seen it before.

What the—?

I stare at the screen, thinking that surely it was a trick of the eye. But, nope. There it is again. Nothing, nothing, and then *poof.* A news helicopter.

The security cameras are running on a loop!

Which makes me wonder what I'd see if I could see the real live feed from the sign.

I don't have to wonder, though. Because I know.

I'd see Blake.

And it wouldn't be good.

Chapter 57

It's pitch-black by the time I make my way up the winding road to the section of mountainside on which the Hollywood sign is perched. A tall wire fence extends across the road, disappearing into the wilderness.

The moon is full, but the foliage is so dense that it hardly makes a dent against the shadows. With the flashlight's narrow beam to guide me, I pick my way up the hill, climbing parallel to the fence as it circles around the sign.

I stop to get my bearings, looking down toward the lights of the city. It's so dark up here that it almost feels like I'm floating in space. I'm not, though. Right now, my feet are more firmly rooted on the ground than they've ever been.

In front of me looms the Hollywood sign, the white-painted wood glowing eerily in the moonlight. Even from the back, it's majestic, and so much bigger than it seems from down below.

I'm still dozens of yards away, and even with the illumination from the moon, I can't see clearly, but I squint at it anyway, trying to find Blake. It's too dark for me to see anything, and I feel a sudden rush of fear that I'm wrong, and wasting valuable time. That this whole nightmare will just go on and on.

No.

That thought is way too much to bear, and I force it out of my mind.

One step at a time, Devi. Just go one step at a time.

Since that's damn good advice, I shine my light near the bottom of the fence, moving slowly until I see a place where the fence doesn't quite reach the ground. It's rough and rocky, and I'm going to get scraped up from head to toe, but I'm sure I can wiggle through.

I'm a little worried that the fence might be electrified, but there aren't any voltage signs, so I try to quash the fear. Instead, I lie down and push my bag through the hole, then try to make myself as skinny as possible as I slide through after it. I get hooked on part of the fence, but manage to free myself. And then, with one more squirm, I'm through.

I stand up, brushing dirt off me, then bend over and grab my purse. I'm using the Prada bag because it was handy and I hadn't wanted to waste time. But I dumped my usual accoutrements out, and now the bag carries only two things: a gun and a knife.

Just what every fashionable young celebrity needs.

I give the bag a pat, and press on. The ground is getting rougher, descending at a steeper angle as I approach the huge standing letters. So far, there's no sign that there's anyone here but me. I look around as I walk, trying to find the security cameras I know are out there. I can't find them, though, and I wonder if my tormentor is watching me now. I suspect that he is. And I wish that the park rangers were.

I don't hear any sound from in front of me, and I finally decide I've been sneaking around long enough. "Blake?" I call out in an overloud whisper. "Blake? Are you here?"

I stand still, silencing the crunch of my feet, and listen for a response. I don't hear anything, though, and a bubble of worry rises in my chest. "Blake!" I call again, louder this time. Why the hell not? If the rangers find me, great. And I know that whoever lured me here already knows what I'm doing.

This time, I'm rewarded with a sound. Not a word, just a sound. A small rustling. I know it could be an animal, but I don't believe that. It's Blake. He's okay. And all I have to do is get to him.

I rush forward, desperate now, stumbling over rocks, scraping my fingers on the ground as I try to keep from falling. I cover the distance quickly and find myself behind the giant *H*. He's not there, though, and so I move along the letters, finally finding him at the far end of the sign. At the *D*.

He's hanging there unconscious, suspended on the curve of the letter, his wrists bound together in front of him and his feet bound tight at the ankles. I'm not entirely sure what's holding him up.

Not that I really care about the engineering; all I care about is getting him down.

"Blake?"

He doesn't answer, but he does moan, and that little sound gives me hope.

It doesn't, however, give me any ideas. I desperately wish he'd wake up. Not only because I'm terrified that he's seriously in-jured, but also because I'm afraid I can't do this by myself.

He's not coming to, though, and I'm all on my own.

I edge closer, trying to get a feel for the situation. As far as I can tell, it's just him and me, but that can't be right. There's some sort of trap here, too. I just haven't found it yet.

What I *have* found is what's holding Blake to the sign. I can just see it as I stand below and shine the light up. A cord tied around the thick girders that support the sign and wrapped around Blake's waist. Cut that, and he should drop free. It's a long fall, but if I can unbind his hands and legs—and if I can wake him up—I know that he's got the training to make the jump.

The support girders form a sort of scaffolding to which each letter is attached. Every few feet, there are little wooden out-croppings, which I have to imagine are to hold cans of paint when the letters are in need of repair. Small cans, I think, since the ledges are tiny. They will, though, provide some foothold.

The letters themselves are seated into the ground with posts at the bottom, keeping them secure through wind, rain, earth-quakes, and the like. I guess it's worked. The sign has been here for decades.

I was a pro at monkey bars in my youth, so I leave my purse on the ground but tuck my knife in one back pocket and my gun in the other. Then I start climbing. It doesn't take too long to reach Blake, and for the first time in my life, I'm truly glad that I don't experience vertigo. Because this is very high. And re-markably windy. As if we're on a magnet for all the winds that blow from the ocean to the desert.

Blake's eyelids are fluttering, so I start talking to him. Basically narrating what I'm doing as I use the knife to saw through the cord binding his ankles. When I move to his wrists, he opens his eyes. "Good morning," I say, trying for light, but probably not managing. I'm sitting on a girder, one arm hooked around a vertical bar for support and my legs hanging over another, as if I were sitting in a very small chair.

My free hand has the knife, and I'm starting to work on the cords on his wrists.

"Where—oh, God."

"Do you remember anything?" I've got his wrists free, and now I start massaging them.

"Devi," he says, his voice harsh and serious just as I shift back a bit to reach his waist. "I was giving him a ride, and he stuck me with a needle. I was out in seconds." He meets my eyes, his expression grave. "Devi, it was Andy."

Chapter

58

His words shock me so much that I quit sawing at the cord around his waist. "What?" I say, but even as I voice the question, I can see how it has to be true. So many little things fall into place. The person from the movie who ordered the bags. Someone with access to Tobias's stationery. His intense crush on me.

I flash with a sudden memory of him on his Treo right after I spoke with Blake about the Greystone Mansion. Right before Mac was killed.

"Oh, God. Is Andy the reason Mac is dead?"

"What do you think?" comes the harsh reply from below. I turn and look down to see Andy staring up at both of us. "Because you should know that *you're* the reason she's dead. You broke the rules, after all."

"You son of a bitch. You played us."

"Not at all. I played the game."

"Played for me to lose, you mean," Blake says. "The Holly-wood Bowl. The carousel horses. All those were wrong, and you knew it. Yet you pushed for us to go there."

"What do you expect?" Andy says. "You weren't even sup-posed to be in the damn game. You brought it on yourself by eating the strawberry. If Devi had eaten it like she was supposed to, I promise you I would have interpreted those clues like a pro."

"So instead you tried to slow us down," Blake said. "Tried to make it take too long. So that I'd die, and you could step in and help Devi work her way to the last clue."

"You're smart, Blake," Andy said. "I don't think I gave you enough credit."

"And Janus?" I ask. "Was he—"

"Very real," Andy says. "I've loved you for years, Devi. And I had to prove I was worthy. So I did my homework. I saw how the protectors and targets who survived ended up together. Mel and Stryker. Jenn and Devlin. And I thought, why not me?"

"Because you're a damn freak?" Blake says.

But Andy ignores him. He's too lost in his tale. "When Mel wanted to get word out about her project, the movie seemed the perfect way. I was *helping* you, Devi. Helping you get your ca-reer back. I insisted that we would only sell the rights if you were attached to the project. *I* saved your career. And I knew that I could save you, too."

"No," I whisper, because it's the only word I can manage.

"I'd met Janus online, years before. Not a difficult thing to realize he was susceptible. And when I began to investigate—when I realized he was the one who'd attacked you so many years ago—well, I knew that he had to be punished. And what better way than for me to kill him in the context of the game? To beat fair and square the one other man who believed he loved you as much as I truly do love you."

"*You* put him in the game? But . . ." I trail off as I remember Mel's comment about how the body of Archibald Grimaldi— the genius inventor of Play.Survive.Win.—was never found. "Oh, dear God. Andy, are you Grimaldi?"

"The one and only," he says with a little flourish. "And I put Janus in as the assassin and myself in as your protector."

"Save the girl," I say. "The knight on the white horse." My stomach is churning, and I'm having a hard time grasping everything he was telling us.

"And Devi would end up with you," Blake finishes. "Not me."

"Never," I say, shaking my head. And to think I thought this man was *nice*.

"Why are you doing this?" Blake asks.

"Because I can." He looks only at me now. "I wish it could have turned out differently."

I shiver and try to fight my fear. We're up on this scaffolding, trapped like rats, and certainly a clear target if he has a gun. Enough talk. Time to get the hell out of there.

For that matter, time to get *him* the hell out of there.

Without second-guessing, I reach behind me and pull out the gun. I whip it around in record speed, but I'm not nearly fast enough. A bullet whizzes by, embedding in the wood just beside my ear, the splintering crack loud enough to burst my eardrum.

Startled, I grasp for the nearest girder, managing to keep myself from falling. The gun, though, slips from my fingers, bang-ing down a bit before landing on one of those little wooden ledges. I reach for it, but it's too far. Not without engaging in some serious acrobatics. And I have a feeling that really isn't such a good idea.

We're sitting ducks up here, though, and I'm not sure what to do next. "Blake?"

"He could have killed us if he wanted to," Blake says. "Go ahead and cut me down."

I'm a little nervous, but I scoot over again. I still have the knife, and I start sawing at the cord around his waist. It only takes a few good whacks, and then it's free. I've pressed my back up against the wood, and I've got my hands on his waist. He's heavy, but I've got leverage, and only need to help him ease down until his feet can touch.

I'm almost there when Blake yells for me to stop. *"My throat,"* he croaks, his voice hard and pinched.

"Oh, right," Andy calls up. "I forgot to mention. If you cut the cord around Blake's waist, his weight will bear down on the garrote around his neck. Should kill him almost instantly once the right pressure point is hit."

"Damn you!" I scream.

"You move, and he slides down. Even half an inch is going to kill him."

I look around and realize he's right. I've got Blake—and right now, his feet are balanced on my thighs—but there's nowhere else for him to go.

I move, and he dies.

Dear Lord, what are we going to do?

"Give me the knife," Blake says. "I'll just cut through the damn garrote."

Since that's a perfectly brilliant plan, I reach the knife up, my fingertips brushing his as I pass it off.

"Not a bad plan," Andy says. "Except I should probably mention the C-4 I packed around this letter's support beams. And that cord around your neck is part of the detonation system. Cut it, and three seconds later you're falling through space."

"You're bluffing," Blake says.

"Could be," Andy retorts.

And there it is. Stalemate.

I really, really, really want that man dead.

Blake must be having similar thoughts, because he whispers to me, "If I'm holding your wrist and dangling you, can you reach the gun?"

"You mean if I weren't in a thousand little pieces because of the explosion? Yeah, probably."

"I don't think he intends to blow us up," Blake says. "He said we'd be falling through space, remember?"

"Either way, we're dead at the end."

"Maybe not."

"Blake . . ."

We're talking low, and I see Andy shifting toward us. I don't know if he can hear us or not, but I can tell that he wants to.

"He said three seconds," Blake said.

"I say numbers all the time. That doesn't mean I'm being literal."

"Do we have another chance?"

That one, I don't have an answer for.

"Do you trust me?"

"Yes," I say, without hesitation.

"Then take my hand. I'm cutting the cord."

And then, before Andy can figure out what we are up to, Blake does just that. As soon as he does, he starts falling, taking me with him. His hand is tight around my wrist, but otherwise I'm free-falling. The gun is right there, and I grab it. The odds of actually hitting Andy are slim, but I fire anyway. And as I do, the mountain below us seems to explode. I slam back into something hard—and the skin on my arm feels like it's being ripped off—but Blake never lets go.

And then we really are falling, the sign crashing down above us. Everything happens in a haze of dust and soot and debris. And when everything clears, I find myself dangling over a mountain, tethered to earth only by Blake's hand on my arm. His hand, I see, is tight on one of the straining girders from the now collapsed *D* in *Hollywood*.

"I can't hold you much longer," he says. "I need you to climb up to me."

"I'm trying," I say. But he's holding my injured arm, and the pain is too great. I can't move. I can't do anything.

I feel myself start to slip, and cry out for Blake. I have an image of myself splatting on the ground hundreds of feet below us, and that is a reality I really want to avoid.

"Take that," Blake says, and I look up to see my black Prada tote dangling right in front of me.

I tilt my head more, and see Mel among the debris at the base of the sign. She's holding fast to a rope to which she tied my purse. "Use it as one of those firefighter lifts," she says. "Get your free arm and head through it."

She lowers it down a little bit more, and I squirm through, never letting go of Blake in the process.

Slowly, she helps us work our way up, until we collapse on the dirt. Solid ground never felt so good.

"What was it you were saying about not wanting to do *North by Northwest?*" Blake asks, and I have to laugh. Because, really, the idea of hanging off of Mount Rushmore is nothing compared to this.

Blake couldn't keep his hands off her. He was amazed she was alive. And humbled that she was his. That she'd risked so much to save him, and that they'd finally won so completely.

Andrew Garrison—born Archibald Grimaldi—was dead. And that was the big news of the day.

"How did you find us?" Blake asked Mel as the police took charge of the scene.

"Stryker called me a few hours ago. He found out that the building where Janus lived had been owned by Grimaldi years ago. Okay, that's fine. But now it's owned by a trust. And that trust is controlled by Andy." She sighed. "I tried to get a hold of Devi right away, then got worried when I couldn't reach either one of you. Lucas let me in the house, and I saw the computer. After that, it didn't take long to figure out where you were."

"Remind me to give Lucas a raise," Devi said.

Mel laughed. "Well, he only did it because you'd told him who I was and what was going on."

"I still can't believe he was Grimaldi," Devi said.

"I know," Mel agreed. "But once we started to look at it, it made sense. He'd gotten poisoned when he helped Jenn, for example. But in retrospect, I think he did it to himself." She made a show of slapping her neck. "Bam. A poisoned dart."

"And he did the same thing with the knife and Janus," Devi said. "It's really unbelievable. He seemed so normal."

"He was brilliant," Mel said. "But he was fucked up, too. And obsessed. Obsessed with his game. With making it harder, wilder, better. I think he faked his death so that he could bring it into the real world. No one could argue with his decision if he wasn't around to fight with. And no one would be looking to lay the blame on him if he was dead."

"And he was obsessed with Devi," Blake said.

"Yeah. In a big way. And since he was a risk-taker by nature, he took a big one to try to get her."

Blake turned to her. "Another crazed fan. Are you okay?"

She smiled and nodded. "Yeah. I'm actually fine." The smile widened. "We really won, Blake. It's over."

Somehow, he knew that she meant more than just the game. The fear, he knew, was over, too.

"If we won," he said, "shouldn't we get a prize?"

She pulled him close for a kiss. "I've got everything I need already."

EPILOGUE

"**S**o, come on, you two," Letterman says. "Tell the truth. That stunt on the Hollywood sign. That was just a big PR campaign for the movie, right?"

I laugh. "Now, David. You know we can't reveal trade secrets. Especially not on opening weekend."

He looks at Blake. "Oh, come on now. Toss me a bone. Something."

Blake just shakes his head. "Maybe it's time to show the clip," he suggests, and the studio audience applauds madly.

"Yeah," David says with his trademark grin. "And we've got a little surprise for you." The last, he says to me, and I frown as the video screen drops down. Because this isn't supposed to be a surprise. My PR folks are very against surprises in the late-night arena.

But David's right. Because this isn't the clip from the movie we'd messengered over that morning. Instead, it's Blake's interview from earlier in the year.

The interview. The one that started all the trouble between us.

I'm not particularly happy with David for playing it, but I can hardly show it. Not in front of an audience the size of his.

So I laugh. "What?" I ask. "Trying to drum up ratings with reruns?"

"Not when I've got this," he says, in that deadpan way he has.

And now he's pointing at Blake, who even as I watch is going down on one knee. The audience is way more astute than I am, because they're already on their feet, stomping and clapping.

"Devi," Blake says. "Marriage may not have been on my radar earlier this year. But it is now." He looks me in the eye, and the studio, the audience, and the noise melts away. "I love you," he says. "Will you marry me?"

I nod, because suddenly my voice isn't working. But I try again and manage a squeaky little *"Yes!"* before tossing myself in his arms.

And that, of course, is when the crowd goes wild.

Up Close and Personal
with the Author

Well, it's time for me to sit down and interview myself again . . . a melancholy moment, as *The Prada Paradox* is the last book in the "Play. Survive. Win" trilogy, and thus the last chance I'll have to interrogate . . . er . . . *interview* myself in this way. So here we go:

ME: Can you tell us what inspired this book, *The Prada Paradox*?

ME: Um, *that's* your opening gambit for hard-hitting journalism? I'd think you'd pick a question where the answer isn't so obvious.

ME: Obvious? What's obvious about it?

ME: I mean, duh! It's the third book in a trilogy. I was hardly going to write a ranching story, right?

ME: (deep, heavy, exasperated sigh.) Fair enough, Miss Sarcasm. But I was referring to the fact that this book is set in a different location—Los Angeles rather than New York. Any particular reason?

ME: Okay, that's a decent question. I take back my snark. The book is set in Los Angeles for two reasons, the first being that it's the natural setting for the overall backdrop of the story (the film industry). Certainly, the book could have been set in New York (the actors could have been on location), but as to that, the second reason applies: it was time to mix it up a little, and Los Angeles fit—fast-paced, fun, and fashionable.

ME: Alright, then. Let's narrow the question a bit. How did the idea for doing the third book against the backdrop of the *Givenchy Code* movie come about?

ME: Much better question—

ME: (dripping sarcasm) So glad you approve.

ME: —and the answer is really quite easy. It's typical in romantic trilogies, each new story stars a different hero/heroine. The romances in these stories certainly followed that pattern, but the ultimate question of who was pulling the strings of the game remained open, starting in book one and continuing through the trilogy. Because of that open question, I really wanted to bring the series full circle. Not just answer that underlying question, but truly circle the series back on itself. At the same time, I didn't want to have Mel and Stryker starring again—they'd had their story! But if someone else was doing their story . . . if a movie was being made . . . Honestly, it was just one of those brainstorming thing!

ME: And didn't you study film for a while, and even work in the industry?

ME: Ah, this is the part where you show off your investigative skills? Yes, my undergraduate degree is in film, and I practiced law in the L.A. area for a while, did some entertainment-related work, and also worked as a production exec for a small film company.

ME: So you lived in L.A. Have you been to all the places in the book?

ME: For the most part, yes (though, ahem, some literary license has been taken, though I won't say where or how!). And I had a very good friend play research assistant for me. Things have changed in L.A. in the years I've been gone, so my friend Stephen Carver suffered mightily to go to Beverly Hills and Universal Studios for me, sending back pictures and descriptions. It's a tough job, but somebody has to do it!

ME: Pictures, huh? So that "grafitti" in Beverly Hills is real?

ME: The "Don't Panic" sign? Absolutely! I have a jpg!

ME: And that seems like a good place to wrap this interview. Once again, you didn't panic, even in the face of my hard-hitting interview.

ME: It was tough, but I muddled through . . .